HER LAST WORDS

MARTINA MONROE BOOK 8

H.K. CHRISTIE

ALSO BY H.K. CHRISTIE

The Martina Monroe Series —a nail-biting crime thriller series starring PI Martina Monroe and her unofficial partner Detective August Hirsch of the Cold Case Squad. If you like high-stakes games, jaw-dropping twists, and suspense that will keep you on the edge of your seat, then you'll love the Martina Monroe crime thriller series.

The Selena Bailey Series (1 - 5) — a suspenseful series featuring a young Selena Bailey and her turbulent path to becoming a top-notch private investigator as led by her mentor, Martina Monroe.

The Val Costa Series —a gripping crime thriller with heart-pounding suspense. If you love Martina, you'll love Val.

The Neighbor Two Doors Down —a dark and witty psychological thriller. If you like unpredictable twists, page-turning suspense, and unreliable narrators, then you'll love *The Neighbor Two Doors Down*.

A Permanent Mark A heartless killer. Weeks without answers. Can she move on when a murderer walks free? If you like riveting suspense and gripping mysteries then you'll love *A Permanent Mark* - starring a grown up Selena Bailey.

For H.K. Christie's full catalog go to: **www.authorhkchristie.com**

At **www.authorhkchristie.com** you can also sign up for the H.K. Christie reader club where you'll be the first to hear about upcoming novels, new releases, giveaways, promotions, and a free e-copy of the prequel to the Martina Monroe Thriller Series, *Crashing Down!*

Cover design by Odile Stamanne

www.authorhkchristie.com

First edition: April 2023

ISBN: 978-1-953268-15-0

012225h

For my dear friend, Karma

1

TWO YEARS EARLIER

I had never watched anyone die before. Based on what I had seen in the movies, I had expected the act to be more violent. *More disturbing.* Like maybe he would have twisted in agony while pleading for my help. Or clutched at his throat as the drugs stole his last breath. *None of that.* There wasn't even a look of surprise or a realization something was off. The man had simply climbed into his car and lain back. His eyelids fluttered before he tilted his head and drifted away. It was pretty anticlimactic, if you asked me. With no gory scene or obvious signs of foul play, the manner of death would likely be *undetermined.* Or so I hoped.

As I stared at the man with thinning gray hair and tan skin wearing a conservative, white, button-down dress shirt tucked into his khakis, I almost felt sorry for him. *Almost.* He had no idea what was coming for him, and from my observation, he never would. Unfortunately, that was how it had to be. He couldn't suspect a thing, nor could there be any witnesses. I knew not to stare at my handiwork for too long or check for a pulse. *As much as I want to.* No, I had to have faith the drug did its job and he was dead or would be soon. To an unsuspecting stranger, he looked like a man sleeping in his car. No reason for anyone to stop and inquire about his wellbeing. By the time he turned ashen, alerting a well-meaning passerby, it would be too late.

Would the authorities assume it was an accidental overdose or realize something was amiss? *Homicide.* That was the worst-case scenario. But even if law enforcement thought a crime had occurred, they wouldn't find any evidence. He tossed the only clue into the trash.

His downfall was twofold.

First, he'd been a vile man. Second, he was a creature of habit and went to the same coffee shop every morning, Monday through Friday. He sipped his latte as he strolled along the boardwalk before chucking his cup into the bin and heading to his car to start the workday.

Every weekday.

Like clockwork.

It was almost too easy. All I had to do was watch him for a few weeks, track his habits, and grease a few palms to get access to his morning cup of joe. Considering the coffee shop was mostly run by teenagers working their summer vacation, all it took was a hundred bucks to get one of the teenage boys to let me wear an apron and serve a few customers under the guise of surprising my boyfriend.

In hindsight, it was silly how nervous I had been. When I first approached the young barista, my hands shook and sweat trickled down my back. I told him it embarrassed me to ask, but that I wanted to surprise my boyfriend, who just moved to the area. At first, the teen was wary of the odd request, but I assured him I had worked as a barista when I was in college and knew the inner workings of the popular coffee chain. Relief filled me when the teen, albeit reluctantly, agreed to my plan. To sweeten the deal, I gave him five twenty-dollar bills and, just like that, his reluctance was gone. The boy had to serve a lot of lattes to make that much dough.

The moment I handed over the cash, my nerves calmed.

Not that I could ignore the fact the boy and a few other workers could identify me. Although if asked for a description, they would describe a redhead with too much makeup and all-black clothing. Nothing to worry about. Not anymore. I had spent too much time worrying about making mistakes or what other people thought of me.

When my world tipped over, my outlook shifted. I replaced concerns for my personal welfare with worrying about protecting the ones I loved. Honestly, I hadn't thought it would lead me on this journey, but when left with no other options, what's a girl to do? The only thing she could do was to ensure those who did bad things had bad things happen to them.

I took one last look at the not-so-sleeping-beauty before I glanced around the busy street and strolled past the car with the dead monster inside. At the first streetlight, I hurried across with a few dozen other tourists. I meandered down the pier without a care until I hit the end. Staring out at the azure blue sea with gentle waves and the sun shining down, I thought, *What a beautiful day for justice.*

2

MARTINA

Dark brew dripped into the blue and gold CoCo County Sheriff's Department mug. Performing this ordinary task five days a week for nearly three years had become a habit for me. It shouldn't have provided any significance, but it did. It was a symbol of normalcy. The routine of working at the sheriff's department with Hirsch and the Cold Case Squad.

When I had first started working cold cases, it didn't always feel comfortable. There were new and old faces. New and old challenges. My time at the sheriff's department had been interesting, exciting, and, at times, frustrating. Finding the missing and tracking down murderers to ensure they paid for their crimes was rewarding. But the politics and dirty cops, I could do without. The coffee machine stopped dispensing. And as I grabbed my mug, I thought, *I know this mug and this coffee machine like they were old friends.*

With a bit of sadness, I knew my time with the Cold Case Squad may become my past earlier than I had expected. But to be fair, I did not know when I started how long this gig would last. The only constant was change.

Hirsch approached, not looking too happy.

"Good morning."

"Happy Monday," he said gruffly.

What was wrong? Was he not sleeping? Was it the baby? "How's Kim?"

His grim demeanor brightened. "She's great but getting a little anxious."

When I was pregnant with Zoey, I was a nervous wreck. In some ways, the jab of her kick to my bladder felt like yesterday but also like a million years ago. Alas, my girl was almost eleven years old and posturing to rule the world. When I had learned I was pregnant, the idea of the birth made me nervous, along with every component of becoming a parent. Would I do everything right, or wrong, or maybe a little of both? I liked to think that I had done okay so far.

"How are the Lamaze classes?"

Hirsch cracked a smile. "I think that's what's freaking her out. All the vivid details from the teacher of what's going to happen when she goes into labor. Not to mention she's focused on the stacks of books she's been reading. I think she's over-whelmed. She may not be the only one."

His words sounded worried, but his baby blues shone. He was excited for his first child.

"Don't worry so much. You and Kim are going to make great parents. Plus, you have a village of babysitters waiting for the little critter to arrive. Zoey's angling to be your number one babysitter."

"Isn't she too young?"

Yes, I thought she was too young to take care of an infant, but maybe in a few years, she could help. She had never been around babies, but considering Kim was her favorite "auntie," she couldn't wait for the baby to arrive. "For now, but she can't wait to meet the baby, and she's already been talking about all the things we should get for the baby and how we should visit often so that they can bond."

Hirsch tittered. "She must have been talking to Kim."

Smiling, I said, "She has." Hirsch's wife, Kim, was a good friend and had become Zoey's favorite shopping and nail salon partner.

"Without Zoey and the baby, I think I would struggle to find a reason for what we do. Without the hope and that brightness, I'm not sure how much longer I could do this."

What was up with him? I knew the gravity of the job had weighed on Hirsch. The politics, the paperwork, and the unending workdays. "Did you have your meeting with Sarge?" I had a feeling that was the reason for the grumpy demeanor.

"I just came from his office."

We had been waiting to hear about the fate of the Cold Case Squad ever since they had elected the new sheriff into the office. Sarge was happy to give up the temporary position, but we knew little about Sheriff Baldwin. So far, he seemed okay, but one of his campaign promises was to clean up the department and start rooting out the rotten apples.

In some ways, it was our own fault for putting the Cold Case Squad's existence into question. We had taken down several high-ranking members in the county. From a mayor to a sitting sheriff and a few detectives. There had been corruption, there had been lies, and there had been murder. We knew shining a light on the misdeeds could cost us our jobs. But it didn't stop us. Serving justice *was our job*.

And despite previous praise for closing high-profile cold cases, the public wanted to know why the active homicide closure rates were dropping. Half the press claimed all funds should go to active cases and the Cold Case Squad should work fresh ones. Statistically, fresh cases were more likely to be solved than cold ones. We couldn't beat the statistics.

And since they had made no mention of my contract, which was ending in seven weeks, a pretty clear picture had been painted. Although I didn't think Hirsch was as convinced. "What did he say?"

"He said they're continuing to discuss budgets and the plan for a new image for the sheriff's department. They haven't made any decisions about the squad or your contract."

That wasn't good news. As the only civilian contractor, I would be the first to go when they started making cuts from the Cold Case Squad or folding the squad into the other departments.

Not only had the critics questioned the low homicide closure rates, but also why the Internal Affairs Bureau hadn't been the ones to take down the crooked cops in the department. IA, like the other departments, was under a microscope. Not that I thought IA hadn't done a good job. I didn't know much about them and hadn't been involved in any of their investigations since I was a civilian. But the cases we brought to light were decades old, and there was no way the current IA team would have discovered the truth without our help.

It was as I figured. "I'm meeting with Stavros next week to discuss what a transition back to the firm will look like and the nature of my role."

"Don't you think that's premature?"

"Do you?"

Hirsch and I knew how each other operated. He had to know I was planning. He knew I had a daughter to support and couldn't leave my employment status to chance. Even if the sheriff's department wanted to renew my contract, if they waited too long, I would have to notify them I wasn't open for a contract next year. I needed to secure my spot back at my firm, Drakos Security & Investigations.

"Let's not give up yet. Come on, let's go talk to the squad.

Vincent called me last night and said he found something interesting on the Jars case."

"What is it?"

"I don't know. Let's go find out."

Hirsch grabbed his coffee, and we headed toward the squad room. After we practically ran into Sarge, the big man said, "Martina. How is it going?"

Sarge was my mother's boyfriend. Lately, they'd been talking about moving their relationship to the next level. Mom hadn't been specific, but if my gut was right, it meant they would move in together.

The last few years, I had fought to create a new normal, a normal that I loved, but my instincts told me it was all about to change again. "Doing well. Yourself?"

"Okay. It's never a dull moment around here. I'm glad I ran into the two of you. I just came from the sheriff's office, and he has a request."

Hirsch and I exchanged glances. We had received requests from the sheriffs in the past, and neither one of us had liked it much. But we tried to give the new sheriff the benefit of the doubt and assumed he was nothing like Lafontaine. "And what's that?"

"There's a case he wants you to reopen."

Well, there were worse possibilities.

Hirsch said, "What's the case?"

"Don't know. He wants a meeting to discuss it. From his enthusiasm, something tells me it's important."

I tried to contain my displeasure. Perhaps this was a last test to see if the Cold Case Squad were worth their keep? Admittedly, I was tired of being tested. "When is the meeting?"

"Fifteen minutes. Sheriff's office."

Hirsch said, "We'll be there."

I exhaled, blowing strands of hair out of my eyes. *Happy Monday, indeed.*

3

HIRSCH

Sitting opposite Sheriff John Baldwin, I contemplated which case he needed us to reopen. Martina and I had discussed different high-profile cases we'd seen in the news over the last ten years and had considered a few. But we were walking in blind. My least favorite way to walk in.

I hadn't had many interactions with Sheriff Baldwin since he took office a few months earlier, but he seemed fair, cordial, and, best of all, he mostly stayed out of our business. It was how I preferred it, but to be honest, I wasn't sure what I preferred anymore. Kim was due in less than a month.

In a month, I would be a father. And I didn't want to be a dad who only played with the kid on the weekends and barbequed on Fourth of July. I wanted to take in every moment. Every diaper, every first. I didn't want to miss my daughter's childhood. *My daughter.* The most terrifying two words I could think of.

How could I be present in her life with my long hours and dangerous job? No matter how hard I tried, I could never get rid of the image of the spouses and children of the murdered from my memory. The tiny eyes and teardrops, wondering where daddy was. I couldn't put my daughter or my wife through that — not if I could help it.

After I'd introduced Martina to Sheriff Baldwin, he said, "Thank you both for meeting with me. I wanted a chance to explain my motivations for the request. Full transparency."

Refreshing.

Martina said, "We appreciate that, Sheriff. That hasn't always been the case around here."

He nodded. "Understood. I assure you I intend to run a clean ship. You won't find any skeletons in my closet, and I want to make sure nobody else in our department has any, either."

Good news? Bad news? Did that mean he would divert our resources to internal affairs? "That's good to hear."

"I've been tracking the Cold Case Squad's record over the past few years. It's incredible. To be honest, I wish we had your talent in homicide and missing persons. Perhaps we should check with our forensics lab and see if they can clone the two of you and the rest of your squad?" He delivered a reassuring smile.

This new sheriff was certainly a breath of fresh air, but was he dropping clues he'd be moving us out of cold cases? What if he sent me back to homicide? Being woken up in the middle of the night to attend a crime scene. Working around the clock until we'd exhausted every lead. I couldn't do it.

Even if the squad was no more, I couldn't forget all the outstanding work the team had accomplished. And I knew every member of the team would continue to do the same outstanding work and bring justice to find the missing wherever they landed. "Wouldn't that be something?"

Martina gave me a little side eye.

"With that being said, I assume you're very busy. But before I get to the details of the case, I want to say thank you. Thank you for all the exceptional work the Cold Case Squad has done, and thank you for accepting the case I'm about to share with you."

I tipped my head to indicate I understood. We hadn't technically accepted the case yet, but I think the sheriff knew we didn't have a choice, and he was trying to butter us up.

Sheriff Baldwin continued, "The case is the death of Matthew Baldwin. My younger brother."

My heart sank. The sheriff's brother? Surely, with a brother in law enforcement, they had done a thorough investigation. But I could understand wanting answers. My brother had been murdered, and the case remained unsolved for the last twenty-five years. The circumstances around my brother's murder made it nearly impossible to solve unless someone offered up new information.

Sheriff Baldwin straightened his spine. "I wanted to be open with you. This is personal for me. I'm not asking for miracles. A solid team of detectives investigated the case, but I'm simply asking for you to take a second look."

No pressure. "Understood, sir. What can you tell us about your brother's death?"

"Matt died two years ago. He was forty-seven, working as a scientist in biotech. He had been married for twenty years and has two children, ages eleven and thirteen. My niece and nephew. This has been hard on all of them."

"I can only imagine."

"The cause of death was a heroin overdose."

"Accidental?" Martina asked.

"The medical examiner listed the manner of death as undetermined. But I knew my brother, and he never used hard drugs. He dabbled back in his college days, but nothing more. We saw each other a few times a month. We were close. I would have known if he had a drug problem. And he was a scientist, so the idea that he accidentally gave himself too much doesn't work for me."

"Do you know if there was anyone with a motive to hurt Matt?"

Sheriff Baldwin raked his fingers through his gray hair. "No. Neither him nor Gina, Matt's wife, had been unfaithful. They had no money problems, and he had a good job. He was a family man. He was beloved. There was no one with a bad thing to say about him. Matt had no reason to dabble in drugs or other dangerous recreational activities."

"I'm assuming family, coworkers, friends, neighbors, and past flames were interviewed during the original investigation?"

"Yes. Not one person had a bad thing to say about him."

He was a saint? *Doubtful.* "Did he have any new friends or hobbies before his death?"

"The investigators didn't find any. The detectives theorized if it wasn't murder, maybe my brother used drugs recreationally, or it was a onetime thing. He tried it and it went wrong. But I don't think that's true. It doesn't fit. He was smarter than that."

Even intelligent folks do dumb things on occasion. "Do you believe he was murdered?"

"I've thought a lot about this. I've been on the job for thirty years, and I tried to use my experience to think about it pragmatically. If I didn't know Matt, I would probably consider it an accidental overdose with the remote possibility of murder. But my gut is telling me Matt's death was not an accident. Someone killed my brother, and I want to know who, and more importantly, why. Everyone you talk to will tell you they loved my brother. He was smart, friendly, fun. There wasn't a single person who would say a bad thing about him."

Matt Baldwin would be the first.

"We'll do everything we can to find the truth about what happened to your brother. You say you want full transparency.

I'm assuming that means we can come to you for an interview after we have gone through the file?"

"Of course. Anything you need, and I mean anything. I'm here to help find the truth about my brother. Between the three of us, you're my last chance. If you could take down a sitting sheriff, you can find the truth about my brother."

I said, "We will do our best. And on a personal note, I understand. My brother was murdered, and the responsible person was never caught. I understand the need to understand who and why."

The sheriff gave me a knowing look. "I read that in your file. It's why I trust the two of you will do all you can. In the case file, I've added a few fresh notes on his wife, his kids, the family, and work. The original investigators took diligent notes during the interviews as well. They had to have missed something. Otherwise, we would know what happened."

If a thirty-year veteran of law enforcement thought his brother's death was a murder, he was probably right. He seemed like a sensible man. We would find the truth. I hoped Sheriff Baldwin could handle it.

4

ANDREA

Buried in a pile of contracts, I glanced up at the sound of footsteps. One of the more competent paralegals in the office approached my desk. I said, "Hi, Georgia. What's up?"

"I just needed the Alexiore CMO contract. Do you have it?"

"Yep, it's in here somewhere." Digging through the pile, I looked for the manufacturing agreement between my company and the contract drug manufacturer. I had to admit, when I started law school, I didn't think my job would mostly comprise reviewing contracts and negotiating terms. It was boring. But it was fine. I had more important things to do and didn't need to waste my energy pulling all-nighters preparing for trial or negotiating with district attorneys. My gig as a corporate lawyer reviewing contracts for biotech firms was my preferred speed. It gave me plenty of time for extracurriculars.

I found the contract in question and handed it to Georgia. "I haven't looked at it yet, but here it is." I was a little relieved. If Georgia reviewed the document first, it would make my job even easier.

"Thanks," Georgia said, but she hesitated instead of walking out of my office, as if the file wasn't the real reason she had stopped by.

My gut stirred. What was it? More layoffs? The paralegals always seemed to know the office gossip first. Not that I didn't have a bunch of money stashed away. I didn't do much traveling or make extravagant purchases. But I needed a job because I had expenses that cropped up from time to time that required significant capital, and I wanted nothing jeopardizing that. "What is it?"

"Oh, it's nothing to worry about. I just wondered if you had heard?"

Here it is. "Heard what?"

"Do you remember Matt Baldwin from Research?"

My pulse sky-rocketed. "Vaguely. Why?" I knew exactly who Matt Baldwin was, and from what I understood, he was six feet under, his corpse rotting as we spoke. Good riddance is what I had to say about that guy. Everybody else thought they had lost a genuine hero when he died. His loving wife. His doting children. His coworkers. They were crushed. He was a brilliant scientist who had been adored by all. *Not by all.*

But why was she bringing him up?

"Well, I just heard from Lynden in HR that the police are reopening his death investigation. You know, they found him dead and his brother, the new sheriff, doesn't think it was an accident, so he's handed the case over to the Cold Case Squad. The same team that solved all of those high-profile missing persons cases. The sheriff said he intends to bring his brother's killer to justice. It's kind of sad, though, right?"

Sad? "What do you mean?"

"Well, I think it was pretty obvious Matt died by suicide or of an overdose. Apparently, the family is having a hard time accepting the facts. They insist there was no way he would have taken his own life. Obviously, it's too hard for them to accept. It's sad. I hope the family finds some peace."

That's what she meant by sad. Yes, it was very sad for the family members left behind after a suicide. Especially when your loved one was forced to take their life in order to end their suffering caused by someone else. The gaping hole left behind can never close. That I knew firsthand.

"You're right. It's sad. I hope the family finds some closure." Closure. As if that existed.

"Me too. But it must be hard. They didn't even know he liked to party. And why did he take so much? He's a scientist. He should have known better. But I guess we never really know anybody, right?"

"So true."

Georgia still wasn't budging.

"How did Lynden find out the case was being reopened?" I asked, curiosity getting the better of me.

"Well, she said the sheriff's department contacted her to arrange for the cold case investigators to come by the office to re-interview people."

That didn't ease my concerns, and despite my mind telling my body to calm down, my heart was beating like a humming-bird's. "Did they say who they planned to interview?" It wouldn't make sense to interview me. Our paths barely crossed. We hadn't worked together long before he died. We barely knew one another. Not that I didn't know who he was and what he had done.

"Lynden said anyone who worked with him. They're setting up a conference room for the interviews. Why? Did you want to talk to the police about him?"

Shaking my head, I said, "No, I really only knew him by name and in passing. After he died, everyone talked about him in the office for weeks."

"Oh, I know. I mean, I feel sorry for his family and every-thing. But I don't see why we need to be put through interviews again. It's so nerve-racking. I just wish he'd been a little smarter about his recreational activities, and then his family wouldn't be grieving, his children without a father, and endless searching for answers I don't think the police will find. My gut says overdose."

Yes, you'd think he would've been smarter — but he wasn't. That much I did know about him.

"Well, anyhow. I'll take this contract and let you know if there are any issues."

"Thanks, Georgia."

After she left my office, I hurried over and shut the door. My hands shook as I closed the blinds. Trying to convince myself there was no need to worry, I scurried over to my phone and dialed. My logical brain was reminding me there was no way they would learn the truth. There were no witnesses, no evidence, and *no regrets*. Only justice. And I needed to keep it that way.

5

MARTINA

STUDYING THE LARGE, modern building, nestled amongst a mostly residential neighborhood in Berkeley, I wondered how a man who had worked in the sciences for twenty years with a loving wife and family with no history of mental health issues or drug abuse could end up dead from a heroin overdose. The medical examiner's report didn't find any older track marks to indicate he'd been a secret user. In fact, the ME had found no puncture marks at all, where Matt, or anyone else, could've injected the drug that killed him. If somebody killed him, they didn't inject the drugs. How did they get it into his system?

At first review, I agreed with Sheriff Baldwin. Matt's death was suspicious and didn't fit with an accidental overdose.

As we headed up the steps, I asked Hirsch, "Did you ever consider becoming a scientist?" Hirsch was bright and a little nerdy despite his Ken doll appearance that often made the ladies swoon.

He cracked a grin. "Not even once. Although in school I did like science. Especially the chemistry labs. It was fun to mix things together and watch things bubble or change colors. Science is cool. It's probably why I enjoy talking to Dr. Scribner and Kiki so much. Their work is fascinating. Science can do so much, from identifying a perp to fighting cancer to unlocking the secrets of the universe."

"True. Well, let's use that enthusiasm as we interview the scientists. Asking them about their job will loosen them up."

"Let's do it."

With that, Hirsch pulled the handle on the door and walked into the massive atrium with an ornate glass ceiling. During the warmer months, I guessed natural light shone down, illuminating the lobby.

We walked up to the receptionist. "Hello, my name is Martina Monroe, and this is my partner Detective Hirsch. We're here to see Lynden Kitter in HR."

"I'll let her know you're here."

I stepped back and lowered my voice. "You know, our original thought was that we should talk to anybody who worked with Matt Baldwin, but what about the peripheral people? People who he'd chat up in the break room or the receptionist. The receptionist always knows what's going on, right?"

"Absolutely."

The receptionist hung up the phone. "She'll be right out."

Hirsch gave her his most charming smile. "Thank you. And what's your name?"

The young woman blushed. "My name is Rita."

"Nice to meet you, Rita. How long have you worked here?"

"I started about six months ago."

"You like it?"

"Everyone's really nice."

"That's good to hear."

A woman in a tan pantsuit with short, dark hair and a necklace made of large, colorful orbs approached. Cozying up to the receptionist for information would have to wait. "Hello, I'm Lynden. You must be Ms. Monroe and Detective Hirsch?"

We nodded, shook hands, and exchanged business cards before she said, "I've set up a conference room for the interviews. I figured it would be easier for people to come to you. To give you a home base."

"We appreciate that."

As we shuffled through the hallway, we passed a room full of cubicles and offices and what looked like a break room. Lynden opened a door and led us inside the conference room. The room was large with a table and twelve chairs, whiteboards, and a projector screen on the wall. "Can I get you anything? Water, coffee, tea, fruit juice. We have snacks. Anything you need. Don't be shy."

Hirsch said, "I would love some coffee."

"Me too."

"I can take you over to the break room, and you can pick out whatever you'd like. We have a couple of machines."

We set down our things and followed her into the break room. She explained the mechanics of the coffeemakers, and I gladly accepted a large mug to fill up. While we stood there waiting for coffee, I asked, "How long have you been at Vaxxmore?"

"Oh boy. I'm one of the first employees. About nine years now. We've grown significantly since then."

Chances were Lynden knew everything that went on at the company. "It must be a pretty nice place to work?"

"Oh yeah, it's great. We're all like a big family."

Coffee brewed and mugs in our hands, I said, "All set."

Lynden escorted us back to the conference room. From my periphery, I spotted the eyes of the employees watching before turning away and whispering with their coworkers. Lynden must have notified them of our visit.

Back inside, which I presumed was not for our comfort but a means to contain us, we sat down, and Lynden joined us. "Here is the list of people you had requested to interview today. It's everybody who worked for and with Matt. Is there anybody else?"

"That should be sufficient for now. Unless you can think of anyone who could help us with our investigation. We would like to ask you a few questions, too."

She shook her head. "I can't think of anyone."

"Do you have Matt's employment records we can review?"

"Oh, no. I wish I had known. We moved our older files off site to a storage facility. But I can get them here by tomorrow."

"We would appreciate that."

"Did you have much interaction with Matt?"

"Occasionally. Mostly in a social capacity, like at the company holiday party or in the halls, and when he was opening requisitions for new employees."

"Any disciplinary issues or complaints against him?"

"No, there were never any disciplinary actions against him."

Lynden's hesitation and verbiage piqued my curiosity. "No complaints against him?"

"He was very popular."

Was she avoiding my question? "And he was happy here? He didn't think they overlooked him for a promotion or was unhappy with the pay or work environment?"

"No. He was one of our best employees."

"Okay, well then, I suppose we can get started with the first interview."

"All right, I'll bring them right in."

AFTER INTERVIEWING four of Matt's coworkers and three members of his staff, we had learned nothing new. All reported Matt was a great supervisor, scientist, coworker, and friend. Was this turning out to be a dead end? If Matt's death wasn't work related, and none of his family or friends had motive to kill Matt, then who? And why? Something wasn't adding up.

Our last interviewee of the day held her arms stiffly by her side, and she didn't meet my gaze as she walked in. It wasn't unusual to be nervous when being interviewed by law enforcement. Trying to warm her up, I said, "Hi, you must be Hannah?"

Her light brown eyes met mine. "Yes."

"I'm Martina, and this is my partner, Detective Hirsch."

We shook, and she glanced quickly at Hirsch.

"Please take a seat."

When she sat down, I noticed her fingertips were vibrating on the table before she tucked them into her lap.

"Thank you for meeting with us. We've reopened the death investigation of your previous supervisor, Matt. We want to ask you questions about your time working with him. Do you have questions for us before we get started?"

She shook her head.

"How long have you worked here?"

"Five years."

"And what do you do?" Hirsch asked.

"I'm an analytical chemist."

Not warmed up yet. I looked over at Hirsch.

"Science has always fascinated me. What exactly does that mean?" Hirsch asked.

"Well, once they come up with new drug targets, I run assays. Like tests to determine how pure they are or how potent they are."

"What kind of tests?"

"Well, I run a lot of gels, Western Blots, ELISAs, and chromatography. Chromatography is a process for separating components of a mixture. To get the process started, the mixture is dissolved in a substance called the mobile phase, which carries it through a second substance called the stationary phase. Sometimes I use a special instrument for the separation, sometimes..."

She studied our faces, must have seen we had no idea what she was talking about, and hesitated before explaining further.

I said, "Wow. It's like a unique language. Very cool."

She relaxed. "Sorry, that was probably more than you were asking."

"It's fascinating. Thank you. It sounds like you like your job?"

"I do."

"Did you like working for Matt?"

"He was okay," she said, rather quickly.

"Did you ever have any issues with him?"

She shook her head.

"He always treated you fairly?"

She nodded quickly. "He did."

Something was definitely off, but I couldn't figure out what. "Was he ever inappropriate with you?"

"What do you mean?"

"Did he flirt with you, or touch you when you didn't want him to, or make suggestive comments?"

Hannah's eyes were wide. "No, not with me."

Not with me? Then who? "Can you tell me about the others who worked with Matt? Like Dana, Jeff, and Donavan?"

She stiffened. "And Sarah."

Sarah? "Sarah worked for Matt?"

"She did."

"Does she still work here?"

"No. Sarah died."

Something in my gut stirred. "When was this?"

"About three years ago."

It surprised me Lynden hadn't mentioned Sarah. We

asked for a list of everybody who had worked for him. Did she omit Sarah because she was no longer alive? Were there others?

"Were you and Sarah friends?"

"We were."

"That must've been really hard. I'm sorry for your loss."

"Thank you." She fidgeted in her seat before saying, "She didn't like him."

"Sarah didn't like Matt?"

She shook her head again.

"Do you know why?"

"Are you allowed to look at her records?"

Her records? We'd need a warrant if the company didn't willingly hand them over.

Hirsch said, "We can do that. Can you tell us why Sarah didn't like Matt?"

She stared at Hirsch and back at me. "No. I have an experiment I need to get to. Can I go?"

"Sure, absolutely, please. You've been very helpful. Thank you."

She got up and flew out of the room.

With Hannah off to the lab, I said, "That was strange."

"Sounds like we need to look into Sarah."

The door creaked open, and Lynden ambled in. "How did the interviews go?"

"They went well. Thank you so much for organizing all of this. We have one more question for you."

"Oh?" Lynden asked, with raised brows.

"Who is Sarah?"

Lynden grew still. "Sarah Nesbit. Such a tragic story. She died a few years ago. Suicide. About a year before Matt."

"Was she having any issues at work?"

"I'll have to check, but nothing rings a bell."

"When you request the records from offsite, please make sure that Sarah's are in there."

"Of course, I'll make a note of that. And I'll get those records to you as soon as possible. No later than tomorrow afternoon."

Something told me Matt Baldwin's sterling reputation had a few scuffs.

6

MARTINA

TURNED out not everybody loved Matt Baldwin. Looking at Sarah Nesbit's employment file, including her complaints about harassment from Matt, it was clear the previous investigators hadn't gotten the complete picture. The accusations were surprising, considering everyone who was interviewed had said he was beloved. Professional. One of the good ones. Did they lie, or were they really not aware of his true character?

Sarah's first complaint:

> I, Sarah Nesbit, am writing to make a formal complaint against my supervisor, Matt Baldwin. On several occasions during my employment, Matt has made inappropriate and odd comments such as, "Where do you want to go on our big date?" When I inquired, "What are you talking about?" he would claim he was kidding. Yet, the comments regarding our dating continued. At first, I rolled my eyes and let it go. But then he started coming up to me and giving me unwanted massages. I told him I didn't want a

massage, and he replied, "Sure you do. It'll feel good." I pushed his hands off and said, "No. I don't want a massage. Please don't touch me again."

But it didn't end there. On several more occasions, he repeated the actions, and I told him if it happened again, I would report him to HR. He said, "Fine. No need to be so mean about it. All I wanted to do was make you feel good." A few months passed without incident, and I assumed the issue was resolved. But one night, while I was alone in the lab, working on an ELISA, he creeped up behind me and put his hands around my neck and then down to my shoulders and he rubbed them.

I hadn't even heard him walk into the lab. The action terrified me, and I froze. After a minute, he crept back out of the lab. Feeling unsafe, I abandoned my experiment and packed up my things and went home. I never thought I would feel unsafe in the lab and wasn't sure what to do. I had already expressed to him how uncomfortable he was making me. But since he put his hands on my neck, I'm now afraid of working with him.

My stomach churned. Sarah made Matt sound like a first-rate creep. The actions she described, with the sneaking behind her in the lab, were likely a message to Sarah that she was powerless. And it sounded like she got the message. Assuming Sarah's account was true, hands on the neck was a bright red flag that Matt was an abuser. It was enough to make me think about interviewing his wife again.

The next complaint was even more bizarre.

I, Sarah Nesbit, want to complain formally about retaliation from Matt Baldwin. Since my complaint and change to a new supervisor, Matt has been taunting and teasing me in front of everyone. He is telling everyone that I broke up with him and that he is heartbroken. This has been going on daily — for weeks. I try to ignore him, but he doesn't let up. And nobody says anything. The constant harassment is making my work environment hostile and scary.

How *weird*. Why would a married man with two children and twenty years her senior think it was okay to taunt and tease her in front of everyone? To make comments they had been together and she no longer liked him and they'd broken up? Why didn't anyone say anything? If I had been Sarah, I would have clocked him. But I wasn't Sarah. Sarah had only been twenty-five years old at her first job after graduating from college.

The final complaint was unnerving.

I, Sarah Nesbit, want to make a formal complaint against Matt Baldwin for continuing to threaten and intimidate me. He talks about my appearance and body in front of others and gives me dirty looks. He bumps me in the hall and says, "Sorry." But it's rough, and I know it wasn't an accident. The most recent incident happened when I was in the back lab weighing out reagents. He entered the small room and then stood, blocking the door while I continued my task. He didn't

*say a word until I was ready to leave. I said,
"Excuse me."*

*He responded. "You're excused." But he didn't budge.
I said, "I would like to leave. Can you please move?"*

He said, "On one condition."

I dared to ask. "What?"

"You kiss me."

*The request shocked me. I said, "No." But he
refused to move. He then knocked the reagents out of
my hand and pushed me against the cooler and shoved
his face up against mine, kissing me and grabbing at
my body. He left after about thirty seconds.*

*My sister told me all of this is illegal. And it is
assault. You need to do something about him. If he's
doing this to me, he's likely done it to others or will do it
to others in the future. I fear he will retaliate for this.
If the company does nothing to stop him, I will obtain
legal representation.*

My heart broke for Sarah. She was brave, yet clearly scared at the same time. Matt should have been arrested. Someone should have stopped Matt well before the final complaint.

Looking at the date of the last complaint, I saw that it was one month before Sarah died. Yet, Sarah had been complaining for almost a year and had worked at Vaxxmore for three. What else had she endured before she said, "enough is enough"? And what had happened in the month since her final complaint and her suicide? Was it really suicide?

There wasn't any record of the complaint against Matt in his own employment file. The notes from HR and Sarah's file stated the claims were unsubstantiated and noted that Matt said Sarah had misinterpreted his actions and he had the utmost respect for her.

A shiver went down my spine.

The thought of a young woman alone, with nobody to believe her about his actions and how he made her feel, was unconscionable. The acts toward Sarah weren't as brutal as some crimes, such as rape, but it was the same MO. Men don't rape only for sexual gratification. It's typically because they want to punish, control, and dominate women. Leaving the victims and survivors to be fearful, confused, ashamed, and lose all sense of control over their body. From Sarah's words, I deduced Matt had accomplished just that — and likely contributed to her death.

Hirsch said, "Find anything interesting?"

"Well, let's just say that if Sarah had been alive at the time of Matt's death, we'd be questioning her. From what I can tell, she's the first person I've seen who may have had a motive to kill Matt."

"You're kidding?"

"No joke. She made multiple complaints to human resources about his actions and behavior toward her. All ignored, and all said she'd misinterpreted the situation and was being too sensitive. Even though she repeatedly asked him to stop doing what he was doing. He kept on taunting her and then it escalated to physical assault."

"There's more to Matt Baldwin than we thought."

Based on Sarah's notes, everyone in the lab knew how Matt was treating Sarah. But the only person who even mentioned Sarah's name was Hannah. "Are you surprised nobody mentioned it during the interviews?"

"Maybe they didn't know the extent?"

"Hannah knew. And HR knew."

Hirsch tilted his head. "How many complaints are against him?"

"Four over a year. Sarah's last complaint was a month before she died. Makes you wonder why Lynden didn't mention Sarah and all her complaints against Matt, doesn't it?"

"Maybe the Vaxxmore lawyers tried to cover it up so the company wouldn't be liable for Sarah's death. Or to protect Matt. It's also possible Sarah's complaints are false."

I didn't think so. What would Sarah have to gain by complaining about a senior member of the company? If anything, it could actually hurt her. It was a sad fact that many women who complained about harassment in the workplace were told to "put the experience behind you and change jobs, or it could ruin your career — you don't want to be labeled as a troublemaker." The victims being the ones forced to change their jobs, their behavior while the perpetrators went on with their lives, their reputation intact.

Handing over the complaints, I said, "Do you really think a company dedicated to helping humankind by creating medicines to make the world a better place would cover up this kind of harassment?"

Hirsch took the file and said, "I'm pretty sure that kinda stuff happens in all industries," before studying Sarah's complaints against Matt.

Considering we had taken down members of law enforcement, why would anyone think scientists would be above coverups and corruption? Was it the white coats? Everybody seems to trust a person in a white coat. It was like they were magically smart, authoritative, and to be trusted.

Hirsch threw some twisted expressions and raised brows. He set the papers down. "We should do a full background on Sarah. Talk to her friends, family, and re-interview Hannah."

"But if Sarah's dead, how does that help our investigation?"

"Everyone else has painted Matt as a golden child, a man who could do no wrong. We have evidence that not everybody believed that was true. I have a hard time believing Matt would only behave this way toward one person. There's likely someone willing to talk to us and tell us the truth about Matt, like Hannah. And there may be others who Sarah confided in, like her sister. She even says so in her complaint."

"That's a good point." I glanced down the table at Vincent, who looked like he was deep in thought, staring at his laptop screen.

"Hey, Vincent."

He glanced up. "Yeah, boss?"

"Do you have time for a background?"

He picked up his laptop and walked over to us. "What's the name?"

"Sarah Nesbit."

"Give me a few minutes," he said as he tapped away on the keys.

"What is that gut of yours saying, Martina?" Hirsch asked.

"That Sarah is the key to what happened to Matt. Maybe it's not that somebody murdered him, but maybe he felt guilty for what he did to Sarah and felt responsible for her death. Or he was afraid he could be exposed."

"Well, if he's as good a man as everybody says, then perhaps he felt guilty. Perhaps his actions, whether or not they were intentional, led to her death."

"Possibly."

But something wasn't adding up for me. We needed to talk to the wife again to see what Matt was really like at home. Maybe a second interview would reveal the cracks in the plaster. I had a hunch that Matt's picture-perfect life was anything but.

"What are you thinking?"

"We need to re-interview the family. We start with the wife."

He smirked. "Oh boy, you've got your bone."

"That's right. And I'm not letting it go until we find the truth."

7

ANDREA

MY FAILURE TO concentrate on work put me behind schedule. And I didn't want to fall behind any further. Mostly because I didn't want anyone questioning why I couldn't focus. As it was, I planned to take a three-day weekend to go to the cabin. But my mind kept diverting back to why the sheriff's department reopened Matt's case. Was the only reason because his brother had the power to do so, or did they have new information?

When the case fizzled, I was confident that would be the end of it. Had I been wrong? My mission wasn't complete, but all the planned activities were put on hold while the investigators continued poking around. After all my planning. All the money spent. All the time and energy. All the steps I had taken to get there. Would it be all for nothing?

Get it together, Andrea. I needed to put the situation out of my mind. This would all go away. It had to. They couldn't find anything. There was no evidence pointing to a motive or a suspect.

I knew when his brother was elected sheriff of CoCo County the situation could get sticky. But I hadn't expected for him to hand over the case to his star cold case investigative team.

They'd solved some of the county's toughest cases. It had been all over the news. As far as I was concerned, Martina Monroe and Detective Hirsch were the only things stopping me from completing my mission.

A knock on my door broke up my thoughts. Georgia and her bouncy blonde hair had returned. "Hey, what's up?"

"I was checking to see if you're done with the Blackwell contract?"

Done with it? I hadn't gotten past the first paragraph. That was one downside of having an incredibly boring job. When I needed to escape my personal life, work was no help. The content was too boring to steal my attention. It was almost like white noise instead of a loud crash. My skin was itchy. My nerves were in overdrive. "Not yet. But I'll have it done by the end of the day. I might head home to work on it. I'm getting a bit of a headache."

"Is there anything I can do to help?"

"No, Georgia, it's fine. I'll look at it. Don't worry about it."

"Can I get you anything for your headache?"

"You're so sweet. I just took a couple of pills, but thank you."

"I hope you feel better."

"Thanks. I'll email you the contract when I'm done."

"Perfect. Have a good afternoon."

I exhaled, wondering how long the investigators would be snooping around. At least they weren't in the office. No need for them to discover my true identity or why I took this job six months before Matt *tragically* died. Tragic. He was the worst of them. The ones who pretended to be something they weren't. The ones pretending to be the loving, charitable family man but really were simply wolves in sheep's clothing. I was glad he was dead.

My phone rang. *Great.*

"Andrea Puerto. How can I help you?"

"Yes, hi, Andrea, it's Ted. I was wondering if you had finished with the Blackwell contract yet?"

Seriously? I told him I would have it done today and *I would do it today.* "It's still in progress. Working on it right now. But I'll send it to your paralegal by the end of the day. Don't worry about it."

"Okay, I just wanted to make sure it's still on track. It's a pretty big deal."

Eye roll. "No worries." I hung up the phone. A big deal? *Please.* Everybody in this office thought because they had a PhD or were good at chemistry, they were the most important people on the planet. That every new project or milestone could make or break the future of the universe. But it couldn't. Beneath the façade of improving people's lives and bringing forth the medicines of tomorrow were the shareholders' expectations. The team of upper management with their milestone and strategic deals. It was all about milestones. Gotta hit the milestone or we don't get our funding. Which really meant they wouldn't get their bonuses. No new boat this year. *Tragic.*

Another façade. The healthcare industry making billions, pretending to care about the public's health and safety when really the executives were more concerned about padding their pockets as shareholders smiled when they hit certain milestones. *Woo-hoo.* Drug passed Phase II. Stock goes up four points. Everybody cheers. The drug fails the phase III trial. *Boo.* Stockholders are unhappy, and the stock dips five points. But that's okay because the smart ones already pulled out, knowing that the drug wasn't likely to work. And don't get me started about fen-phen and the opioid crisis. All preventable. All repeating history. All caused by the big shots in the pharmaceutical industry's own disregard for human life. And I thought *lawyers* were bad. At least we didn't pretend to be noble.

Staring back at my computer screen, I thought maybe I would power through and force myself to concentrate. Close my office door, put on classical music, and focus. Forget about how those two investigators could bring my entire world crumbling down. But I had finally found a purpose, and I damn sure would not let them take it away. Glancing down at my empty coffee mug, I grabbed it and headed for a refill.

In the break room, I spotted Lynden with two visitors. My heart raced. They both had the telltale signs of law enforcement. Defensive stances and taking in every detail in the vicinity. Why were they back? The two investigators turned to focus on me. The man was six feet with dirty blond hair and gorgeous blue eyes. Unfortunately, he also had a ring on his finger. The woman, about 5'7", with dark hair, amber eyes, and a smooth complexion, gave a warm smile.

"Hi, Lynden. You two must be Detective Hirsch and Martina Monroe? The ones investigating Matt Baldwin's death, right?"

I approached, wearing a friendly smile.

We shook hands.

"My name is Andrea Puerto. It's nice to meet you. I work in legal — contracts."

The very sexy detective said, "It's nice to meet you. Did you know Matt?"

"No. I only started working here a few months before he died. So sad." I said it with as much sincerity as I could muster.

Martina looked down into my cup. "Looks like you're here for the same reason we are — caffeine fix."

"Yep, another contract to get through this afternoon."

"Well, it would be a crime to stand in your way." They stepped away from the coffee machine, and I placed my mug under the spout. With buttons pressed, the brew dripped in.

Lynden said, "We can meet in my office or the conference room. If there's other people you'd like to speak with."

"We have a few follow-up questions for you as well as Hannah, if possible."

Hannah? She had been friends with Sarah. According to Sarah, she was one of the few decent people in the lab.

"Sure, no problem. Let me just check if there's a conference room available." Lynden hurried off.

"Any luck in finding out what happened to Matt?" I asked innocently.

The hot detective said, "We've discovered a few interesting things that we're trying to explore further."

"That's good. Well, if any roads lead you to contracts, my office is down the hall."

"We appreciate that."

I nodded and scuttled back to my office. What had they unraveled? Had they already figured out that Matt was not the perfect man everyone pretended he was? If that were true, I might actually be in trouble.

8

MARTINA

LYNDEN DIDN'T LOOK as relaxed or friendly as she had two days earlier. Perhaps the fact we were back and specifically wanted to question her had diminished her confidence. Lynden smiled like she was at the dentist. "So, Detective, Ms. Monroe. How can I help?"

I said, "For starters, I'm curious to know why you didn't mention the complaints from Sarah Nesbit against Matt."

Lynden shut her eyes and exhaled. "I didn't think it was relevant. But you're right. I should've mentioned it. None of the complaints were substantiated, so I figured it wasn't relevant. Sarah had complained, but there were no witnesses, and Matt insisted he had done none of the things that Sarah had accused him of."

"So, the company took no actions based on Sarah's complaints?"

"Well, because of the accusations, we thought maybe it could cause tension between Matt and Sarah to continue to work together, so we had Sarah work for a different manager. It would give both of them a fresh start."

Staring Lynden directly in the eyes, I said, "Based on the

complaints from Sarah, it sounds like it didn't fix the issue. In fact, it sounds like it caused retaliation and others witnessed it. The strange declarations to the lab that they had broken up and that she didn't like him anymore. His claims of heartbreak."

"Matt insisted he was just teasing and trying to lighten the mood."

I glanced over at Hirsch. He wasn't buying it either. "Did you find that type of teasing to be appropriate for the workplace?" Hirsch asked.

Lynden paled. "It wasn't the best choice for Matt to use those particular words. His manager, Frank, had a word with him, and he stopped the teasing."

"So then, the complaints were substantiated?"

"Well, not exactly. He said that she was exaggerating, and those were the words that he'd used, but she misinterpreted them. He promised to be more careful about what words he used in the future."

My gut said Lynden wasn't being straightforward with us. "What about the last accusation that he physically assaulted her? She could have had him arrested. What do you have to say about that?"

She lifted her hands in the air, as if she didn't have a good explanation. "He said it never happened, and there weren't any witnesses."

"Let me guess. The company took no actions after that complaint?" Hirsch asked with a sternness that let Lynden know none of this was acceptable. The company had been irresponsible in handling the situation.

"Like I said, we couldn't prove that it really happened."

"Did you talk to Matt and ask him if the actions occurred?"

"Of course we did. He denied everything. He said that Sarah had it out for him and he didn't know why. He insisted he had always been friendly to her."

Whatever Matt had tried to sell, I didn't buy it and was shocked Lynden and the company had. "Did Matt have any explanation as to why Sarah had it out for him?"

"He said he didn't know and that it was really strange. We had no problems with Matt and any other employees before."

"What would Sarah have to gain by submitting false complaints?" The answer was absolutely nothing.

"I didn't say they were false. They were unsubstantiated."

"But no actions were taken. She still had to work alone in the lab with him. Don't you have a duty to make sure your employees are safe?"

"Well, yes, of course." Her voice wavered.

"Why do you think Frank never mentioned any of this when we interviewed him?"

"I can't speak for Frank."

Hirsch folded his arms across his chest, letting Lynden and I know he meant business. "How I see it, and I've been in this job for a long time, is that you withheld this information about Sarah and the complaints against Matt on purpose. My partner point blank asked if Matt had any issues with any employees of Vaxxmore, and you said no. At first, we thought maybe it was just an HR thing — maybe you forgot. But it sounds like Frank also covered this up, and I'd like to know why. I don't believe for a second that you thought it was irrelevant."

Lynden's hands shook. She put them onto her lap so that we couldn't see, but I already had. "Honestly, we didn't think it would make a difference in the investigation."

"We?"

She lowered her head. "Before you came to interview the team, upper management, including our legal representative, discussed whether to mention Sarah and the complaints against Matt. We all decided that it had no bearing on the investigation and all it would do was tarnish Matt's reputation."

Rage filled my being. "That's a lot of concern for Matt's reputation. What about Sarah? What about all the complaints that were all but dismissed? He physically assaulted her at your company. She had no reason to complain about Matt unless what she said happened and it had made her feel uncomfortable and unsafe. I think you and I both know that women who complain about sexual harassment in the work-place don't get crowned the winner. The most common advice given to them is to find a new job and put it behind them as to not tarnish their own employment records by being labeled as a troublemaker. Sarah had nothing to gain by complaining other than a safe work environment. It could only hurt her career, not help her. But it's obvious your company was more concerned about Matt's reputation, one of your founding members of the company, than about a twenty-five-year-old woman's reputation and her safety. Did I get that right, Lynden?"

Lynden placed her face into her hands and rocked. Maybe I'd been harsh, but it was reality. She may have inadvertently contributed to Sarah's death. Although it seemed unlikely that sexual harassment alone could have driven her to such a drastic step — ending her own life. We still had to interview her family to find out what had contributed to her suicide, but Lynden and the rest of the company should be ashamed of themselves for failing to protect Sarah.

As Lynden cried, Hirsch shook his head at me like I'd gone too far. Maybe, but perhaps it would get her to play straight with us. After a moment, Lynden wiped her eyes with the backs of her hands and sniffled. "You're right. We should have done more to help Sarah. But unfortunately, this happens a lot. There were no witnesses and there was a senior member of the team who contradicted her story."

"I understand how difficult that can be. But you still had a duty to make sure she was safe, even on the off chance the accusation was false."

She nodded. "I did what I could with what I had. After Sarah's last complaint, we put together a specialized sexual harassment seminar for the group, so they understood that all those behaviors weren't acceptable by the company."

"Did it help?"

She shrugged. "Sarah made no more formal complaints. But a few weeks later, she started missing work. Said she was sick. Then she died," Lynden said sadly.

"Did she say why she was calling in sick?"

"She said she had the flu, but I wondered."

"This was Frank's team. What role did he play?" Hirsch asked.

"He met with Sarah. He talked with her and tried to let her know he would do everything he could to help. I think they had a good relationship."

Hirsch said, "I want to interview Frank again. You can let your upper management know that we need you to be forthright with all future investigations because any detail could help us find out what happened to Matt. Omitting information isn't advised and could be construed as obstructing justice, which comes with jail time."

"Of course. I apologize for not being more forthright earlier. We really thought it wouldn't affect the investigation. Sarah's not here anymore. We figured there was no harm."

"That's not for you to decide."

Full on frazzled at that point, Lynden eked out, "Do you want to speak with Frank or Hannah first?"

Hirsch and I exchanged glances. "We'd like to talk to Frank."

9

HIRSCH

HAD the detectives not pressed Matt's company harder during the original investigation? Or had they not spoken to Hannah? If it weren't for Hannah, we would never have learned about Sarah Nesbit and her complaints against Matt. I just couldn't believe that a young woman would take her own life because she was being harassed at work. Surely, she had to have other mental health issues to take her life. Something wasn't right there. We were missing something. I just didn't know what it was.

Frank Musker strolled into the conference room. Martina and I stood up and shook hands. "Detective. Ms. Monroe. Good to see you again."

"Please have a seat. We have a few follow-up questions about Matt."

He nodded.

Based on how long it took Lynden to bring Frank into the conference room, I would bet money that she explained to him we knew about Sarah.

"I'm going to shoot straight with you. We're not pleased. My partner and I were here two days ago, and we asked you and

Lynden, your head of human resources, if there had ever been any complaints against Matt. You both said no. Do you remember telling us that?"

Frank's cheeks flushed. "I do, and my deepest apologies. We really didn't think the complaints had anything to do with Matt's death."

"Are any of your staff trained investigators? Retired homicide detectives?"

Frank shook his head, as if defeated.

"This is the part where you stop holding back information. My partner and I have solved every case that we have investigated. We will find the truth. With that being said, do you think you can answer our questions honestly and accurately?"

"Yes. Again, I apologize. We should never have withheld the complaints. We didn't want to give Matt a poor reputation."

"We appreciate that," Martina said, her voice dripping with sarcasm.

"Tell us about Sarah. Everything. Please leave nothing out."

Frank glanced down before beginning to speak but stopped and stared at the wall. "Sarah was an angel. She was smart, charismatic, a real go-getter type. Great at her job." Frank hesitated. "During her early months at the company, there had been some banter in the lab. Comments about Sarah and other women. She didn't appreciate it and made it known. She came to me and said that she was uncomfortable with the conversations that were going on. Specifically, about the discussions on women's bodies. I told her I would take care of it."

"Was that before or after her first official complaint?"

"It was well before. This was just a few months in. But then she came back to me again. She complained and said Matt was the ringleader, even though she told him to his face she didn't like the comments and thought it was unprofessional. And I have to admit that, at first, I didn't think there was anything wrong with it. And I admit to partaking in some of that banter. I was guilty too. But I knew it bothered Sarah, so I told the team to cool it."

Martina sighed loudly. "And did they *cool* it?"

"It seemed to fuel the fire. To be honest, this was my first time in a leadership role like this, and I wasn't equipped to handle the situation. In almost every staff meeting, I told them to knock it off with the locker room talk and repeated that it was making some employees uncomfortable. But Matt claimed it was just Sarah and that she was being too sensitive."

"Do you think she was being too sensitive?" Martina asked.

"At first, I thought maybe. It's kind of how things have always been. Most of them came out of academia. Academia is far worse than the environment we had in our lab, but I guess it still wasn't good enough, and I understand that now. I deeply regret not taking more of a stand against it after seeing what it did to Sarah."

"What did it do to Sarah?"

"When she first started working at Vaxxmore, she was bright-eyed, optimistic, happy. Someone who was going places, you know? But as the environment grew uncomfortable for her, and she submitted the complaints, she became more withdrawn. She didn't want to go to group lunches or to after work happy hours."

"What caused her to file a formal complaint?"

"She told me she was fed up with me not doing anything that made any difference. And that's when she went to HR. I made the decision that it was best to keep Matt away from Sarah. Sarah was the only one who had complained. Everybody else went along with things, which I think made it harder on Sarah. She felt like she wasn't being believed or that the old boys' club was winning, and we didn't care how the younger women in the lab felt."

The insight Frank had on Sarah was surprising. He seemed to know a lot about her and how she felt. He said she kept coming to him. Maybe they had a closer relationship than he originally thought. "So, you assigned Sarah to a new supervisor?"

"Yes, but then Matt was upset. He told me it made him look guilty. I guess he took that frustration out on Sarah. She told me what he'd said. She said it was weird, and she was right. Eventually, after weeks of it going on and him not letting up, I had a talk with him and explained if he didn't knock it off, that it would affect his bonus and his performance rating for the year."

It was as if we were seeing a different side of Frank than we had previously. He was sad and full of regret. It was obvious he had cared for Sarah. But how much had he cared? "And then it stopped?"

"It did, but then..." He hesitated again, shaking his head in disbelief. "When she came to me and told me what he did in the back lab, I was furious he had hurt Sarah. And I didn't enjoy being put in the position to discipline senior members of my staff again and again. At that point, Sarah was terrified of him. I told her to not work in the lab unless she had someone other than Matt with her."

Sarah had to find her own protection?

Martina cut in. "So, you believed Sarah?"

"Absolutely."

"Lynden said there was no way to back up her claims, and that's why there were no actions taken against Matt."

"We didn't have proof, but I knew Sarah. She wouldn't have made that up. It just wasn't who she was."

We were still missing a piece of the puzzle. "It sounds like you and Sarah were close?"

Frank sank down into himself. "We had been. It started out innocently enough. I was there for her. She was really upset about what was going on with Matt and so I tried to comfort her and be someone for her to talk to. I hated seeing such a bright light dim because of his constant harassment."

"Why wasn't he fired?" Martina asked, interrupting.

"If I could've proven what he did to her, I would've fired him."

Eyeing Martina, I said, "Back to Sarah and your relationship. You said that she came to you when she was upset."

"She told me she'd cry at lunch. She felt powerless and weak. It started chipping away at her. I tried to distract her from it and let her know there were other people who believed in her and thought she was a brilliant scientist with a brilliant future and then..." He fidgeted with the gold band on his left hand. "A line was crossed. She was such a special person and the way she looked at me. It was flattering, and I didn't discourage it."

"You had a relationship?" Martina asked, brows raised.

"We went out to lunch a few times, just the two of us. Mostly innocent. But then we attended a conference, and we spent the night together. The entire conference, we were inseparable. But after we were back home, I told her it was a mistake and it couldn't happen again. I'm married, and I had to honor that. She told me it wasn't a mistake and that she was in love with me. She said she wanted to be with me. I told her that could never happen."

The missing piece of the puzzle. The man she loved rejected her and then discarded her. "When did you tell her things were over?"

He stared down at the floor. "Two weeks before she died."

Martina's eyes widened. I did a quick head nod. Between the daily harassment and then her lifeline, a man she'd grown to love, rejecting her... "When was the last time you spoke with Sarah?"

Frank looked up at us. "She called me the day before she

died and told me that the only thing she ever wanted was for me to be happy and that she hoped I had a good life." Tears formed in Frank's eyes. "I never thought..." He shook his head and wiped at the corners of his eyes before taking a breath and straightening up in his seat.

"How did Matt react to Sarah's death?" Martina asked.

"He didn't seem bothered by it. He just kind of said that's too bad or something insensitive like that. He held a grudge against Sarah for all her complaints. I don't think it was because they were false. I think it was because he didn't like being told he wasn't allowed to do something. And he was hell bent on proving he could do whatever he wanted. And that's partly my fault."

"Did you love Sarah?"

"What is love?" he asked, as if he didn't believe in the notion.

"Love is caring about another person so deeply that their pain is your own. For example, I have a wife at home eight months pregnant, and I would do just about anything to keep a smile on her beautiful face."

Frank shrugged. "Well, I wouldn't blow up my entire world for her. It's just not something I would do even if... I loved her that way."

Could Frank have a motive to take out Matt? He had made his job more difficult, and he had hurt Sarah, a woman he felt deeply for.

"Thank you for meeting with us again. This has been very helpful."

He got up and turned. "Will this be public?"

"Not unless it needs to be."

"My wife doesn't know."

"Like I said, if there's not a reason to bring it up, it doesn't need to leave this room."

He nodded and quietly exited the conference room. I turned to Martina. "Wow."

"No kidding. What is this place? Lying to the police? Harassment? Affairs? Frank has to be twenty years older than Sarah, right? What else will we find if we keep digging around?"

"The CoCo County Sheriff's Department doesn't look so bad now, does it?"

"Well, we have found no killers at Vaxxmore — yet. So I think CoCo County can keep the trophy."

"Point taken. We should do a full background on Sarah — go deeper. It sounds like she didn't have any known existing mental health conditions that could've led to her suicide. Maybe the combination of the daily bullying from Matt and the rejection from Frank was a major contributor."

Martina said, "Are you thinking if we find out more about Sarah, it might lead to more women who had complaints against Matt?"

"I think so. If there was another victim of Matt's out there, maybe Sarah knew her. Maybe it was one of his victims who killed him. The murderer did use poison, which is fairly common with female killers."

"You're right. We keep following the path of Sarah's death, and we'll probably get closer to the truth."

I was about to speak when Hannah walked into the room. She looked just as nervous as before. "Good to see you again, Hannah."

"Hi."

"We've looked into Sarah's employment and found that she had many complaints about Matt. Did you know about that?"

She nodded.

"We've been told that the harassment from Matt had been going on for a long time."

"It had, but she wasn't alone. He harassed others, too. She was the only one with any guts to say anything about it."

"He treated you that way too?"

"He treated all women like that. He was a pig."

Ouch. Hannah was no longer holding back. Good for us, bad for Matt.

"Do you know why nobody said anything? You're the only one who even mentioned Sarah."

"Everyone else is probably just too scared to lose their jobs. Everyone knows Frank was protecting Matt."

"Why would Frank protect Matt?"

"No idea. But it seemed like Matt could do whatever he wanted and nothing bad would ever happen to him. Well, until someone killed him."

From what Hannah had said, I had a feeling there were a lot more people with motive to end Matt than we had originally thought. Every woman who had ever worked with Matt could be a potential suspect.

10

MARTINA

As I had suspected, Matt Baldwin was no saint. Hannah confirmed it, as did Frank. There was another side to Matt. One that most people either didn't talk about or wouldn't admit to themselves. People like Matt usually had flaws in their facade, which was why I couldn't wait to re-interview Matt's wife and ask her if she knew about the complaints against him and what it was really like to live with Matt.

There were several telltale signs of an abusive father and spouse, but sometimes you have to dig hard to get the survivors to divulge the details to complete the picture. Did he run the house like a dictatorship? Did his family have to cater to his every whim? Did he expect women to take traditional gender roles? My guess was Matt thought he was superior to all females and could do whatever he wanted to them.

It was interesting how just a few days earlier we had zero suspects or motive for murder, and now it seemed as if there could be multiple. How had the original investigators missed all of this? Were they afraid to pry apart Matt's life in fear of what his brother might do if it tarnished the Baldwin name?

We pulled up to the home of Gina Baldwin and her two

children. During the last visit by the original investigators, she'd played the role of a grieving widow. Could she keep up the act? Was it real? "Ready for this, Hirsch?"

"You bet."

He opened the door and paused, but stopped and answered his phone. After a quick, "Hold on a sec," he spoke into the phone. "Hey. What's up?" His eyes widened. "Are you sure?" Nodding, he said, "Okay, I'll be right there." Hirsch turned to me with a mix of terror and excitement in his eyes. "Kim's having contractions."

"Is she going into labor?"

"She's having contractions. She needs to go to the hospital."

"All right, I'll drive."

"The interview?" he asked.

"Give me two seconds. I'll tell Mrs. Baldwin we'll be back later." Before I hopped out of the car, I said to him, "It'll be okay."

As I approached the front door of the rather stately home, the door opened. "Ms. Monroe. Is everything okay?"

"Yes. But I'm so sorry, my partner's wife has just gone into labor. I need to take him to her. Would it be okay if I came back in about an hour?"

"Yes, of course, that's fine. Tell your partner good luck."

"Will do."

Back behind the wheel, I turned to Hirsch. "Are you ready for your life to change?"

Worry was etched all over his face. "I don't know. I think so."

With a knowing smile, I drove safely to Hirsch's house.

WITH HIRSCH and Kim at the hospital, I returned to the Baldwin home. This was probably better anyhow. Going alone would allow me to speak to Mrs. Baldwin woman to woman. Sitting at her dining table, I accepted the tea she had offered. "Thank you again for being so accommodating."

"How is the detective's wife?"

"She's with her doctor. No word yet when the big event will happen."

"Is it his first child?"

"It is."

"Is he nervous?"

"Absolutely. Hirsch has been my partner for nearly three years, and this is the most nervous I have ever seen him, and we've been shot at," I said with a smile.

"I'm sure. I remember when I learned I was pregnant with Penny. I was so excited and so was Matt. We hadn't been trying long, so we knew she was a miracle."

With Gina Baldwin sitting across from me looking pensive, I said, "I felt the same way with my Zoey. She was a surprise miracle."

"Sometimes those can be the greatest gift."

"Indeed." Pausing, I knew I had to get to the hard part. "I'd like to ask you some follow-up questions about Matt."

"Of course."

"I have to warn you, some questions I may ask are a little sensitive."

"Oh?"

"We interviewed some of Matt's coworkers and the head of HR. Did you know Matt had complaints against him?"

"Complaints? What complaints?"

Gina didn't know, or she was a talented actress.

"There were several complaints of sexual harassment against your husband."

Gina's brown eyes widened. "Sexual harassment?"

"Yes, there were multiple complaints."

With her hand on her chest, she shook her head. "I didn't know. What did they claim he had done?"

"Mostly verbal harassment, bullying, and taunting as retaliation after the complaints. But there were a few instances where he'd gotten physical with a female employee."

"Physical?"

"Unwanted massages and then he forced a kiss upon her."

She gasped.

Actress? I didn't think so.

Gina's cheeks were crimson, but I couldn't tell if she was angry or about to burst into tears. "Do you ever think that we don't *really* know anyone at all?"

The question made me think she knew exactly who her husband was, and he wasn't the perfect man she had previously described. "Do the allegations against Matt surprise you?"

"A little." She wiped away a tear. "I suppose. But not as much as they should."

"During the first round of interviews by the original investigators, everyone had claimed that Matt was beloved — no enemies, and no faults. Second round of interviews, almost everyone said the same thing except one. That person led us to the discovery of complaints against him. Upon further investigation, I'd say it wasn't a secret Matt wasn't so perfect."

Mrs. Baldwin sipped on her tea. "Perhaps no one was asking the right questions."

"Perhaps, but from what I have found, I have a feeling Matt's behavior wasn't contained in the workplace, but more of a pattern of how a person behaves at work, at home, and in the outside world. But also somebody with enough authority to get away with it."

"You know his brother is the sheriff?" she asked with

sarcasm. "You know the implication, right? There's no protection when your husband has a brother in blue."

My logical brain had told me Gina had likely been a victim of domestic violence, but I didn't always like being right. "The sheriff was clear to us he wanted full transparency on the investigation. Whatever it is we find, even if his brother doesn't come out looking like a hero. But we haven't given him an update yet. How do you think he'll respond to the complaints lodged against his brother?"

She shrugged. "I don't know. He had to have known what his brother was like. John's a good guy. I used to wonder how it was they came from the same family. From the outside, they seemed alike in appearance, but when John talked about honor and loyalty, he meant it. When Matt said it, I'm not so sure he did."

"How did Matt treat you? When I ask that, I mean, did he treat you as an equal partner in the marriage? Did you have a say in how the money was spent, how the home was kept, and how the children were raised?"

She laughed bitterly. "Well, you do know how to ask the right questions, don't you?"

"I've been doing this for a while. I'm currently on contract at the CoCo County Sheriff's Department, but my firm specializes in helping victims of intimate partner violence leave their abusers. I'm well versed in the more subtle signs and the red flags of an abuser."

She glanced up at the stairwell. "The children are upstairs. I don't want them to hear. I tried to shield them as much as I could." Returning her attention to me, she said, "Matt was in charge of everything. He dictated what we ate, what activities we took part in, and what classes and sports the children would partake in. He didn't see me as an equal or like I was an actual person. My job was to take care of his home and raise his children and do whatever he wanted. I wasn't a friend or a partner. We were young when we got married, and I didn't know any better. Do I miss him? No. I mourned our relationship long ago. And now, watching the kids in his absence, I'm actually glad he's gone. I thought I had been shielding them, but I was wrong. Since Matt has been gone, it's like everybody in the home has let out the breath we'd all been holding. The kids can now choose their activities. Aaron quit basketball, which he hated, and is now playing soccer. Penny quit piano and now is taking art classes. They're so much happier."

So many parents stayed in bad relationships to avoid hurting the children, but it was inevitable. Kids were like sponges. "Now they get to be themselves."

"Yeah. For me, I'm still trying to figure out what that looks like."

"Did he ever physically harm you?"

She shook her head. "No, he never did that. But do I think he could have? Yes, but I mostly just did what he said to keep the peace for the kids. I didn't want them to see a man hit a woman. I didn't want Aaron to think that's how a man should behave because it isn't."

Tears escaped Gina's eyes. Her husband had kept her like a prisoner, and it was clear she was glad he was gone. Motive? *Yes.* Means? *Unclear.* Opportunity? *Absolutely.*

11

MARTINA

"Where's your other half?" Vincent asked with a puzzled look on his face.

"He's with his other half. Kim started having contractions."

"No kidding. Kim's in labor?"

My phone buzzed. "Speaking of the devil." Answering, I teased, "Papa Hirsch, is that you?"

"It's me. But not a papa yet. Doc says it's Braxton Hicks."

I would have to wait a little longer before I cradled a newborn again. I had been so looking forward to it; I hadn't held an infant since Zoey was one. "Is the doctor sending you home?"

"We're home now."

"Consider it a trial run."

He sounded tired. "I guess so. How did things go at the Baldwin house?"

"Enlightening. It was as we suspected. Matt's bad demeanor toward women didn't end in the workplace. He ran his home like he was the captain of a ship full of prisoners."

"Bad for anyone who came across him, but good for us. We now have a better picture of who this guy was. Are you going home soon?"

It was only two-thirty. "No, I'm going to catch up with Vincent and follow up on a few things."

"Do you think you can manage without me? Kim's a little shook."

Hirsch could be so silly. "Absolutely. Stay home and take care of Kim. We've got it under control."

"Thanks, Martina."

"Tell Kim I said hello and to hang in there."

"Will do."

After putting away my phone, I turned back to Vincent. "False alarm. The baby is going to cook a little longer."

"That's good. It's too early, right?"

"It is. She's not due for another four weeks."

"Then good. And I have some news for you. I finished the preliminary background on Sarah Nesbit."

"Anything interesting?"

"I don't have medical records, but I do have names and addresses for her family members and the report from her suicide."

"Is it bad?" That was a dumb question. Suicide was always bad. It was tragic that someone could lose all hope for brighter days and think the only way to end one's suffering was to end their life.

"It wasn't pretty. Bathtub. Razor blades. You get the picture."

After a silent prayer for Sarah, I asked, "Who found her?"

"Sister."

Heartbreaking. "Any indications of foul play?"

What if Matt had killed Sarah as the ultimate revenge? At that point, I'd put nothing past him. Or did Frank kill her to keep their affair from coming to the surface?

"The report said there was no sign of forced entry or signs of a struggle."

Doesn't mean someone, like Frank, couldn't have coaxed themselves inside, slipped her something to knock her out, and then staged the suicide. "What about the toxicology report?"

"Blood alcohol was 0.15."

Yikes. She was twice the legal limit for impaired driving, which meant she was pretty intoxicated. "Do you have the crime scene photos?"

"Yep."

Vincent hurried to the table, then ushered me over to the bulletin board and pinned up the photos. "Here is the entry to the cabin. No sign of forced entry. No shoe prints. The hallway is clear. The only sign something was off was in the bathroom. These are her clothes on the floor and then..."

He stopped describing the scene when the image of Sarah in a tub filled with water and her blood was displayed. She appeared as if she was sleeping. Moving closer, I studied the close-up photo the medical examiner took of the wounds on her wrists. They were a straight vertical line. Sarah, or someone else, knew what they were doing. Had Sarah been sober enough to make a straight line?

Pointing to the photo, I said, "If you were as drunk as Sarah, could you have made that straight of a cut?"

Vincent stepped closer to study the picture. "That's a good question. Maybe. Maybe not. Do you think she didn't take her own life?"

Unsure. Based on what we learned from Frank, I thought she could have, but then again, if Frank killed her, his testimony was unreliable. "Not sure. Looking at all angles."

"Got it. Well, let me know if there's anything else I can get you. If you need extra hands or boots on the ground, put me in, coach."

"Based on our interviews today, we need to look further into Sarah Nesbit's life. We need to talk to anybody she may have confided in about what was going on with her. Like her sister. We should set up an interview."

Before I could continue, the door to the squad room opened and Sheriff Baldwin strutted in. The room fell into silence with all eyes on the sheriff. Not a single sheriff had visited our squad room since its inception. "Sheriff Baldwin, this is a surprise."

"Hi, Martina. Where's Hirsch?"

"His wife went into premature labor. Everything's fine now, but they're at home resting. Is there something I can do for you?"

"I was hoping I could get an update on my brother's case."

"Sure. We have an update and some leads we're following."

"That's not very specific."

I turned around, and the rest of the squad room remained focused on us. "Would you prefer we talked in your office?"

The sheriff furrowed his brow. "Sure." On the way out, he said, "How bad is it?"

"It's not pretty."

He nodded and led me into his office. Seated behind his desk, the sheriff said, "I knew my brother wasn't perfect. I meant it when I said he didn't have any known enemies. I didn't know any of them, but I knew how he was. He wasn't always respectful toward people. Full transparency, Martina. I want to know what happened to my brother, even if that means you expose some of his dirty secrets. It sounds like he had some. Like I told you and Hirsch before, I'm not like LaFontaine. I just want the truth. I'm not in the business of covering up crimes, even if it makes my brother's or my family name look bad."

Time would tell if we could take him at his word. "We've learned there were several sexual harassment complaints against Matt. Two of the complaints were actual physical assaults where he could have been arrested. There was one particular woman at work who he put most of his energy into. She was the only one who ever made a formal complaint against him. Everybody else, from what we could gather, was too scared to say anything."

"Have you interviewed this woman?"

"No, she died by suicide the year before Matt's death."

The sheriff leaned back and ran his fingers through his hair. "How old was she?"

"She was twenty-five."

The sheriff stared off, as if processing the information. "I can't understand why he would do something like that. He had everything. Why would he treat a young woman like that?"

"I don't know, Sheriff. But I also spoke with Gina after we confirmed the harassment complaints. It sounds like Matt's need for control over women and everybody in his life didn't stop in the workplace. He controlled his wife and his children down to what they wore, what activities they participated in, and what food they ate. Classic abuse."

Sheriff Baldwin shook his head. "In my line of work, I should've seen the signs. I should've known. I should have said something. Did he ever get physical with Gina and the kids?"

"Gina says no. She said she did whatever he told her to do so the children wouldn't see him be violent. She didn't want Aaron to follow in his footsteps. But Gina knew he was capable."

The sheriff sat silently, staring down at his desk, as if trying to come to terms with what I had told him. "I appreciate what you're doing. I know as well as you that most people don't get killed for no reason. Especially somebody like Matt. Somebody wanted him dead. Maybe he did bad things, but he didn't deserve to die."

Agreed. If Matt broke the law, he should be in prison, not dead. "We're looking into the young woman's death. We'll question friends and family to see if she confided in them or found more of Matt's victims. Perhaps there was somebody else who may have had a motive to kill Matt."

"Thank you."

His silence and distant gaze were all the evidence I needed to know our talk was over. I showed myself out.

If Sheriff Baldwin was good police, like my gut said he was, he had to have known his brother was into something dirty to end up in the crosshairs of a killer.

12

ANDREA

Outside the Bay Area, my mind softened, and my nerves calmed. Going to the cabin always made me feel better. Mom and Dad hadn't returned since Sarah died. Most people don't want to visit the scene of where their daughter's lifeless body was discovered. For me, it brought me comfort, and I felt closer to her. Or maybe I thought she was still there and would remain trapped until she was ready to go to her forever resting place. I was undecided on whether ghosts existed. Either way, there was a force that continued to pull me there.

Sarah had called me that day. Three hours before I found her. Through sobs, she told me she loved me and that she wanted me to know I was the best sister. Her words were slurred, and I knew she had been drinking. The call frightened me. As soon as I ended the call, I left work and rushed to the family cabin in Tahoe. It had taken me three hours.

Upon entering the home, I yelled, "Sarah! Sarah!" My voice echoed throughout the cabin as I ran from room to room. I jogged downstairs and saw the light on in the bathroom. The door was open. The cabin was quiet. Too quiet.

With dread, I stepped closer and into the bathroom. My baby sister lay with her head turned to the side, eyes shut, as if she were sleeping. The bath water was crimson. Her left hand resting on the edge. It was ice cold and stiff to the touch.

As I backed away, my mind couldn't process what I was seeing. It took me ten minutes before I could find the energy to call for help.

I knew she was dead.

The medical examiner said she likely died two to three hours before I arrived. If I'd paid closer attention, I would have known that her impromptu trip to the cabin that day was a sign. She was devastated and saying things like her world no longer had meaning. I argued and told her things would turn around. She had a bright future ahead of her and could find a new job. She could even move. The world was hers. Something in me knew I should have called in sick and gone with her. If I had, she'd still be alive.

I owed it to her to make things right.

The cabin fueled my passion and gave me my purpose. Nobody should have to go through what she had. My sister had paid for those creepy old men's sins with her life. And I intended to reclaim those fees.

It was through Sarah's death that I found my purpose. Sure, I had gone through the mourning phase where I was angry and I was sad and I was heartbroken. But I knew I couldn't just leave things how they were. I couldn't be there to stop Sarah before she took her life, but I could make sure what happened to her would never happen to any other woman at the hands of those men. Sarah would've liked that.

My only concern at this point was that the investigators were getting a little too close for comfort, and I didn't like their second visit to the office.

At my destination, there were two other cars in the driveway. *Good, they're here.* About to park, my phone buzzed. A number I didn't recognize. Car set to park, I said, "Hello."

"Is this Andrea Puerto?"

"Yes, who is this?"

"My name is Vincent Teller, and I'm with the CoCo County Sheriff's Department."

At that moment, it felt like the forest was spinning and I was in a dizzying tornado of branches and bark. I stumbled out of my SUV and started panting.

"Ms. Puerto?"

Steadying myself on the side of my car, I said, "Yes, this is she. How can I help you?"

Staring at the gravel driveway, I told myself to get it together. *Act normal. Don't ruin everything you've worked so hard for.*

"I work with Detective Hirsch and Martina Monroe. They're investigating the death of Matt Baldwin, and we've learned that your sister Sarah worked with Matt. The investigators would like to talk to you about Sarah. Is there a time you could come down to the station and speak with them?"

The trees were closing in on me. Soon, they would push me down into a hole until I sank so far there was no way out. *Pull it together, Andrea.* "Sure, of course. What time would be good?"

"The investigators are available any time. What's best for you, ma'am?"

"I'm out of town right now. I'll be back in the Bay Area on Monday. Does Monday work?"

"Perfect. Is there a specific time that would be best for you?"

"Three o'clock."

"Great. I'll let Martina and Hirsch know. You have a good day."

He hung up before I could whisper, "You too."

With every ounce of energy, I pushed my shoulders back and headed toward the front door. I stopped, turned around, gazing at the surrounding forest, my vision clear. The mission was too important. It must go on. I had to stop the detectives and their investigation.

13

MARTINA

AFTER FILLING Hirsch in on the details of Sarah Nesbit's autopsy and showing him the photos, I waited to see if he had the same questions I did. He looked perplexed and said, "Any chance it wasn't suicide?"

Of course, Hirsch would question it. He was the best investigator I had ever worked with. Based on the circumstances in Sarah's life, her manner of death should have been questioned. "I think we should look into it..."

Before I could say more, Vincent approached. "Hey, Hirsch. How's Kim?"

"She's doing well. A little anxious and is fussing around the house with her mom, making sure everything is ready for the baby. I keep telling her to rest, but she flitters around the house cleaning windowsills and the oven. They call it nesting."

"It's perfectly normal. She'll be fine," I assured him.

Vincent said, "I'm glad everything worked out."

"Me too. What's up?"

"I found something kind of interesting."

"Oh?"

Vincent said, "Reviewing Sarah Nesbit's autopsy report, it

got me curious. So I pulled the autopsy and crime scene photos for Matt Baldwin."

Vincent never ceased to amaze me. He was an exceptionally dedicated researcher, and his ability to make connections was impressive. "Any similarities?"

Vincent shook his head. "No. Totally different. But it really got me thinking. Matt Baldwin was a man with no history of drug abuse, yet he dies of a heroin overdose. They found him in his car the morning of March ninth. Dead. No injection sites found, which means the heroin had to be ingested. It's highly unusual, right?"

"Absolutely. Did you find something else?" I wasn't sure where Vincent was going with this. We had thoroughly reviewed Matt Baldwin's autopsy and crime scene photos, and other than his manner of death and questions about how the poison was ingested, it was rather unremarkable.

But we knew Vincent loved his theatrics. He typically gave us the minute details in a dramatic fashion that, on more than one occasion, ended up cracking a case wide open. I hoped this was one of those times.

"Well, I thought it was super weird. How and who could poison a middle-aged man? Food and drink are really the only options."

Hirsch leaned back in his seat. "Are you thinking the wife could have poisoned his food? He was an abuser. She had a motive. They found him in the morning on a weekday in the parking lot of a strip mall where his favorite coffee shop was located. And no coffee cup was found in his car, so the original investigators presumed he never made it inside or he drank it inside the shop. The staff didn't remember serving him but said they were busy, and it was possible they had. If they hadn't served him, he had to have ingested the poison either at his house or on the way to the coffee shop from his house. It could be the wife. It fits."

It was an original theory, but the forensics team didn't find any trace of heroin inside the Baldwin home or in his car. There was no trace of it anywhere other than inside of Matt Baldwin.

"That was what I thought too — at first. But think about it. If you were a killer barista with half a brain, you would tell the police you didn't serve Matt. And you'd get rid of the cup after he passed out. I don't think you can rule out a barista."

It was an interesting idea. "That's something to consider. According to his wife's original statement, he stopped at the coffee shop every morning on the way to work. He'd take it to go and then toss the empty at work. If someone knew his routine, they could have spiked it. It could have been a patron as opposed to a barista. The notes said he often used the drive through when he was in a hurry."

"We should re-question the staff at the coffee shop. Maybe he'd made enemies there or... a romantic connection gone sour?" Hirsch suggested.

It was definitely a lead to pursue. When I had read the original investigation reports, I didn't think too much of his habit of going to the local coffee shop every day, considering the staff had been thoroughly questioned by the original team of investigators. But if a patron had spiked the drink, it would fit. But who was it? At that point, who killed Matt and why was wide open. Had we yet to uncover an affair? There had been no evidence, but then again, the original investigation also said he was picture perfect with no enemies. "I think it's time we disregard the original investigation and act as if it's brand new. I think little of the original investigation is reliable."

Hirsch nodded. "I agree."

"Exactly. Except for one little detail we should take and run with."

A twist?

"What do you mean?"

"The ME didn't make a mistake. Matt Baldwin died by an overdose of heroin that was likely ingested through food or beverage. It's pretty unusual, so you'd think his case was rare, right?" Vincent sat down on the table and folded his arms across his chest. "I searched for similar causes of death, poisoning by heroin ingested from food or beverage. And you want to take a guess what I found?"

"It's not so rare?"

Vincent said, "Oh no, it's rare. By my count, there were exactly three in the state of California the year Matt died. All under hauntingly similar circumstances."

Three deaths with the same cause. Could that be a coincidence?

"Are you thinking what I'm thinking?" Vincent asked with a gleam in his eyes.

Doubtful. "What's that?"

"Serial killer."

Another serial killer case? I did not think that was how the case would play out. Did we have to consider the possibility that Matt was a random target and all the leads up to that point were dead ends?

Who were the other victims? What had drawn Matt and the two others to their deaths? Maybe this information was why the original investigative team never found the truth. It was rare to be a victim of a serial killer or to be murdered by someone you didn't know. Was it karma that killed Matt Baldwin?

14

HIRSCH

ANOTHER SERIAL KILLER CASE? Martina was to blame for this. She had a way of attracting the most difficult and off-the-wall cases. Since I started working with her, I'd investigated some of the craziest cases of my twenty-year career in law enforcement. It was like somehow the universe brought them to us. I was sure if I asked Martina about the phenomenon, she'd say it was a gift.

My biggest concern was that if we caught a serial killer case, it could drag on for months, if not longer. It would require more time than I had to give. Once Kim had our baby, there was no way I could leave her alone with a newborn while I was out hunting serial killers. If anything, this job had taught me what was most important in life. There were others who could replace me on the case and investigate the murders, but nobody could replace Kim and the baby.

When I married Kim, I made a vow to her and myself that my family would always come first. They were my top priority. Yes, I had grown soft in my old age. Or maybe it was Kim. I'd fallen in love with her and everything changed. And I had fallen in love with our baby, even though I had never seen her except for the strange black-and-white skeletal outline on the sonogram photos.

In a few weeks, I would have two girls. And as far as I was concerned, it was my number one job to protect them. If Kim went into labor before Matt's case wrapped up, other members of the team would have to take over. And I would just have to deal with that. I couldn't stand to leave a case unfinished, but I was a changed man. "Okay, let's hear it. What are the details? I'm assuming you have them."

Vincent hopped off the desk. "I thought you'd never ask. Please join me at the whiteboard, and I will draw you some pictures. Everybody loves pictures, right?"

Martina said, "You have my full attention, Vincent."

That elicited a grin from Vincent. He was clearly excited to show us what he had found. He had become one of our biggest assets in the Cold Case Squad. He had a sharp intellect and a good sense of judgement.

Vincent drew a timeline and placed three tics. He labeled the first tic March, Walnut Creek, Matt Baldwin. The second tic labeled June, Santa Monica, Kyle Weston. The third tic labeled September, South San Francisco, Larry Henderson.

He turned around to face Martina and me. "One murder. Two murders. Three murders. Equals serial killer. All three men were middle-aged and died from an overdose of heroin they ingested. None had a history of drug abuse or even of dabbling. All three were professionals with families and no financial problems. Matt Baldwin, who we are familiar with, died in Walnut Creek, and they found him inside his car." He pointed to the third tic. "They found Larry Henderson dead in his car in South San Francisco. Both men are middle-aged, working in the pharmaceutical industry."

Martina said, "You're kidding."

Vincent said, "No jokes around here. Not today."

"Did you check employment records? Maybe they knew each other?"

"No overlap, but they were both scientists working in the same area of study. So, it's possible they knew each other through conferences or other professional affiliations. I haven't found a connection yet, but I'm not done looking into it. But both were from the Bay Area, so it's entirely possible."

This case was getting stranger and stranger. "How about our second victim, Kyle?"

"Someone killed Kyle in Santa Monica and left him dead in his car. He works in finance. He was some bigwig executive. Like the others, no history of drug abuse, and he's a middle-aged married man with two kids."

Martina stared at the board. "There is no way these three aren't connected."

"Agreed. But how is our killer targeting these guys? What is the motive?"

Vincent said, "That's the million-dollar question. I'm still working on getting some background on Kyle and Larry. Both cases are unsolved. I've left messages with the homicide teams who handled the cases. I'm hoping the detectives can share notes."

"Do any of them have a criminal history?" I asked.

"No criminal history. From what I gathered from the notes in the database, there were no obvious motives for their murders."

Martina said, "There has to be a connection among these three. We need to find it. There is just about zero chance this is a coincidence, right?"

"Stranger things have happened, but I'm inclined to agree. Did you only check California?" I asked.

Vincent's jaw dropped, and he acted offended. "You underestimate me. Of course, I didn't. But the national search is taking a little longer. I'll let you know when the team is done."

Studying the board, I tried to draw conclusions from the three deaths. But without further background, it was impossible. Although... "You know, all three locations aren't that far apart."

Martina said, "They're all drivable from the Bay Area."

I said, "Exactly. The killer might live in the Bay Area. It would make sense. It would take, what, five, maybe six hours to drive from here to Santa Monica. Easy peasy."

"Okay, so working theory is our killer is based in the Bay Area and is targeting these men for reasons to be determined. That likely rules out Gina Baldwin. Another big question is how are they poisoning the three victims? And how are they getting the heroin?"

I said, "Working theory is food and drink. Heroin is pretty easy to score. Especially in the Bay Area. Does that rule out the whole coffee shop angle? There's no way the same killer works at a coffee shop in all three locations."

Martina said, "Maybe. Maybe not. It could be they work at one or frequent one of them or all of them. Or if they stalked Matt ahead of time, they knew he went there every day and slipped it in. The killer could have stalked the others and learned their routines and somehow slipped the drugs into a food or beverage."

"You don't think it was random?" Vincent asked.

"I don't think so."

Martina said, "Same MO. I don't think it was random."

"Let's wait to hear from the other homicide detectives. Hopefully, when we compare notes, we can come up with a story of what happened to these three guys." There had to be something more than their gender and age range to connect all three victims. And that was exactly what we had to figure out.

15

ANDREA

WITH A HEALTHY DOSE of Xanax in my system, I strutted through the reception area of the CoCo County Sheriff's Department. Detective Hirsch and his partner, Ms. Martina Monroe, wanted to interview me about my sister — no problem. I was completely ready to tell them all I knew regarding Sarah and her demise, as well as what those men had done to her. I was an open book — mostly. It would be my responsibility to make sure they knew only what they needed to. Reaching the desk, I said, "Hello, I'm here to see Detective Hirsch and Martina Monroe."

The woman with black-framed glasses and a hairstyle from 1970 gave a crooked smile. "Hello. I'll need to see your identification."

No problem. I pulled out my ID and slid it over the desk to the old woman.

What things had she seen during her time at the sheriff's department? Based on her age, she had grown up in a world dominated by males who thought they could take what they wanted whenever they wanted it. How men ever thought they were superior to women was a mystery to me. Maybe it was a fake it until you make it situation? My guess was she had been called 'baby' and 'sweetheart' and 'toots' by condescending men all her life with no one saying boo about it. Surely there were stories she could tell. We all had a story.

She handed me a clipboard and said, "And I'll need you to fill in your information on the visitor log."

While I filled in my details, I said, "Have you worked here long?"

She laughed, as if it was a funny question. It wasn't. "Oh, yes. Twenty-five years now. After my kids left the house, I decided I wanted to get a job. I've been here ever since."

"Do you like it here?"

"It's a great place to work."

Sure it is. It was a fact that no less than 40% of the families of law enforcement officers were victims of domestic violence. How nice of an environment could it be when at least 40% of your coworkers terrorized their families?

"You can have a seat. I'll call them."

She slid my ID back over to me, and I thanked her and sat in the uncomfortable visitor chair. Tapping my fingers on my thigh, I studied the reception area. There were plaques on the wall and slogans showing the sheriff's staff, there to serve and protect. *Sure.*

Footsteps approached, and I turned toward the entrance of the office area. Sure enough, the sexy detective and his partner arrived. After I stood up, I smoothed out my skirt and headed toward them.

"Ms. Puerto, it's good to see you again. Thank you for coming down. It really helps us out."

"Anything I can do to help," I said in a cheery tone.

They led me into a small conference room, where they sat me down and offered me beverages. But I wasn't foolish enough to give them my fingerprints or DNA. "No, I'm fine. Thank you."

"The reason we asked you to come down here today is that during our investigation into Matt Baldwin's death, we found that there were several complaints against him by your sister, Sarah."

Oh, I knew every single thing that horrible person had done to Sarah.

Detective Hirsch said, "Were you aware of the complaints?"

"My sister and I were very close. We didn't have secrets. She told me what Matt had done to her. He destroyed something that she had worked so hard for. She was excited when she graduated from college and landed her first job. She loved science and working in the lab. He ruined it. He taunted and bullied her. He touched her and he assaulted her," I said, a little angrier than I meant to, but how could I not?

"Do you recall how long the harassment had been going on?"

"From what Sarah told me, it started a few months after she started working there. She said it just kept escalating, and complaining only made the situation worse. Everything she did to stop him made it worse."

Martina said, "It's awful what happened to your sister. I'm so sorry she had to go through that. Matt should have never gotten away with it."

Maybe this woman wasn't so bad. "I agree." But in the end, he didn't get away with *anything*.

"Did you know of anybody else she had problems with in the office?"

It sounded like they had found out about Frank. He was a piece of garbage. He used my little sister and then threw her away like she was trash. "She had an affair with Frank that didn't end well. At least not for Sarah. He washed his hands of the whole thing with no regard for my sister."

"Can you tell us what she told you? The only details of the affair we have are what Frank told us."

I must admit, I was a bit surprised Frank had told them anything. He'd been so adamant that Sarah keep quiet about their affair. Of course, he didn't want his wife and kids to find out. Frank was practically the same as Matt. Neither gave a damn about Sarah. "She told me they'd gotten close, and they spent time together at work. He told her he genuinely cared about her and wanted to help her through the issues with Matt. They started sharing stories about their lives and hobbies. When they went to a conference together, one thing led to another, and the relationship turned physical. Sarah had fallen pretty hard for him. Like really hard. Like the hardest I'd ever seen. I told her to be careful and that he was a creep. That he was married with kids and that men like him didn't leave their wives. But she insisted he was different and that she hadn't wanted it to happen, but it was what it was." I shook my head. "She was young. At twenty-five, she didn't quite understand how the real world worked. She'd fallen for everything he'd told her."

"You're older than Sarah, right?"

"Yes, that's why we have different last names. We have different fathers. I'm ten years older than Sarah. I *was* ten years older than Sarah."

They nodded, as if they'd gotten all the answers to their questions. "How did the relationship between Sarah and Frank end?"

"A little while after they got back from that conference — where they spent several nights together — he told her it had to end and that it had been a mistake. He said he cared for her, but they didn't have a future."

"How long was that before she died?"

"It was about two weeks beforehand. It devastated her. Sarah felt stupid and used. She was in a really bad way, between what Matt had done to her, making her daily life a living hell, and then Frank discarding her like that. She was destroyed. They did that to her."

Martina frowned, and I deduced she was an empathetic woman. "You were the one to find Sarah."

"I was."

"Did you know she had planned to take her life?"

"I knew she was in a bad way, so I had left work and drove straight to the cabin, but I was too late."

"Do you believe she took her own life?"

Interesting. They weren't questioning me because of Matt Baldwin. They were questioning whether Sarah had really died by suicide. I could use that in my favor. There was more than one way to make a man pay. With blood or his life. It didn't always have to be the same outcome. But just as much of a punishment. "It really surprised me."

"It surprised you even though she was *destroyed*?"

"Sarah never mentioned any plan to kill herself, and I really didn't think she believed in that kind of thing. We were raised Catholic."

"Do you think it's possible someone could have killed her and made it look like a suicide?" the handsome detective asked.

They were smart ones. That would pose a challenge. "It's possible. If someone had been with her before or after I spoke with her, then they absolutely could have."

"Who do you think may have wanted to hurt your sister?"

"Obviously Frank or Matt, right? Matt was furious she had complained, and there was Frank who wanted to silence her. What better way to silence someone than to kill them?" I said, straight-faced.

"Do you have any reason to believe he killed her? Did he make any threats?"

"Whether they killed her with their own hand or if they didn't, either way, they are both responsible for her death. I'm not sure if they did it themselves, but it may be something to look into. The original investigators didn't think it was very credible that they had been responsible, but I knew my sister and, from what I heard of Matt and Frank, they were both capable of horrible, horrible things. Even murder."

Martina looked at me skeptically. She wasn't buying my story, or was she simply studying me and wondering what else there was for me to tell them? She said, "You started working at Vaxxmore a few months before Matt died. Is that correct?"

"It is."

Kudos. They were asking the right questions, but it wouldn't do them any good. "What made you choose to work at Vaxxmore after Sarah's death?"

They were good, but I was smarter. And of course I thought they would ask about this. It was the right thing to ask. I knew this duo's reputation, and I was prepared. "We don't work in the same departments or cross paths very often, but being where Sarah worked the last three years of her life makes me feel closer to her. It's the same reason I still visit the cabin. I know most people feel the opposite. They can't stand to be at the crime scene or have such heavy reminders of their lost loved ones, but for me, it makes me feel close to Sarah, as if she's still with me." I may have sounded like a loon, but I didn't care what these two thought of me.

The two investigators looked at one another, as if asking each other if they were done. The two acted as if they could communicate without words at all. That must be how they could solve all those cases on the news. Would they be able to solve this case if there was only one of them? That was an interesting avenue to consider.

Detective Hotty said, "Thank you so much for coming down today. We'll reach out if we have any more questions or find anything that could shed light on what happened to Sarah."

"I appreciate that, Detective. And you too, Ms. Monroe."

"You're very welcome, and we're very sorry for your loss."

"Thank you." We said our goodbyes, and they escorted me outside. Before heading to my car, I said, "Good luck with the investigation." After what I had planned for them, they would need it.

WALKING BACK to the squad room, I couldn't shake the feeling something was off about Andrea. Her reason for working at Vaxxmore didn't jive. And it was weird that we had met her in the Vaxxmore office and she didn't mention she was Sarah's sister. Why had she held that information back? Why keep it a secret?

Her rage toward Matt and Frank was obvious, even though she tried hard to conceal it. This told me she was not likely to be forthcoming with information. Her responses appeared to be contrived. I didn't trust her. Maybe she had mental health issues. Maybe mental health issues ran in her family. Perhaps Sarah's suicide was because of undiagnosed depression?

Inside the squad room, I said, "What did you think of Andrea?"

Hirsch scratched his chin, as if contemplating what his opinion of Sarah's sister was. "I wasn't too suspicious until she tried to explain why she worked at Vaxxmore. It's weird."

"It is unusual. Especially since I don't think anybody at Vaxxmore knows Andrea is Sarah's sister."

"I don't think so either, and that's strange. But maybe she

wants to keep it quiet so people don't bring up Sarah and bum her out."

"True. But to play devil's advocate, if she isn't working there to be closer to her sister, why would she work at Vaxxmore?"

Vincent strolled over. "How did the interview with the sister go?"

"It was interesting. She knew about everything."

"Why is that interesting?" he asked, perplexed.

Hirsch said, "Because she works at Vaxxmore but didn't work there until after Sarah died. That's odd, right?"

Vincent scrunched up his face. "That's weird. Did you ask her why she wanted to work there?"

"She said it was so she could feel closer to her sister. She says she also visits the cabin where Sarah died for the same reason." I hoped Vincent could provide some insight since he was a young person. Maybe that's what young people did? It was pretty unusual.

Vincent shrugged. "If she wanted to plot revenge against Matt or Frank, it would get her close to her victims. If I was planning to kill somebody, I would want to understand their routines and their habits, but I don't think I would go so far as to work with them. Or would I?" He stared off, as if contemplating how to commit the perfect murder.

If I were plotting to kill, I wouldn't start working with my target either. The police almost always interview and investigate those closest to the victim, like their friends, family, and coworkers. It wasn't a smart move. "If she took the job to plot her revenge and concoct a murder plot, she'd put herself at the top of the suspect list, along with all the other friends, family, and coworkers. It's not very smart, and she seems pretty clever to me."

Vincent raised his pointer finger, rather dramatically. "True, but then again, she hasn't been interviewed until now. And the only reason you interviewed her now was to determine if there was reason to believe Sarah didn't die by suicide. Not to determine if she's a suspect with a motive to kill Matt."

He had a point. "True. And after what she told us, I think she has a motive for killing Matt. Revenge. She blames him and Frank for her sister's death. And it's strange that she didn't tell anyone Sarah was her sister."

"Strange enough to kill?" Hirsch asked.

"I don't know, but we need a full background on Andrea Puerto. Let's figure out what she's all about. Let's check her alibi and whereabouts around the time of Matt's death. Although we still don't know how he ingested the heroin, or how she could have poisoned him. It might rule her out."

"Are we now considering Andrea killed Matt but not the other two?" Vincent asked.

That was a fair question. Whoever killed Matt had also likely killed the other two men. Andrea didn't exactly fit that profile, but not all killers fit a defined profile.

"Unclear at this point. We'll do a background and keep gathering information on the other two murders."

"And since Andrea implied that Matt and Frank were responsible for her sister's death, we'll need to check out both men's alibis for the time of Sarah's death."

One murder was tricky to solve. Three, four with Sarah, was even more so, especially when spread over a large geographical area. We would spend the next several days in the car tracking down leads. Hirsch had a wife who could go into labor at any time. Maybe I should suggest Vincent to be my travel buddy.

"How likely is it Frank killed Sarah?"

"Honestly, I don't know. Andrea spoke to her sister three hours before she died. You would think that Sarah would've mentioned if Frank was visiting — if she knew he was coming. He could have followed Sarah to the cabin and ambushed her.

There was no sign of forced entry, but Sarah likely would have let Frank inside without a fuss."

"True."

"Sarah died during regular work hours. If either Frank or Matt were responsible, Vaxxmore HR should have records of their absence. We can also re-interview Frank. We need to ask him about any conferences or affiliations Matt was involved in anyhow."

Vincent said, "If it helps, I can call ahead to HR and ask for Frank and Matt's alibi for Sarah's death before you head back for interviews."

"That would be helpful, and while you're at it, can you set up another time for us to interview Frank and Lynden?"

"You got it, boss."

Vincent hurried off, and I sat down next to Hirsch. "Does something feel off about all of this?"

"I think there are still a lot of unknowns. Once we talk to the other detectives and confirm how Sarah died, it might paint us a clearer picture."

Fingers crossed.

17

MARTINA

Seated across from Frank, I noted that he appeared relaxed. Not on edge. At least not yet. His office was tidy, with large windows and plenty of seating. We hoped to interview him in his office this round to make him comfortable on his own turf. If he was at ease, perhaps he would tell us everything we wanted to know. "Thank you for meeting with us again. We have a few questions we think you can help us with."

"Of course, anything I can do to help."

Hirsch said, "First, we'd like to ask you more about Sarah."

Frank's face grew pale. *Guilt.* Was he guilty because he killed her or guilty because he broke her heart after leading her on for months — or years? "We would like to know where you were on the day of April third, the day Sarah died."

His body relaxed, suggesting he had a solid alibi. Well, at least we could check him off our suspect list. "I was here at work. You can ask several people. I was in meetings from morning until late that night with the rest of the leadership team, preparing for an investor meeting the next day."

When Vincent had called to request the records from the HR department, Lynden informed him they didn't keep diligent attendance records. So, it was possible that one or both of the men could have called in sick that day without a record, which meant we had to confirm alibis for both Matt and Frank the old-fashioned way. "Who was with you in those meetings?"

"All the executives. The heads of each of the departments. A few of them have offices down the hall. Or you can check with our admin. She manages all of our schedules."

If he were in meetings all day, Frank couldn't have driven to the cabin three hours from the office to kill Sarah. "It would be helpful if you could write down the names of the people you were in meetings with."

He nodded and pulled a notepad in front of him and began scribbling on the paper. He slipped the paper across his desk, and I took it. Glancing at the paper, I noted he'd provided names and their titles. If he hadn't killed Sarah himself, could he have hired out the deed? "Do you recall seeing Matt in the office that evening?"

"He wasn't part of those discussions in the late afternoon and evening, but you can ask the lab personnel. They're likely to remember. The day was memorable since she hadn't called in sick but was a no show. We didn't learn about her death until the next morning."

"Will the lab personnel be able to verify if Matt was here the day Sarah died?"

"Do you think someone killed Sarah?"

"We're being thorough. Vaxxmore had two employees die within a year of each other. We want to make sure we investigate every connection."

"I never thought to question whether or not it was really suicide."

"Did she seem suicidal to you?"

"I hadn't thought so. But she was really down and had been missing a lot of work."

Frank seemed distracted, as if his thoughts were in overdrive. "But who would want to hurt Sarah?"

Hirsch cleared his throat. "Do you mean other than Matt?"

Frank shrugged. "I know Matt did horrible things to Sarah, and it made me furious, but I don't think he would've killed her. Were there signs of a struggle at the crime scene?"

"No." It was a valid point. There was no way Sarah would have let Matt into the cabin without a fight. There would have been signs of forced entry and some sort of struggle. But there had been none. We were being extra careful and verifying Sarah died by suicide and not by murder, but I was starting to think it was, in fact, suicide.

"Do you know Andrea Puerto?"

He cocked his head, as if trying to figure out how he knew the name. "I think she's in legal. I'm not sure if we've had any dealings together. Why?"

"Did you know she is Sarah's sister?"

The only way I could describe Frank's face was frozen — too stunned to move. Finally, he stuttered, "No. She is? I hadn't made the connection. I knew Sarah had an older sister... and it's Andrea who works here? Down the hall?"

"Yes, she started working here about six months after Sarah's death."

"That's weird, right?" Frank asked.

"I don't know. Do you think it is?" I asked, trying to lure a useful response.

"Well, yes. Why would she want to work here after Sarah died?"

Studying him, I said, "She said it makes her feel closer to Sarah."

Frank squished up his face, as if he thought it wasn't a legitimate reason, and then he said, "Sarah talked about her sister. And you know, I think she said her name was Andrea. I never put two and two together. I should say something to her, right? Condolences."

"No, I think it's best you don't. She knows about you and Sarah. And she's not your biggest fan. And as long as we're investigating, we would prefer you don't mention this to others at the company."

He nodded, still dazed by the revelation.

"During our interviews, someone made a comment that you were protecting Matt because he had something on you. What is that?"

He shook his head and picked up the water from his desk and took a sip. "He had nothing on me, but I know he suspected Sarah and I were closer than we should've been. But I wasn't protecting him. My hands were tied."

"How so?"

"He was one of the earliest employees. He helped build the company. Without hard evidence, I didn't have the power to fire him. It would have been an executive decision."

"Did you bring the complaints against Matt to the executive team?"

"I did. They said without evidence, no disciplinary action was justified."

Was Frank sincere? He was a cheating, lying man, by his own admission. "Thank you for that." Assuming it was true. "We have a few more questions about Matt and his professional affiliations and any conferences he may have attended in the last year or two before his death. Do you have all that information?"

"I could find it, or I can ask the finance team to pull the expense reports for the professional memberships and conference fees. All of those items are paid for by the company, so he would've submitted expense reports to be reimbursed. I can have them put that together for you. Do you think it's related to his death?"

Not wanting to divulge too much, I said, "We're exploring all angles. Please request the expense reports."

He jotted down a note.

I said, "Did you know anybody by the name of Larry Henderson?"

He shook his head. "Never heard of him. Why?"

"He worked for a pharma company in South San Francisco. Do you remember Matt mentioning him?"

"No."

Interesting. Was it possible there was no connection? With no further questions for Frank, I said, "Thanks for talking with us today. Like I said, please keep Andrea's connection to Sarah quiet until the investigation is over. We figure there's a reason she never told anybody she is Sarah's sister. We want to honor that."

"Of course."

We exited Frank's office and approached Andrea's. In the door frame, I waved.

"Ms. Monroe. Detective Hirsch. This is a surprise." Her cheeks flushed, and she stood up. "What can I help you with?" she asked quickly, as if she were nervous.

Why was she nervous? "We just have a question or two for you. Do you have a minute?"

"Sure, of course. Please come in."

We entered her office, and I shut the door behind us. We had wanted the visit to be a surprise, so she couldn't rehearse her answers.

"What is it?" she asked. Her voice had a slight shake to it.

She was much more calm and collected at the station — because she had been prepared?

"Where were you, two years ago March ninth? It was the day Matt Baldwin died."

She sat back in her chair and said, "I was in Hawaii that

week. Girls' trip. I recall returning from the trip and learning of his death."

"I'm sure you have travel records of that."

"Of course. I can send them to you if you'd like?"

Too smooth. Was she innocent, or was it something else? "I'd appreciate that."

If we confirmed her travel records, and that she'd actually been on the flight she booked, it would be an airtight alibi. She had a solid motive. But it was looking like she wasn't our killer. One less suspect.

"Anything else I can help with?"

"No, that was it. It was good to see you again, and thank you for taking the time to talk to us."

She smiled triumphantly.

Something was off about Andrea Puerto, but I couldn't quite put my finger on it. If she hadn't killed Matt, why had she been nervous? She was hiding something. But what? Something completely unrelated to our case? Unclear. Either way, I would find out.

18

ANDREA

Heart racing, I watched as the detective and Ms. Monroe exited my office. Why did they need my alibi for Matt's murder? I hurried over and closed the door before shutting my blinds. Rushing to my purse, I dumped the contents on the floor as I found my bottle of Xanax. After too many frustrating attempts to get the cap off, I popped two and washed them down with the water that had been on my desk.

As I sat on the floor of my office, I breathed deeply, trying to slow my heartbeat. Why had they thought I killed Matt? Perhaps I had pushed them too far when I alluded to the idea that Matt or Frank had killed Sarah. But really, what I had done was give them my motive for wanting Matt extinguished. That was obviously not what I had intended. What else did they know?

After I steadied myself and returned the contents of my purse back inside, I sat myself down in the chair. There was no reason to worry. I reminded myself, *You're a warrior, Andrea. Not a scared baby*.

My phone rang, and I jumped. So much for self-soothing.

Confirming it was someone friendly, I put on a smiling face and picked it up. "Hello."

"Hi, Andrea, it's Georgia. I saw your door was closed, and I didn't want to barge in, but I have a question about the Blackwell contract."

"Oh, sure, anything you need. I just had the door closed because the detective and Ms. Monroe were here just a few minutes ago. Come on over."

"Oh, really? I'll be right over."

I straightened my blouse, took a deep breath, strutted over to my window, and opened up the blinds and the door. Georgia was there within seconds. "Hi."

She scooted inside. "The detectives were here again?"

"Yes. Have you heard about why they keep coming back?" I asked.

"I thought maybe you'd know, since they were talking to you."

"They asked if there were any contracts Matt may have been involved in, but there really weren't any. You haven't heard anything around the office about what's going on with the investigation?"

"No. But I know who might."

"Who? Can we ask?" Was that too eager? I didn't want to appear too eager but needed to know what was going on with the investigation.

"Let's go into the break room."

I wasn't sure if the detective and Ms. Monroe were still around, so I was hesitant. "Oh, it's not a big deal."

"Are you sure? It'll only take a second. I'm dying to know what's going on. Come on. Hannah is in the break room. We can ask her. The detectives have interviewed her several times now."

Hannah was a friend of Sarah's. She had been at the

funeral. Nobody in the office who attended the service could recognize me because I had changed my hair color, and I'd avoided most of her coworkers who had attended the service. I was amazed any of them had shown up, since nobody seemed to be concerned about her when she worked with them. They let that man harass and bully her until she went home in tears each day. And I couldn't even think about Frank. He would get what was coming to him. "I guess I could use some coffee anyway."

"All right."

We shuffled into the break room. Sure enough, there was Hannah. She worked for Matt and was friends with Sarah. She was young. I knew Sarah liked her. One of her only genuine friends in the lab. Hannah said, "Hi, Georgia. I don't think we've met?" Hannah asked it, as if she weren't sure.

"I'm Andrea."

She hesitated and then said, "Have we met before?"

"I don't think so. I work in legal." Something about her gaze made me think she knew exactly who I was.

"Did you see the detectives were back?"

"I did."

"Any idea what's going on with the investigation? Or why they keep coming back?"

She shook her head. "I haven't heard anything, but they're obviously on to something. They've been back three times now."

"They must think the murderer is here," Georgia said, with a spookiness in her voice for effect.

"You think?" I asked, trying to deflect the train of thought.

"He must be. Why else would they keep coming back?" Hannah asked.

"That's a good point." I needed to get control of this investigation ASAP. The Hirsch-Monroe team was good and could probably solve most cases. I needed to break them up. Throw a wrench in their plans. And for that, I needed Detective Hirsch out of the picture.

HIRSCH

Vincent stood at the whiteboard, pen in hand. "All right, give it to me."

The three of us had been on conference calls for the last few hours, discussing the Kyle Weston case with the homicide detectives in Santa Monica and the Larry Henderson case with detectives from South San Francisco in order to find a common link between the three murdered men that could point to a killer's motive. "Both Matt and Larry were members of the American Chemical Society, subscribed to BioSpace, and most notably, we think, is that they both attended the TIDES conference the year before they died."

"Maybe they met someone at the conference? A woman? Or they met and did drugs together," Martina suggested.

It was all speculation. "We need to dig deeper and find out."

Vincent continued to record the facts and open questions on the whiteboard. He said, "I'm guessing Kyle Weston didn't attend the conference or have any shared affiliations with Matt and Larry."

"No. He worked in finance, so it wouldn't make sense he would. According to the original investigators, the people in his life said he was a nice guy. Married. Two kids. No known enemies. That's it."

Vincent smirked. "Well, we've heard that before. And then we learned about Sarah. I don't think we can trust it."

"And the detectives who investigated Larry's death were certain the wife had him killed. Said he was an abusive jerk at home and at work. She'd even filed for divorce."

"True. But they couldn't find any evidence. Maybe there is someone who knew Matt and Larry. Both were abusive men. But we have no other connections yet, other than the two of them were working in the same industry and went to the same conference. What can we draw from that?" Martina asked.

It was a great question, and I didn't have a response, yet I pondered if the result for Larry and Kyle would be the same as for Matt. When we re-interviewed witnesses, would their statements change the second time round?

There was no way to get out of re-interviewing the families, friends, and coworkers of Kyle Weston and Larry Henderson. How could I swing it? I didn't want to be driving all over the state while Kim could go into labor. There was no way I would miss the birth of our child and force Kim to welcome our daughter into the world by herself. She wouldn't be entirely alone. Her mother would be there, but that wasn't good enough. Kim and I created this life together, and we would bring her into the world together.

Martina walked over to the board and stared at it, arms crossed. "We're missing something."

Vincent said, "No kidding. We're missing a motive."

Martina said, "What if there isn't anything else we can do? If there's some deranged killer out there targeting married men with children who work in professional environments, it may be someone who doesn't know the men personally. Maybe the killer was denied a promotion or was expelled from college and could not realize his dream of a 2.4 children white picket fence corporate job life. This may not be personal. It may be the work of a psychopath who is targeting men who have the life he wishes he had."

"Oh great, that's all we need. If that's the case, we may break our winning streak. Looking for a psychopath unrelated to the victims is the equivalent of searching for a needle in a haystack."

"I'm not ready to admit that it's a psychopath. My gut tells me there's something else here. I think we need to go down to Santa Monica and interview the friends, family, coworkers, and associates of Kyle Weston and do the same for the people in Larry Henderson's circle. At least the interviews for Larry will be easier. South San Francisco is just over the bridge."

"You're right, and that should be our next stop. I'm not buying the psycho killer idea either. However, your friend Agent Holley sure was helpful in the kidnapping case."

Vincent grinned widely. "So, you need my friends in high places. Once again, I understand when all hope is lost, you come to me. Of course, I'll help you. For I am Vincent. That's what I do," he said with exaggerated gestures.

Normally, I didn't mind Vincent's theatrics, but I was worried about how I could do the job and wasn't in the mood. Thankfully, Martina stepped in and said, "It's not a bad idea. Getting a profile on the killer may be helpful. If it's a stranger, their motive could be a myriad of reasons. Maybe the killer had a father in the corporate world and worked too much and wasn't around enough and then was abusive when he was home. Maybe he's killing his father over and over again."

The idea was solid. "It's possible. Vincent, can you put in a call to Agent Holley and request a full profile?"

"I will, but I'm running out of favors, so I'm not sure how

long it will take. I'll call now." Vincent scampered out of the room, and Martina approached me.

"Everything okay?"

Sometimes it was a great thing that Martina could read me and everyone around her. Other times, it was unnerving. "I'm worried about leaving Kim."

"No worries. Vincent can go with me to Santa Monica. He's got good instincts, and he asks the right questions."

It had finally happened. I was going to be replaced by a kid half my age. Was that my fate? "It's a good idea. He'll be helpful."

"You sure you're okay?"

"I don't like to leave you hanging like this."

Martina sat down and, I swear, stared straight into my soul. "Hirsch. Your wife is eight months pregnant and could go into labor any day. She's what's important to you. Never apologize for that."

"I don't like letting people down."

"You're not letting anybody down. Think about it. You're the boss. You set the tone around here. If another member of the squad's wife was going into labor or they were about to have a baby, would you want them here working, or would you want them home with their spouse?"

She had a point. "I would want them to be with their family."

"Exactly. You're leading by example. Showing the team not to feel guilty about leaving work to take care of their own family. Yes, our job is to bring answers and justice to families, but at the end of the day, our family comes first, right?"

"You're right. You're always right, Martina."

"Can I get that in writing?"

I chuckled. "Not on your life."

But Martina *was* right. I had to stop beating myself up about this. When I married Kim, I made promises to her and myself. My first wife only saw me when work was slow, and I never made her a priority. I knew better now. Kim deserved a husband who was there for her, and our child deserved her father. I didn't want to miss a moment of that child's life. How would I do that with this job?

The door to the squad room opened, and Vincent walked in. "I just got off the phone with Agent Holley. She's pretty backed up but said she could start working on it in a few days."

"Awesome."

Vincent looked pale.

"What's wrong?"

"As I was walking past reception, Gladys said there was a note for you, Martina."

Martina narrowed her eyes. "A note from who?"

Vincent shrugged and handed her a white envelope. Martina stared at it and then looked up at us. "I should put on gloves."

"Don't think it's from a secret admirer?" Vincent asked nervously.

"Unfortunately, it's never a secret admirer. It's usually the opposite." Martina walked over to the table and set the envelope down. It was a small white envelope with black block letters that read Martina Monroe.

She put on a pair of gloves with a snap and said, "Here goes." She picked up the envelope, retrieved a notecard from inside, and read. Her cheeks turned crimson, and there was fury in her eyes. "This needs to go to forensics."

"What is it?"

"It's a threat." She growled and then read it. "Dear Ms. Monroe, if you don't stop the investigation into Matt Baldwin, you will lose your partner, Detective Hirsch, and so will his pretty, blonde wife."

How DID the author of the note know I had a pretty, blonde wife? Was the killer watching us? Or was this another sick jerk messing with us? But who? We hadn't done a press conference to announce the reopening of the case. The only people who knew the case was active were the family, friends, and coworkers who had been re-interviewed. Would one of them want to taunt us? Or was the killer among them and afraid we were getting too close?

Vincent said, "I'll take it over to Kiki's lab and ask her to put a rush on it."

"Thanks, Vincent." Vincent ran off again, while Martina turned to look at me. "What are you thinking, Hirsch?"

"For starters, I don't like the fact the author knows I have a pretty, blonde wife."

"Do you think they're watching us? That's the only explanation, unless there are any pictures of you and Kim online?"

"There was a wedding announcement when we were married last year, but nothing since then."

"Maybe the author did a quick search and found the wedding announcement. Or more concerning, they're watching you and Kim and... maybe me and my family. Look, I don't want anything to happen to you or Kim or anyone else. How do you want to handle this?"

In all my years, I never had a family member threatened, certainly not my wife. One thing I knew for sure, it was unacceptable. "We can't back down now. It's like negotiating with terrorists. And we don't negotiate with terrorists."

"We could strike back to draw them out."

Not a bad idea. "We could hold a news conference announcing that we're looking for Matt Baldwin's killer and for anyone with information to come forward. We'll be very clear the entire sheriff's department will do everything in their power to find the truth and bring justice to Matt Baldwin's family."

"Do we want to mention the other two victims?"

"Not yet. We don't want the public to know we've made the connections."

"What if the threat is real? What if our perp comes after you?"

"I can take care of myself, Martina."

With a raised brow, she said, "Last time I checked, you can't outrun a bullet."

"When was the last time you saw me try?" I said, trying to lighten the mood, but it didn't even work for me.

Vincent reentered the squad room. "What did I miss?"

After a brief explanation, I said, "Anything we should add?"

"No, it sounds solid, but aren't you concerned about him or her following through with the threat?"

It was likely a scare tactic, but it wasn't something I would take a chance on — not when my wife and child could be in danger. "Why do you think it's me they're after?"

Martina leaned against the wall and nodded, as if she'd figured it out. "Our killer is after men. That's probably why you're being threatened and not me. This person, this killer, has killed three men and who knows how many more. That's why they're targeting you, Hirsch. I think our perp could be a female who hated these men, maybe even all men, and they don't want to be exposed. We scared her. I don't know how, but we did."

"Any idea who it could be? So far, our top suspects — the wife and Sarah's sister — have alibis that check out. Rock solid. Is it possible they hired out the kill? It's possible a hired gun took a road trip and took out these guys."

Vincent's team confirmed Andrea was on the flight to Maui, as she had claimed, had checked into her hotel, and had taken the flight back. It wasn't her. And Gina Baldwin's home had been searched for any heroin during the original investigation and, according to the toxicology reports, the lethal dose of heroin was most likely ingested after leaving his house. At which time, Gina had been volunteering at her children's school.

"When did Agent Holley say she could work on the profile?" We needed something solid to narrow down our suspects. But Vincent was right. We couldn't completely rule out Gina Baldwin and Andrea Puerto. They both had serious reasons to teach Matt a lesson, but not the others. My instincts told me they weren't the killer, nor had they hired out the job. If we hadn't found the connection to Larry and Kyle, I wouldn't be so sure.

"Not until next week."

"Let's talk to our media liaison and set up the press conference."

"Hirsch, what about Kim?"

"I'll see if her mom and dad can come stay with us until this gets resolved. Her mom is already at our house every day." That would be step one. If the threat escalated, I'd ask the sheriff for a twenty-four-hour patrol on my house.

"Good. You, okay?"

How would Kim respond to all of this? Since we had been together, my life really hadn't been on the line. I had been in a few dangerous situations, but I hadn't been shot at or landed in the hospital since we got together. Thankfully, Martina and I had the upper hand on the bad guys we went up against — most of the time. "I'm worried about how the news will affect Kim. What if the stress causes early labor? She's not one to rest and take it easy. As it is, I can't get her to stop cleaning."

Martina sat down, facing me. "What if you let us take over the investigation? You stay home with Kim. That might help calm her nerves."

Give up the case already? I supposed I could work from home, but that might make Kim even more nervous. "I'll think about it. Let's see if Kiki and the team can pick up any fingerprints or anything distinguishable from the note that could lead to the author. Why do killers like sending notes so much?"

"The killer is toying with us. Let's look at it as a positive. It could help the FBI create a more accurate profile."

Martina, the optimist.

"True. I'll call Jess and tell her we've had a development. Maybe she can bump us up the queue. Oh, and we need an official request, Hirsch."

Vincent, the young man who kept us on our toes.

Rubbing the back of my neck, I didn't like how this was turning out. Each step in this investigation was trickier than the last. "I'll fill out the request this afternoon. The sooner we can get a profile on the killer, the better."

"We don't have any suspects. Which means we need to question the families and friends and associates of the two other victims ASAP. We need to find that connection."

"I agree."

"Vincent, Hirsch and I talked earlier and think you could

help me do the interviews down in Santa Monica. What do you think?"

His eyes lit up. Vincent was new to fieldwork but had a knack for it, and he liked it. Technically, it was outside his job description, but he could handle it. "Sure, absolutely."

"I'll make the arrangements. We'll fly down this weekend, after the press conference."

"Okay, cool."

Jayda and Ross strolled into the squad room. "What's got you three so tense? What have you gotten into now?" Ross asked.

"Hirsch got a threat."

"From the Baldwin case?"

Martina nodded.

"Have you told the sheriff yet?"

"No, we just received it and sent the letter to forensics."

"We've got your back if you need anything. If anyone messes with one of the squad, they mess with all of us."

"Thanks, Ross."

The worry must've shown on my face. Martina said, "Don't worry about the case. The entire squad has your back. Our number one priority is you and Kim."

"I know. It'll be fine. Thank you." I hoped that was true. But the ball of nerves in my stomach was telling me I had every reason to be worried, and I was.

21

MARTINA

Out of sight from the camera lenses, I listened as Sheriff Baldwin pleaded with the public. "The CoCo County Cold Case Squad has reopened the Matthew Baldwin murder investigation. Two years ago, my brother Matt was found dead in his car. He had been poisoned. I'm asking for all of your help to bring his killer to justice. Somebody out there knows something about what happened to my brother. I am offering a $25,000 reward for any tip that leads to the arrest of the killer or killers responsible for Matt Baldwin's death. My team, led by Detective August Hirsch, will not stop investigating Matt's death until we catch the person responsible. There is a hotline for tips relating to his murder. That is all. Thank you." He stepped down from the podium and exited the media room.

I hoped the sheriff's plea did the trick.

After briefing the sheriff about the threat against Hirsch, the sheriff seemed certain that it was a hoax but agreed that whoever sent the threat needed to be stopped, and if the note came from the killer, that person needed to know the sheriff's department wouldn't stop until we found them and brought them to justice.

We followed the sheriff back into his office. With the door shut, he said, "I hope that gives us the result we need. I had originally wanted to keep this quiet considering there are a lot of cases that have been unsolved, and it doesn't make me look too good to prioritize my brother's case ahead of so many others. I know how it looks."

Hirsch said, "Sir, if we can't find your brother's killer, then whose should we find? No one person is more important than another. And how would it look if we couldn't bring justice for one of our own? I assure you, we won't stop until we do."

"I appreciate that, and I'm sorry this killer has threatened you, but considering it was just a note, it's likely nothing to worry about."

I wasn't as sure as the sheriff and had hoped Hirsch would stay home with Kim. But a day later, with no indications of actual danger, he agreed with the sheriff that it was likely an empty threat. But considering this warning was coming from who I believed to be a three-time killer, I didn't like playing fast and loose with my partner's life.

"What's next for the investigation?" the sheriff asked.

I said, "Vincent and I are going to follow the pattern of Matt's normal routine and question everybody again, as if it were the first time around. After that, we'll investigate the third victim in South San Francisco and then round it out with an investigation into the second victim in Santa Monica. In order to find the killer, we need to know why they targeted these men."

"I agree. Hirsch, you're hanging back?"

"Yes, sir. My wife is eight months pregnant, and she's freaked out by the note. I don't want any undue stress to come upon Kim, so I'll come into the office and work with the team while they're out in the field. I know Martina and Vincent and the rest of the team will ensure a thorough and efficient investigation."

The sheriff sat down behind his desk. "That's smart. Sometimes this job can eat you up. You can lose sight of what's most important to you. You're a good man, Hirsch, and a damn fine detective. I appreciate everything the two of you are doing to help find my brother and the other two men's killers. You let me know if you need anything, and you'll get it."

"We appreciate that. We're hoping the FBI profile will provide an accurate picture of who this killer might be, but not until next week."

"Understood. I knew I chose the right team for the job. You have my deepest gratitude. No matter what you find."

"Yes, sir."

"Thank you, Sheriff."

We said our goodbyes and headed back toward the Cold Case Squad Room. "Are Kim's parents okay staying at the house until she goes into labor?"

"They're more than happy to be there. But I hate what this is doing to Kim."

"You know, Hirsch." I stopped him at the break room because I needed a refill on my caffeine, and I wanted a private chat with Hirsch. "This is just the beginning. How will you handle the next case? The next serial killer. The next dangerous position you're put into. How will you manage all of this? Your life is about to change. Big time."

He raked his fingers through his sandy blond hair. "I've been thinking a lot about that lately. They are my priority. How do I do it, Martina? How do you do it?"

"Well, I have my mom to help with Zoey, but I still do this job. But we also don't have the same job. You have the added task of managing a squad and paperwork and the brass."

"Working with the Cold Case Squad is a lot fewer hours than when you were working for your firm?"

"Yes, and no. Most of the time, yes. In this job, I have

constraints and can only work Monday through Friday. There are no restrictions at the firm, and as you can imagine, I didn't always have the discipline to leave the job at the office or to rush home to be with Zoey. And I'll tell you this much — I regret it. If I could do it all over again, I wouldn't work so much. I would make sure I was there on the weekends and would never miss a play or Girl Scout meeting or all the special moments with Zoey. Jared and I worked opposite shifts so that Zoey didn't have babysitters. I didn't get a nanny until he was gone. We loved Claire, but it's not the same. Jared and I had a pretty good thing going," I said sadly.

"Kim wants to go back to work after the baby is born. Next school year, anyhow. She says she doesn't want to miss anything either, but being a teacher is a part of who she is."

It was the reason I hadn't quit working after Zoey was born. My job was a part of me, but I had learned the hard way I could have missed a lot less if I had the perspective I do now.

"What are you thinking about doing, Hirsch?" I studied him.

He didn't meet my gaze at first. Then he said, "My twenty years is coming up."

That was something I knew, and before we put Lafontaine in jail, both of us were at our wits' end with the CoCo County Sheriff's Department. We agreed neither of us enjoyed working for a crooked boss. Thankfully, Baldwin seemed like a new type of sheriff, one worthy of the uniform.

"You don't have to make any permanent choices. You could take leave."

With a knowing look, he said, "I may not have a choice."

"What do you mean?"

He stepped closer and spoke low. "As of about two hours ago, the budget has been nearly finalized. As much as the sheriff says he's grateful for everything we've done, he's talking about moving our funding away from cold cases and putting it back into homicide and missing persons — active cases."

Surprised he hadn't told me earlier, I tried to suck it up. We were best friends and partners, but I knew he had a lot on his shoulders. It explained his melancholy mood, despite saying he no longer feared for his safety. "How much do you think they'll cut?"

"Sarge says anywhere from eighty percent to all of it."

I knew not hearing anything about my contract renewal wasn't a good sign, but I hadn't realized it was bad news for the entire squad. "When will they complete the decision?"

"A few weeks. The sheriff has to discuss the new structure with the mayor and finalize assignments."

"What would happen to the squad? Would they all go back to active cases?"

A frown appeared, and I worried about him. He said, "Yep."

But not civilian contractors. Me. I knew the day was coming, so I didn't know why I was overcome with sadness. Trying my best to keep my composure, I had to be strong for the team and for Hirsch. I popped a mug from the cupboard, shoved it under the spout, and waited. "You know that wherever we end up, we'll be okay."

"What doesn't kill you makes you stronger, right?"

"Indeed."

"Until the assignments are final, the sheriff doesn't want anyone to know. I wasn't really supposed to tell you either. But Sarge knows I couldn't keep it quiet long. So, we need to keep it quiet."

With a wink, I said, "You got it, boss."

He cracked a smile. "Oh, no. Not you too."

"It's got a ring to it."

"Being the boss isn't all it's cracked up to be."

I knew Hirsch had been struggling, but this was the first

time I realized how much. And I couldn't blame him. All of our lives were changing. I was losing one of the best partners and jobs I ever had. Shaking away the thoughts, I had to focus. We needed to catch a murderer, and soon. Not just for the victims, but also for the squad. We could use one last big win before we went our separate ways.

22

ANDREA

AFTER A KNOWING head nod and wave to Rita, I entered the office. Trying to put the news out of my head, I failed. Why did they care so much? I got that his brother was the sheriff, but the $25,000 reward could be much better spent on pretty much anything other than trying to find who killed that treacherous man. Why wouldn't the sheriff give it up? He was likely the only person who cared Matt was dead. Maybe the sheriff was just like his brother. A disgrace. Perhaps he needed to be taught a lesson, too.

Even more infuriating was that they hadn't taken my threat seriously. Didn't they understand I wasn't some loony with nothing better to do? I had far more power than any of them realized. And I was going to prove it to them. They didn't have to do this the hard way, but it was the path they had chosen.

Heading toward the break room, I nearly ran face first into Frank. "Oh, I'm so sorry. I need to be more careful," he said, flustered.

Yes, he did need to be more careful. Like, more careful than, oh I don't know, shattering a young woman's life? Forcing her to do the only thing she thought may ease her suffering. Fracturing her loved ones when she was gone?

When Sarah died, I felt like a piece of glass destroyed by a bullet, becoming ragged shards of my former self.

With a bright smile, knowing our encounters would be limited, I said, "Not to worry. Have a good day," and continued to my office, as if Frank were already dust.

Even after a lengthy discussion with the group, I wasn't sure how to proceed. But they helped me see the way. The note wasn't enough. Detective Hirsch needed proof — and I would give it to him. He could be stopped, and I would be the person to do it if I had to. I didn't have any reason to believe he was a terrible man, but he was a man, so how good could he be? Detective Hirsch needed an unmistakable message that I was serious. And I had just the scheme to do it.

Behind my desk, I powered up my computer. There were a few things at the office I needed to finish before heading out to complete the next phase of my mission. Just needed to reschedule a few meetings, send a few emails. Sip some coffee. Get in and out.

Georgia appeared in the doorway like she often did. She always pretended to stop by for work, but really, she was one of the biggest gossips in the office. It was good to keep her close. She was an excellent source of information. Too bad the investigators hadn't realized that when they came to interview all of Matt's coworkers. Too bad for Sheriff Baldwin. "Hey, Georgia, what's up?"

"You have a sec?"

"Sure."

She scurried in. "Did you see the news?"

"Yeah, they're playing the announcement on the radio, too."

"I can't believe Matt was murdered. I wonder who did it. But I suppose we'll learn soon enough. Crazy, right?"

"So crazy." Crazy to think they'd solve the case. They wouldn't. We were too clever, and that Cold Case Squad was turning out to be *not so much*. Didn't they realize the reward would only hurt them, not help them? Having to man phone lines with thousands of fake tips would only distract them. It helped us a little, but that didn't mean the detective didn't need to learn a lesson.

"Well, if I knew anything, I would tell them. I can use an extra twenty-five grand," Georgia teased.

"Oh, I know. That would be nice."

"Some of us are putting together a pool to see how long it takes to find the killer. I know it's kind of morbid, but you want in?"

What a weird idea. Had Georgia come up with the game? "Sure."

"Okay, I'll come back later with the grid." She giggled. "It's so bad, but we have to keep this place lively somehow." She hurried out.

As usual, I would win the pool and remain free, and Matt would still be dead.

A few hours later, I packed up my things and hurried out the door, not saying goodbye to a single person. If anybody asked, I would claim a doctor's appointment. Otherwise, nobody needed to be informed of my whereabouts. It was one perk of having a boring job where you mostly work alone, except for scheduled meetings and pop-ins from the office gossip.

Rita smiled and said, "Have a nice lunch," as I sailed by and out of the building.

To an outsider, it would appear I was going out to lunch. My timing was perfect, but that wasn't a new phenomenon. Considering I planned things down to the most minute detail. You have to, to be believable.

Out in the parking lot, I studied the area. There were some people out, likely going to their cars to go out to lunch or their own "appointments." *Good for you, little worker bees.*

Behind the wheel, I started my journey toward a quaint little neighborhood for some sightseeing. The radio was playing one of my favorite songs, and it calmed me beyond the Xanax I had swallowed earlier.

Turning off the highway, I followed the instructions I had memorized from the internet. No paper trail. The information wasn't the easiest to get. But not that hard to get either. Driving past the adorable home, I parked three houses down and quickly removed my navy blazer and threw on a black sweatshirt, ball cap, and ugly, all-black sneakers. Dressed as a normal jogger or someone out for a stroll, I exited my car and prowled down the street.

Nestled near the hedges lining the light blue house with white trim, a low fence, lawn, and planters with red and yellow flowers, I bent down, as if to tie my shoe. Eyes fixated on the front of the home, my pulse sped up when the front door opened.

Crouched down, to conceal my presence, I watched as the glowing blonde with a rather significant baby bump stepped outside and waddled toward the mailbox.

Boy, the detective and the pretty lady had wasted no time.

Mrs. Detective slipped an envelope in the box and flipped up the red flag. She glanced around the neighborhood before tottering back down the path into her home and shutting the door.

In the driveway were two cars.

Was the detective home?

Possibly.

The shades were drawn. Perhaps the note had done the

trick — at least for some of the detective's family. With the house closed off for intruders not to peer in, they couldn't see who may poke around outside. *Oh, dear. Detective, don't you know that works both ways?* I would not be seen, and that was exactly how I had planned it.

23

MARTINA

"Are you nervous?"

Vincent shook his head. "I think I'll be okay. I know the case inside and out, but if you wanted to take the lead, I'd be okay with that."

We were about to meet with Larry Henderson's wife of fifteen years. Larry Henderson died six months after Matt Baldwin. They found him expired in his car, in a parking lot in South San Francisco near his place of work. Cause of death was heroin overdose. What a way to go.

It was Vincent's first witness interview. He had been informed on the case every step of the way, and it was time to get his feet wet handling witnesses. I'd prepped him, but it was his first, and nerves could take over. "I'll take the lead, but jump in if you think of a follow-up question that could be helpful."

"Will do."

It was the most serious and subdued I had ever seen Vincent. He had really grown on me since we had started working together. He was still a goofy kid, but a serious side had emerged over the past few years. One that could be professional when needed and one that could work in gray areas when needed.

We headed up the steps to the home in Burlingame that sat on a winding street built into the hillside. They'd lined the path to the front door with tall grasses and rock formations. Vincent said under his breath, "Nice digs."

"Indeed. Not that having money helped our guy."

After a few raps of my knuckles on the door, the sound of shuffling feet sounded, and the door opened. A woman with natural blonde hair with gray highlights wearing a smart suit and a worried look in her eyes said, "Ms. Monroe?"

"Yes, I'm Martina Monroe, and this is my associate, Vincent Teller. We're both with CoCo County Sheriff's Department."

"I'm Clara Henderson. Please come in." She led us through the home, and I glimpsed the views from the floor to ceiling windows. The glittering lights of the city and the hillside were stunning.

In the dining room, she said, "We can talk in here. The kids aren't home. Please have a seat."

Seated, I waited for Clara to sit before saying, "Mrs. Henderson. I imagine this is difficult."

She shook her head. "Have you been accused of murder? Have you had people believe you murdered your spouse in cold blood? The father of your children?"

When I'd spoken to the original detectives, they'd made it clear Mrs. Henderson was their top suspect. Because Larry was obviously poisoned by someone close to him with access to food and beverage, she was an obvious choice. The difference between Mrs. Henderson and Mrs. Baldwin was that Mrs. Baldwin played the grieving widow as opposed to Mrs. Henderson, who had already filed for divorce when Larry was killed. "I haven't, and I'm sorry for what you have been through."

"Yet here you are." She leaned back in her chair.

"We are. I spoke with the original detectives on your husband's case, and they said you had filed for divorce shortly before his death. Can you tell me why?"

She let out an exasperated sigh. "He was a jerk. He was a jerk to me, to the kids, and to his coworkers. He was even about to be fired from work. I'd had enough. I didn't want my kids to grow up in a toxic environment."

The first investigation had no mention of issues at work. Had we found another connection?

"How was it toxic?"

Her face flushed with anger, as if remembering all the awful things her husband had done. "Well, the first time he hit me, he apologized and bought me flowers. The second time, he swore he had a bad day and it would never happen again. And it didn't for a few years, and then the abuse became more subtle. Telling me what to wear, who I could be friends with, what to eat, and what groceries to buy. The last straw was when I saw him raise his hand to our son, and I thought, no way. I had to leave him, if not for me, for him. He was only seven."

It appeared Mrs. Henderson despised her husband, but it sounded like with good reason. If he was this openly abusive at home and his wife had filed for divorce, chances were he was no saint in other areas of his life, either. "That was brave of you to leave. I have worked with a lot of victims of domestic violence. A lot of them don't have the strength or the means to do so. I'm sorry that you and your children had to go through that."

Mrs. Henderson relaxed. I glanced over at Vincent, who was watching intently.

"You said that he was about to be fired from work. Can you tell me more about that?"

"Sure. Not only did he treat us like garbage at home, but he thought he owned all of us. He thought he owned his female coworkers, too. After three or four write-ups for inappropriate touching and sexually assaulting one of them at the holiday party, he was suspended. The poor girl worked for him. He said it was consensual, but she said it wasn't. She ended up dropping the charges against him, but I know he forced himself on her." Mrs. Henderson averted her gaze and wiped away tears. It sounded like there were a few people who were happy Larry Henderson was six feet under.

"Did you know the name of the victim?"

She shook her head. "No, I didn't know about it until after Larry died." That could explain why she hadn't told the original detectives.

Vincent nodded. "You know of anybody who would want to hurt Larry?"

She laughed bitterly. "There are probably more who wanted to hurt him than didn't. But anybody with a real grudge..." She paused and shrugged. "Honestly, if I were you, I would see me as a suspect as well. I wanted him out of my life forever. But this woman he raped, I'm sure she would have liked a little revenge — or maybe one of her loved ones. I was sick when I found out about it, and I didn't even know her."

"That must've been very difficult for you."

"Not as difficult as it was for that girl."

"There have been some developments in your husband's case."

Her brows shot up. "Oh?"

"We think his murder may be related to a few others."

"Seriously?"

"Yes, we think Larry's death could be connected to another man's death also from the Bay Area working in the same field."

"Like maybe they were killed because of a project they were working on?"

"We're still gathering details."

"Am I no longer a suspect?" she asked with wide eyes.

"Let's put it this way. You're pretty far down on the list."

"It's funny. In life, Larry ruined every day, and even in death, he's also ruined my life. Everybody thinks I killed him. It's not like anybody close to us could blame me, but still. Even my mother asked if I did it. I didn't. I'm not a killer. I swear to you, Miss Monroe, Mr. Teller, I didn't kill Larry."

I glanced at Vincent, and he nodded. "I believe you, Mrs. Henderson."

"Please call me Clara."

"Clara, I believe you. Thank you for meeting with us today. It has been very helpful."

"What else can I do to help?"

"What can you tell us about his daily routine?"

"Well, Monday through Friday was the same. He would get up at 6 AM and go for a jog. He'd be back in and showered by seven and then would drive in and go to his favorite diner for breakfast and coffee. He started doing that because he said that my cooking was terrible. He didn't seem to understand that I had two children to feed before him, and they needed to be at school by a certain time. Cereal wasn't good enough for him. He liked a full breakfast."

Vincent said, "What is the name of the diner?"

"Val's Diner. It's about ten minutes from here and near his office."

Vincent scribbled down on his notepad. "What time did he usually come home?"

"By six-thirty. Dinner was promptly at seven."

"Anything else you can tell us that might help us figure out who did this to him?"

"No. He ticked off nearly everyone he crossed paths with. That probably doesn't help much. Let's just say he wasn't beloved."

Quite a contrast from Matt Baldwin. Perhaps Larry

Henderson had a more difficult time hiding his true self. Rather, he had it on full display. "You've been very helpful. Thank you." I handed her my business card. "If you think of anything else, please call me."

"I will."

She seemed broken by her husband's death — not by the fact he wasn't there anymore, but by the investigation, the suspicion, and the weight of it all. She also had two children to whom she had to explain why daddy was never coming home again. I hated we had to dredge it all up, but it was the only way to find the truth. "We'll let ourselves out."

We quietly exited the home and retreated to the car. I said, "That was interesting."

"It was. Sounds like Larry was a piece of garbage at home and at work. What if it's somebody targeting men in the industry who assaulted women?"

"We had suspected the killer was female."

Vincent nodded.

Productive afternoon, indeed. "Let's go get the name of the woman who accused Larry."

"I'm ready, boss."

24

MARTINA

Seated across from the head of HR, Tara Black, of Cesium Pharmaceutical, I said, "Thank you for hosting us. Like my associate mentioned on the phone, we're reopening Larry Henderson's murder investigation. We're re-interviewing and taking a second look at the evidence."

"That's so good to hear. He was a valued member of our team. We were all so devastated by his passing."

Interesting, considering he was nearly fired for assaulting a coworker at a holiday party. Which oddly wasn't mentioned in any of the original investigation notes. If it were me, I would have the accuser at the top of my suspect list.

"Tell us about Larry."

Tara grinned, as if she were about to put on a performance. "Larry was a brilliant scientist. He worked here for almost a decade and headed up our oligonucleotide synthesis lab. He presented at conferences and wrote scientific papers that were published in periodicals. A bright star. Everyone loved him."

They did? "Did he manage others?"

"Yes, he had a team of about twelve."

"And did he get along with coworkers and subordinates?"

Tara nodded. "Oh, yes. He got along with just about everyone."

Just about?

"Had no issues?"

Tara's smile faded. "There were some misunderstandings with a few of the staff. But nothing serious."

Nothing serious?

I glanced over at Vincent, then back to Tara. "We just came from speaking with his wife, Clara, and she mentioned you nearly fired him for sexually assaulting a coworker at the holiday party. Is that the misunderstanding you're referring to?"

She shook her head and flipped open the lid of her laptop. "He wasn't going to be fired, but we had put him on a performance improvement plan because of the accusations from a few of his female coworkers."

"And the accusation of sexual assault at the holiday party?" I asked. Was the company trying to cover it up like Matt Baldwin's company had? Why?

"It was never proven. She said that it wasn't consensual. He said it was."

Really? "What was the woman's name?"

"Luna Katz."

"Who else accused him of sexual assault or sexual harassment?"

"There were two others."

"And what was done to deter Larry Henderson's inappropriate behavior toward them?"

"He was spoken to. After the second complaint, we put him on the performance plan."

"And what did the performance plan include?"

She peered at the screen. "He was to avoid working alone with women. And he needed to go six months with no complaints."

"What would happen if he didn't fulfill the plan?"

"It could affect his performance rating, bonus, and lead to termination."

"Was the sexual assault Luna Katz had accused him of within the six months stipulated in his performance plan?"

"Technically."

Technically? "Did he still receive his annual bonus?"

"Yes."

"So, he had a complaint, but no further action was taken?"

"Like I said, the assault wasn't proven."

Outrage simmered within me. "What exactly did Cesium Pharmaceutical do to protect women from him?" I asked, with anger in my voice.

"Ms. Monroe, these were three isolated events that were brought to my attention. We have harassment trainings, and we spoke to him, and we wrote him up. There is a process we have to follow here. We can't just fire him because somebody said that he made inappropriate comments. There was no proof that he had done any of the things he was accused of."

Three women had made claims of sexual harassment and one rape, and the company wrote up a plan and didn't even bother to follow through with the consequences? "Did you ask anyone in the office and labs if they had witnessed Larry exhibiting inappropriate behavior toward the accusers?"

"No, we just questioned the women and then questioned Larry."

"Wouldn't it make sense to ask the others in the lab if they saw any inappropriate behavior to see if you could corroborate the women's stories?"

"It's not procedure."

Vincent said, "Not procedure? What does that mean? That if one of your male scientists harasses women, then you just take the man's word for it and disregard what the women say?"

"No, that's not what I'm saying. The procedure is to question the accuser and question the accused, and if it happens more than once, we write them up. And that's what we did. Cesium Pharmaceutical did nothing wrong."

"What about after the third accusation? Luna Katz accused him of sexual assault. How did the company handle that?"

"We questioned him and her about the incident. There was alcohol involved, and it wasn't on campus."

"But it was at a company-sponsored party. You have a duty to protect your employees," Vincent added.

"Luna didn't want to go to the police. We had no choice but to disregard the matter. A few weeks later, Luna quit. The matter was closed."

Closed? No doubt another HR representative prepped by their in-house counsel.

"I would like the names of the other two women who made accusations against Larry Henderson."

"I'll have to check the file."

"Please do." I shook my head in disgust. You would think at a minimum, woman to woman, she would care more about protecting women in the workplace.

She tapped on the keys of her laptop computer as Vincent and I seethed. "The first to accuse him of inappropriate behavior was Jennifer Waverley, and the second was Marcia Mathers," she said.

"What exactly did they accuse him of?"

Peering at her screen, she said, "Jennifer claimed he made comments on her body parts and described what he would like to do to her sexually."

"Where were they when it happened?"

"She claimed it happened in the late afternoon, when it was just the two of them in the lab."

We had heard that story before. What was with these guys? "And Marcia. What did she claim?"

"Marcia described a similar incident. Alone in the lab."

"Do Jennifer or Marcia still work here?"

"Yes, both of them."

"We'd like to speak to them."

"Of course." Tara pursed her lips.

"May I ask why none of these allegations against Larry were told to the original detectives?"

"The detectives never asked about complaints against Larry. Employment records are confidential. We don't just offer them up without cause. Today is a courtesy."

Like Mrs. Baldwin said, it's all about asking the right questions. "The detectives didn't ask if he had any enemies?"

"We didn't consider Luna, Jennifer, or Marcia enemies. They were coworkers."

I peered over at Vincent, who appeared to find the statement as mind-boggling as I did. What motive did the company have to cover up the complaints? Perhaps they were trying to avoid lawsuits. "We'd like to speak with them. Are they here today?"

"Let me check."

"Okay." I crossed my arms across my chest as she hurried out of the conference room.

Vincent leaned over. "I've heard about this kinda thing."

"This kind of thing?"

"The corporate world. Apparently, sexual harassment runs rampant, and everyone just looks the other way. Amanda said she has friends who complain about it constantly."

Amanda was Vincent's long-term girlfriend. We'd met on several occasions. She was friendly and adored Vincent. "Looks like it."

"Maybe someone got fed up and started taking out offenders."

Interesting. "It would fit."

The door opened, and a woman in her late twenties wearing a white lab coat entered. "Hi. I'm Marcia. I heard you wanted to speak to me?"

Standing up, we introduced ourselves before offering her a seat. "We'd like to ask you a few questions about Larry Henderson."

Her face melted from friendly to disgust. "Oh?"

"We were told you complained he harassed you."

Marcia nodded. "I did. Not that it did any good. He could basically get away with anything. I learned the hard way there are no consequences for men in management."

Bitter. Perhaps rightfully so. "Did it ever get physical?"

She shook her head. "No, but that doesn't mean it didn't matter. He made me fear being alone with him. He didn't stop after I complained. He just laid it on thicker whenever he could get me alone. I'd leave work in tears. But nobody cared."

"Did he target anyone else?"

"Jennifer and Luna too. Luna was the smart one. She quit to get away from him."

"How did you know how he treated Jennifer and Luna?" Tara said the incidents happened when Larry was alone with the accuser.

"They told me. And sometimes when it was Jennifer and me alone in the lab, he'd say gross things like how he loved twins and thought it would be fun to date a pair." My confusion must have shown. "Jennifer and I both have long dark hair and olive complexions. People often say we look alike. Twins."

Nodding, I said, "What about Luna?"

"Luna worked in another lab. But she told me what he did to her. He was such a scumbag."

"Did Luna go to the police?"

"She wanted to. But her friend's mom is a lawyer and advised her to let it go and move on. Change jobs."

Why was this the standard line to victims? Why didn't the criminals have any consequences? "So, she did."

"Yes. I should have done the same."

"Do you still talk to Luna?"

"From time to time. She's been doing a lot better since changing jobs."

"That's good to hear."

"Is there anyone else who complained or had problems with Larry?"

"Not that I know of."

"You've been very helpful. If you have questions or think of anything that could help us find who killed Larry, call me." I handed her my card.

She smirked. "Yeah, once you find Larry's killer, I'd appreciate their mailing address, so I can send them a thank you note."

Ouch. And with that, I mentally added Marcia to the list of suspects. We said goodbye, and Marcia exited. Tara returned. "Jennifer will be in shortly."

"Thank you."

We stared at her, but she averted her attention. She was clearly trying to avoid spilling any more company secrets. A knock on the door, and Tara opened it. A young woman with dark hair, who looked quite similar to Marcia, entered. After introductions, we questioned her, as we had Marcia. Her statements corroborated Marcia's and Luna's claims.

"Do you still talk to Luna?"

"Every few months, we meet for brunch in the City. She's doing a lot better. She has a much more positive outlook on life now."

"That's great. Can you think of anyone else who had an issue with Larry?"

Jennifer said, "The three of us were the only ones who ever said anything against him."

"But were there others who didn't get along with him?"

"Not that I know of."

"Okay, if you can think of anything else that could help us find who hurt Larry, we'd appreciate it."

"Doesn't the sheriff's department have higher priorities than investigating some sad creep who died of an overdose in his car?"

These women *hated* Larry and didn't seem to care who knew it. And just like that, I added another suspect to the list.

BACK IN THE SQUAD ROOM, I was about to update Hirsch on the revelations about Larry Henderson when we saw him with his cell phone pressed to his ear. He held up a finger. His face was beet red. He nodded and whispered something before he hung up. He stormed over. "That was Kim. The mail carrier hand delivered a note he found in the mailbox. It was a white envelope with no return address or postmark. The outer envelope had my name on it. Inside, the note said something to the effect of 'I can get to you. Now stop the investigation or you'll be next.'"

My mouth dropped open.

"The killer was at my house, Martina."

"Let's go to your house. You need to be with Kim. Vincent and I will bag the note and bring it back to the lab."

"My house. With my wife and my child."

The look in Hirsch's eyes was frightening. But understandable. This killer would not get away with this. "We'll get them,

Hirsch. They will not hurt a hair on your head — or Kim's. Do you understand?"

He nodded.

I said, "You go ahead. I'll talk to the sheriff and arrange for twenty-four-hour patrol. We'll be over after we talk to the sheriff."

He simply nodded, obviously too furious to speak. One thing I knew for sure. Whoever had threatened my partner *would* live to regret it.

25

ANDREA

SIPPING MY COFFEE, I stared across the living room, admiring her long blonde hair and Disney princess-like blue eyes and fair skin. All she needed was a poofy, baby-blue dress, and she would be a dead ringer for Cinderella. Luna told me on more than one occasion her physical appearance had brought her far too much grief over the years. She tried to downplay her looks by omitting make-up and form-fitting clothing. The course of action was taken to stop unwanted attention, but despite her efforts, it was as if her natural beauty had given the opposite sex the whacked-out idea they had the right to look, touch, and take whatever they wanted without ever asking if it was okay with her.

If I had met Luna five years ago and she explained her dilemma, I probably would have rolled my eyes. But after Sarah's experience, and the stories from the other women with similar tales, I carried a different perspective. It wasn't that they were too beautiful; it was that men were too vile.

All the women sitting attentively in the living room on my family's old brown leather sofas were worth so much more than their physical appearance. But men and society tried to downplay that. Women were to be beautiful and agreeable. Not strong and intelligent. We couldn't change the deep-seated patriarchal ideals overnight, but we could start with a select few.

It was strange to think that before Sarah was gone, these couches and the room were our go-to spots to hang out with family and friends when we were in our teens and twenties. It was the perfect escape from the Bay Area. The cabin was nestled within the forest, with cocoa and marshmallows always stocked in the pantry. We would sit in that very living room with blankets and pillows, snuggled on the butter-like leather sofa while enjoying a roaring fire in the fireplace. Sometimes we would toast marshmallows and chocolate candy bars right inside the house. Indoor s'mores is what we had called them.

Those days were long gone. The cabin served a new purpose. Our sanctuary had turned into a war room. And I was more than a little curious why Luna had called the emergency meeting. Her voice message was obvious: "Girls' weekend, starting tomorrow morning. Be there or be square."

She had said it in a cheerful tone. But we all knew the code. It meant we needed to meet, and it was urgent.

With the heat ratcheting up on Matt Baldwin's case, we had been in contact more than usual. But I was struck by the fact that Luna had been the one to send the message. "We're all here, Luna. What is it?"

Perfectly sculpted brows raised, Luna said, "Jennifer called me yesterday after she got off work. She said that a pair of detectives arrived at her company asking about Larry Henderson and about women who had accused him of sexual harassment and sexual assault. She thought I should know."

Speechless, I made eye contact with the other three women in the room. It couldn't be as bad as it sounded. They couldn't know. "Who were they? What questions were they asking?"

"Martina Monroe and Vincent Teller. They asked if he had

any enemies and if there were any complaints against him. They reopened the case and are looking for his killer."

Technically, Luna had nothing to worry about. But this was an unsettling development.

Rita said, "Sounds like the attempts to stop the investigation into Matt's death failed."

Like throwing blame will help the situation. "Obviously."

"Perhaps more drastic measures need to be taken," Mila suggested.

More drastic? Were we really considering taking out a police officer? It was one thing to poison an unsuspecting jerk, but a detective? I mean, if it had to be done, we'd do it. But there had to be a better way. "Any ideas?"

Mila shook her head. "No. I take it back. I think we need to lie low. If we just stay the course, we'll have nothing to worry about."

We had devised the perfect plan, but considering the investigators were digging into Matt Baldwin and Larry Henderson, I questioned if it was really the work of art we had thought it was. If they had connected all the murders, there was a possibility it could come back to us. But they hadn't. Not that I was aware of. We had been careful, and I could argue that even if they connected the murders, it would be difficult to link them to me or anyone else in that room.

"Does that mean my second target is on hold?" If I couldn't have both, justice wouldn't be served.

Mila scrunched up her face. "Definitely. The last thing we need right now is another murder for them to investigate. Actually, I think the entire plan needs to be scrubbed. Sorry, Andrea, but target two is off."

Target two would not be off. It may be paused, but not off. Not if it was the last thing I did. I had worked too hard to not get the job done. "We can't just pretend the mission is complete. There are more targets. Deserving targets."

"I agree. But we have to put a pin in it for now. Until the current investigation goes away. If it goes away," Rita added.

"It'll end. There is no evidence or ties back to any of us. And when they give up, we'll resume."

Luna said, "We should cease all communications until we're sure the investigation is over. We don't want to put ideas in their heads."

"I respectfully disagree. I think we stay in contact to notify each other of new developments. And I think we should stay the course. But maybe we change things up so that they don't connect them in the future."

Mila said, "I don't know. I think I'm out."

Was Mila chickening out? It had all been Mila's idea. She'd approached me at Sarah's funeral. After her condolences, she said she had a friend, Luna. The three of us talked, and Mila said she had another friend who would also like to have a conversation about finally righting some wrongs. And we had done so with no suspicion falling on any of us. "Out? No one is getting out." How could they think walking away was an option?

Mila tsked. "What are we, a gang of thugs? If people want out, people can be out."

"And do what? Pretend like this never happened?"

"Look, I don't know what you're so worried about, Andrea. Nobody is going to talk. One of us talks, we all go down."

She was right. I was just jumpy and unhappy about the fact the police were making connections. We didn't think they could or would. We needed to think of a new way to make them back off. It would take time and some research, but I would find a solution. One way or another — I would make them stop.

26

MARTINA

Rushing after a quick shower, I paused briefly to check my appearance. There were dark circles under my eyes, and my skin was pasty. Sleep had become a stranger. Ever since the threat at Hirsch's house, I was working round-the-clock and wouldn't stop until I caught this killer.

The previous sheriff had restricted my hours and only allowed forty per week, strictly Monday through Friday. This didn't allow for overtime or working weekends. It was petty retaliation for breaking the rules, but I had to accept the terms or my contract would have ended. I supposed I should be grateful they hadn't booted me back then. The new sheriff was far more understanding of the job and didn't have an axe to grind. Even so, my late hours and weekend work were technically outside my contract. But this wasn't for a case. This was for Hirsch, Kim, and their baby. A contract couldn't stop me from protecting my loved ones.

After a comb through my hair and a quick blow-dry, I was ready.

Stomping down the hall, I grabbed my backpack from the

hook and met the singing duo in the kitchen. "Morning, you two."

Zoey halted her song. "Are you leaving already?"

"You're going to miss out on pancakes," Mom added.

"I'll just have a protein bar and get going."

"Coffee?"

"Is it ready?"

Mom gave me a knowing look. "I'll put some in a travel mug for you."

Zoey said, "How long will you have to work on the weekend?"

"I'm not sure. We're all working as much as we can to get this one finished as soon as possible." I hadn't told her Hirsch and Kim had been threatened. Zoey was sharp and knew that my job was dangerous, but she didn't need to know the bad guys we were hunting were also hunting us, or more specifically, her Uncle August. All I had divulged to my ten-year-old daughter was that it was an important case that we had to solve.

"Are you going to the office?"

"I'm making a stop at Hirsch's house first and then into the office."

"How come you're meeting Uncle August at his house?"

"He's working from home until the baby is born."

"Oh, that's good. I'm sure Auntie Kim is delighted. I can't wait for them to have the baby so I can hold it and then poof I'll be her favorite. I just know it," Zoey said with the utmost confidence.

My confident, bright light of a child. Even though we were working round-the-clock to keep our team safe, I took a few hours the previous night for our Friday night movie night. It was a tradition Zoey and I started a while back after Mom moved in with us. Every Friday night, we would have pizza, ice cream, and watch a movie. Zoey would be eleven soon enough, and then, after a few blinks, she would be in high school. A sleep or two later, away at college. Out in the world by herself. Friday night movie nights were sacred. "I'm sure the baby's going to love you."

"I am too."

Mom handed me a travel mug filled with steaming hot coffee. "Thanks, Mom."

"Any idea what time you'll be home? Maybe for lunch or dinner?"

"Lunch is out, but maybe dinner. I'll call you and let you know."

She nodded.

Mom knew why I was working every moment until the case was closed. She had grown to love Hirsch like a son, and Kim was a bonus. We had the same desire to protect them.

After a quick kiss on Zoey's cheek, I headed out of the house.

Mom had been a godsend living with us, helping take care of Zoey, filling in the gaps left by Jared's departure from our world. Between Mom's support and home-cooked meals, she had made our house a home again. With her and Sarge getting more serious, I knew these days were numbered.

A SQUAD CAR sat in front of Hirsch's house, and another a few doors down. Hirsch and Kim's cars took up the driveway. It was a full house.

Backpack slung over my shoulder, I hurried through the brisk air and knocked. Hirsch opened the door. "Come in here, it's freezing."

Inside, I unzipped my coat. "Patrol here?"

"A couple in the car, a few on foot out back."

Good. I didn't want any undesirables near my partner and his family. "How's Kim holding up?"

"She's rattled."

"We will find them and stop them."

"I know you will. I just hope it's soon."

Kim walked over with her hands planted on her belly. She was glowing, but worry was written all over her face. I gave her a warm hug. "You look wonderful, Kim."

"Thank you. Any news?"

"Not yet, but Vincent will join us soon."

Kim frowned. "The sheriff said he was stopping by, too."

Full house indeed. "There is no way the person who threatened Hirsch will get inside this house. And we will catch them. They won't get away with this. You're safe."

My pep talk didn't seem to faze her. She was a schoolteacher, not a police officer or private investigator. This life was new to her, and it was a heckuva way to be indoctrinated into the spouse-of-a-detective kind of life.

A knock on the door drew our attention. Hirsch stepped over, peered into the peephole, and pulled the door open. "Sir, thank you for coming."

"Of course."

His eyes met with Kim's.

Hirsch said, "Sheriff Baldwin, this is my wife, Kim."

"It's nice to meet you, Sheriff."

"You too. I wish it was under better circumstances. I really do."

"Thank you."

Hirsch said, "Where do you want us?"

"Dining room. I'll hang out with Mom and Dad in the living room."

"Sounds good. I'll answer the door, so if you hear a knock, don't worry about it."

Kim nodded and waddled to the living room.

As we strolled past, I waved at Kim's mom and dad before continuing to the dining room at the back of the house.

"Can I get either of you something to drink?"

I raised my travel mug.

Sheriff said, "No, I don't want to be any trouble."

Hirsch didn't argue. Seated at the dining table, the sheriff said, "Hirsch, I wanted to come here in person to tell you that you have the full support of the sheriff's department. Anything you need to keep you and your wife safe. You got it."

"I appreciate that, Sheriff."

"When I had you open my brother's case, I had no idea it would endanger the team or you or anyone. Between the three of us, I honestly thought that he must have messed with the wrong person on the wrong day. I didn't think it was a diabolical killer who would come after a police officer in order to stop the investigation."

Nobody had.

"During the original investigation, the investigators didn't find any potential suspects," I said.

"No, but I suppose they didn't ask very good questions. Your team has uncovered far more than the previous detectives, and now you're saying Matt's murder is connected to two others. I knew your reputation, but now this. It's a..." The sheriff stopped.

Was he about to explain that it was a shame he was going to disband the Cold Case Squad and no longer fund my contract?

A knock at the door. Hirsch called out that he would get it and hurried over.

"What were you saying, Sheriff?"

His eyes met mine, and he knew I knew. "It's a shame that we don't have more funding, but I think the talents of the Cold

Case Squad will be utilized to their full extent in their new roles."

"I understand it's a tough place to be, Sheriff."

"You'll go back to your firm full-time?"

"That's the plan."

Part of me couldn't process that my time with the Cold Case Squad was ending. The other part was making plans because my logical brain knew I had to.

The previous day, I had called Stavros, the owner of the firm I worked for, and let him know Hirsch was in danger and given the update that it was pretty much official I would come back full-time to Drakos Security and Investigations. We talked about what my workload would be like and how it fit with my desire to spend more time with Zoey. I wouldn't just be going back to my old job, I was going back to a new opportunity. Nothing final yet. There were a lot of details to iron out before I would sign on the dotted line. They say when one door closes, a window flies open. Wasn't that the truth? In my experience, nothing lasts forever, so you have to make the best of your reality at any given moment in time.

"I sincerely hope our paths cross again, and I appreciate everything you've done so far. Could we convince you to go to the Academy and wear a badge?" he said with a small smile.

"Not a chance," I said with a chuckle.

"That's what I thought. But please know that these budget changes and reallocation of funding are no reflection upon you or the team's work. I wish there were a hundred of you and Hirsch. Your firm is lucky to have you."

"I appreciate that."

Hirsch returned with Vincent, who looked startled by the presence of the sheriff. "Hey."

"Vincent, good to see you."

"You too." He gave me a look, and I returned it with a slight shoulder shrug. He took a seat next to me and Hirsch at the head of the table.

The sheriff spoke. "As I was saying, anything you need to keep the team safe, you've got it. Additional patrol. Escorts to the grocery store. You name it."

"That's appreciated, sir."

"Where are we at with the case?" the sheriff asked.

Sheriff Baldwin was a new breed of sheriff. He told us that, and I believed him. He wasn't there to cover up or to make sure that he looked good in front of the cameras. Baldwin was there to help. "Vincent's team will research potential suspects in your brother and Larry Henderson's murders. Tomorrow, we head down to Santa Monica to interview friends, family, and acquaintances of the second victim, Kyle Weston. We're still trying to define common threads to understand the motive behind the murders. We think it will help identify a suspect, or suspects."

"Three murders. One year. Same MO. These guys pissed someone off," the sheriff commented.

"That's right. We've been fortunate that our witnesses are being more forthright this round. Although with Larry Henderson, it was well known that most women he encountered had a motive for revenge. The original investigators put little stock in that fact. Thought the women were harmless. We're not so sure."

"And that's how I know the case is in excellent hands. I'll leave you to it. I'll let myself out."

"Thank you, Sheriff."

With the close of the front door, the three of us turned to one another. "Hirsch, we're going to take him up on his offer. Twenty-four-hour surveillance of your house. Not just a car out front and a couple of guys in the back. Use the resources while we can. We'll call in some extra teams for this weekend. We'll track down anyone who could be a suspect, no matter how remote a possibility. Kiki is coming in this weekend to finish the analysis of the letters. Hopefully, we'll get some fingerprints or something usable to identify the person who left them."

Vincent said, "You're the boss. It's all hands on deck. No one takes a break until we stop the perp."

I couldn't have put it better myself. We would catch the killer or killers, and when we did, they would regret the day they ever crossed our path.

WITH DETERMINATION, Vincent and I strutted toward the Cold Case Squad Room. Vincent said, "I'll check with the team and see if they found anything interesting about Sarah Nesbit, Luna, Jennifer, or Marcia."

"Fingers crossed they found something. If they didn't, we're back to square one for suspects."

"Don't I know it?" Vincent hurried off, and I set my bag down on the chair.

The squad room wasn't normally so quiet. There were usually at least a few people milling around or coming in and out.

The entire team was on-call in the event we needed them. Jayda, Ross, Leslie, and Wolf had all signed up to stop by Hirsch's place and make rounds along with patrol. We were being more than a little cautious, but we couldn't allow any breaches to the security for one of our own.

The door opened, and Vincent entered with two of the researchers who came in for the weekend shift. "Hey, Rosemary. Hi, Linus."

"Hi, Martina. How's Hirsch and his wife?"

"He's holding on, but frustrated. His wife, Kim, is definitely on edge. Not great in her condition. Did you find anything on any of the suspects?"

"Not yet. But we're doing a deep dive into their backgrounds. So far, we have all their current information, but we're going further. Looking for school records, family records, known associates... the whole nine yards."

"It's appreciated."

If they had found nothing on our suspects, then why were they there? When they entered, I had assumed they'd found something. But what?

Vincent led them over to the whiteboard with all the connections between Kyle, Matt, and Larry. The only connections at that point were the fact they were all middle-aged men, married with children. One was in an estranged marriage, but a marriage nonetheless. That and two had been accused of sexual harassment and assault.

We didn't have the full story on Kyle Weston in Santa Monica, but we would soon enough.

The suspects were Luna, Jennifer, Marcia, Andrea, and the wives and potential loved ones who might want revenge. Like Andrea, Sarah's sister. But we didn't know if this murder spree was about revenge or something else.

Vincent led them to the murder board. Rosemary said, "Is it okay if I add to it?"

That piqued my attention. "I thought you said you didn't find anything on the suspects?"

Rosemary pushed up her sparkle-framed spectacles. "We didn't. But we think we found more victims."

More victims. "How many?"

"Two. Both up north. Seattle and Portland."

"How wide was the search for the victims?"

Linus said, "We searched the entire United States. But these are the only five that fit the MO."

I mumbled, "Five victims on the West Coast."

Vincent nodded. "Drivable."

True. Our suspect must be based on the west coast. Could it be the work of one or more? Vincent seemed to pick up on my deep thoughts. "One or more than one suspect."

"It's very possible. A pair?" I suggested.

"Maybe a couple of friends said, 'Hey, we're done with women being assaulted with nobody doing anything about it. Let's take 'em out.' Sounds like a solid motive to me."

But we only had two confirmed assault accusations.

Rosemary said, "I can see it."

"It's premature. We need more info, especially on the new victims."

"Rosemary, go ahead and put up the information you found."

As Rosemary and Linus recorded on the board, I theorized the chain of events. One in Portland and one in Seattle. Had someone been on a road trip starting in Santa Monica, popping off in the Bay Area and then heading up north to Portland before hitting Seattle? No, the kills were too far apart for one spree. These were spaced out.

The team finished and stepped back. "Six months ago, an overdose killed Danny Appleton from Seattle. Two and a half months ago, someone killed Scott Ogden from Portland. As you can see, they have similar biographical information. Middle-aged. Married with kids. Both scientists. Danny was a professor at the University of Seattle. Scott worked in the pharmaceutical industry."

Two and a half months? The killer was active.

Vincent and I looked at each other. "The killer is still killing."

"The threat to Hirsch could be legit."

"Yep." Turning to Rosemary, I said, "What is the status of the cases?"

"Open. Unsolved."

Worry filled me as I realized there was a killer on the loose — and they likely weren't done hurting people.

We needed to call in members of the squad to help with interviews up north. We needed to solve this before they could get to Hirsch or another victim. "Okay, here's what we should do. Vincent, you and I head to Santa Monica tomorrow. Can you call in Jayda and Ross to see if they can reach out to the police department in Portland and Seattle to gather all the details? Let them know we think we have a serial on our hands. One who could be working independently or in a pair. We need them to head north to interview witnesses ASAP."

Vincent nodded.

"Did we get the contact information for Luna Katz?"

Rosemary said, "We have all her information here. She's local."

"Excellent. Good work, team." I grabbed the file on Luna Katz. We needed to get her down to the station for an interview ASAP. Perhaps she had insight into who may have wanted to harm Larry, and we could feel her out to determine if she was that someone. Did Luna have the ability to take out five men undetected? Setting down the file, I dialed Luna Katz. It was about time the two of us had a chat.

28

ANDREA

The room was silent as we devised a plan to ensure none of us ended up on the police's radar. The tension in the air was thick. And the only thing I could think of was an old heist movie where a group of bandits suddenly turned on one another. Would one of them turn on the rest of us? It made little sense to do so. We were all just as guilty. *Guilty of serving justice.* But it happened all the time in the movies and in real life. Where one criminal turned on the other to get a lighter sentence. The sound of Luna's cell phone vibrating on the coffee table made me jump. Luna grabbed it off the table and stared at the screen. "Unknown number."

"Answer it."

"Hello?" Luna's eyes widened. "Yes, this is she." She nodded and looked away. "I'm out of town right now, so I can't come in today for an interview."

An interview. Was it the police calling her?

"Yes, I'll be returning on Monday." And then, "Um. Sure. That will be fine." Luna bit her lower lip. "Oh. Okay. Thanks. See you then." And with that, she ended the call.

"Who was that?"

"That was Martina Monroe from the CoCo County Sheriff's Department. She said she has some questions for me and asked me to come down to the station."

This was not good. Not good at all. "I've met her several times. She's intuitive. Smart. Just stick to the plan, and everything will be fine." Would it be fine? I wasn't so sure anymore.

"I don't like any of this," Rita said.

"No, none of us do, but it sounds like the threats against the detective have done nothing to thwart their investigation. We may need to seriously ratchet up the effort."

"How?"

"I don't know. We change our approach. A new method that won't be connected to the others."

"Like what?" Mila asked.

"Does anyone know how to shoot?"

Rita said, "I know how to shoot. My dad has guns. I could get one."

Mila sighed. "Are we seriously talking about shooting and killing a police detective?"

"What other option do we have?" Did Mila not understand the severity of the situation?

"Don't you think it will bring more suspicion to us? You don't think they'll investigate the murder of a police detective?" Mila was off the couch and pacing around the living room.

"Yeah, I think they will investigate. But that means they won't be investigating the other murders."

"One murder. Multiple murders. It doesn't matter if we're still the ones they'll be looking at."

I offered, "What if we give them a suspect or fake tips to get them chasing their tails?"

"Not a bad idea. But how?"

Rita said, "Call the tip line?"

"What if they trace the call?"

Rita nodded. "Okay, not the tip line. Anonymous letter? Or a rumor? We could start rumors about them. We can give them a suspect."

None of that would work. We should have thought about pinning it on someone else at the time of the deaths. Erroneous evidence that would keep the cops spinning their wheels. Instead, we gave them none, forcing them to look under every stone and pebble. Our plan hadn't been perfect, after all. *Lesson learned.*

Mila said, "I'm not sure how to do that. But let's give it a hard think. But in the meantime, we say and do nothing. Stick to the story and everything will be fine."

"What about the target list?"

"The mission has been compromised. Any more activity and we'll be toast. This is over. Completely over. Done. Too hot to handle," Luna said with conviction.

"This is how all of you feel?" I asked the group.

Rita sunk into her shoulders. "Luna's right. I think anything we do from this point forward will just throw suspicion on us. We should cut our losses and move on."

Mila said, "We cease all activities related to the mission."

They were abandoning the mission. We had come so far and accomplished so much. How could they just turn their backs on it? They may decide to cease all activities related to the mission, but that didn't mean I had to.

29

MARTINA

I never liked to be the bearer of bad news. And Hirsch didn't seem terribly receptive to it either. We knew the killer was still active, which meant the threats against Hirsch and his family could be real. Not that we had taken the matter lightly, but it was one more reason to take extra precaution.

Vincent said, "How did he take it?"

"He's not happy."

"No kidding. But with the security surrounding him, there's no way anybody will get close to Hirsch."

"Exactly."

"Hungry? Need coffee?"

Glancing up at the clock on the wall, I realized it was nearly seven. I had completely forgotten to call my mother to let her know what time I would be home for dinner, and it turned out I wouldn't be. "Let's order in. I don't want to take a break yet, but I'll understand if you need to go home."

"You crazy? I'm here until we catch the perp and we know Hirsch is safe. I'm all in, Martina."

"All right then. I'll call my mom and let her know I'm going to be late."

"I can order a pizza or two."

Zoey would be so jealous. There were few things she loved more than pizza. "That'll work. Order me a garden salad with chicken too."

"You got it."

Vincent toddled off to the other corner of the squad room while I called my mother.

"Let me guess. You won't be home for dinner."

Good guess, considering we usually ate around six-thirty. "I completely forgot to call. Sorry about that. I won't be home until late. Unfortunately, there have been some serious developments."

"Say no more. Zoey and I are having ourselves a great time. No need to rush. You do what you need to do, Martina."

"Thanks, Mom. Can I talk to my girl?"

"Of course."

It had been a while since I worked late like this, and Zoey had been understanding, but I didn't want her to think I would completely forget about her while I was on a case.

"Hey, Mom."

Mom made me feel old and made me miss the days of being referred to as Mommy. "Hi, Zoey. How are things going?"

"Good. Grandma said we can make cupcakes."

"That sounds great. What kind?"

"Chocolate with cream cheese frosting."

My stomach rumbled. The pizza and salad couldn't get there soon enough. "That sounds amazing."

"Working late?"

"That's right. But I wanted to say good night to you. You may be in bed by the time I get home."

"Okay, well, don't work too hard."

Shaking my head at my too-mature daughter, I said, "I'll try not to. I love you, sweetheart."

"I love you too. Bye, Mom."

"Goodnight, Zoey."

Vincent strolled over. "Food will be here in thirty minutes."

"Perfect."

The doors opened, and Rosemary and Linus entered. "You two are still here?" I asked.

Rosemary said, "Of course. All hands on deck. And we found something kind of interesting."

"Oh?" I liked the sound of that.

"We'll just get to it."

Clearly, they had not been trained by Vincent, who liked to have a long, drawn-out, dramatic reveal. Sometimes I wondered if he should be in the theater as opposed to investigating crime, but he was good at that, too. Rosemary continued, "We did a full background on Luna, and nothing really stands out."

Not super helpful.

"But then we were going through all the files and all the research we've done so far on all the victims and suspects and realized we hadn't done a full background on Sarah Nesbit, Andrea's sister, the one who died by suicide. So we did a deep dive on Sarah."

I wasn't sure where they were going with this. Sarah was dead. She couldn't have killed any of our victims.

"Sarah Nesbit went to UCLA, and so did Luna."

It was a big university, so that wasn't terribly surprising.

"And?" Vincent asked, rather impatiently.

Ironic.

"Well, not only did their time at UCLA overlap, but they also both majored in biology, and that's not all. They shared an address, a dorm room."

Vincent and I exchanged glances.

"You're kidding?"

Rosemary shook her head. "Nope. They knew each other.

They lived together. That's more than a little coincidence, right?"

"I'd say so."

"Let me get this straight. Sarah is a scientist who worked in pharmaceuticals. She accuses her boss of sexual harassment and assault. She later dies by suicide, and the man she accused of assault dies less than a year after Sarah. And her old college roomie also works in pharmaceuticals and was a victim of an assault by her boss. And both men are dead within six months of each other. Murdered."

Vincent said, "Whoa. There is no way that's a coincidence. You know how we were thinking maybe the killer is a person with a vendetta against a certain *type* of person? Maybe not a type — it might be personal. If she had kept in touch with Sarah over the years, maybe her assault and Luna's own traumatized her. And then Sarah died, and she snapped. Luna might be our killer."

Entirely possible. "When will the FBI profile be available?"

"Jess said it's gonna be a couple of days. She's trying to clear her schedule and will come by on Wednesday."

It would have been nice to have it sooner, but beggars couldn't be choosy. "It makes sense. If anybody would have a motive to kill Matt and Larry, it would be Luna. Because, like Andrea, maybe Luna blames Matt for Sarah's death. She decides revenge is the way to go. But while she's at it, she takes out the guy who assaulted her and got away with it. Well, until she took him out."

"But what about the other guys? Did she know Kyle or Danny or Scott?"

"I have a feeling we need to keep digging. Thanks, Rosemary. Thanks, Linus. This is really helpful."

Dang it. We needed eyes on Luna. "We need to get Luna in here ASAP."

"But she said she's out of town."

Or on the run. "Rosemary, can you check to see if Luna has made any travel reservations for this weekend? Airline, bus, car, or hotel — anything to indicate where she may be right now?"

"We'll check right away."

Was it really possible that a young female scientist had gotten fed up with all the misogyny, sexual harassment, and assaults against other females in the industry and went on a killing spree to teach the abusers a lesson? Matt died because of what he did to Sarah. Larry died because of what he did to Luna. It seemed far-fetched, but so far, it was the only theory that made sense.

Vincent and I needed to get down to Santa Monica and talk to Kyle Weston's friends, family, and acquaintances *and* find a connection to Luna.

<hr>

BELLY FULL, I wiped the corner of my mouth with a napkin. About to stand up and grab another mug of java, I paused as the door opened. It was the busiest night the Cold Case Squad had seen since its inception. Jayda, Ross, and Kiki sauntered in. I said, "How are things at the Hirsch residence?"

Ross said, "The place is like Fort Knox. Nobody will get to Hirsch and Kim or her parents. We heard the killer was active. That's not good news. But they're like bugs in a rug. It'll take a tank to get to them."

Well, that was something. "Hey, Kiki. You find anything?"

"Unfortunately, no. We tested for fingerprints and DNA from the seal, but whoever wrote and delivered the note wore gloves and didn't lick the envelope."

Vincent said, "What about the card stock? Was there anything unusual about it?"

"Another dead end. It's very common and sold in every Target in America."

Now we knew the killer had shopped at Target. That narrowed it down to just about everybody.

"Thanks, Kiki."

"Sorry it wasn't more helpful. I'm heading home now, but call me if you need anything."

"That's appreciated."

Jayda said, "What's next? Vincent called and said you need us."

"Vincent and I are going to Santa Monica to interview witnesses in the death of Kyle Weston. We need to locate and interview witnesses in the Danny Appleton and Scott Ogden cases up in Seattle and Portland as soon as possible. Any chance the two of you have the travel bug?"

Jayda chuckled. "I do, but not to hunt down suspects. But yes, I can clear my schedule and be on a plane Monday morning. Does that work?"

"Absolutely."

Ross eyed the leftover pizza and said, "It's for anybody?"

"Absolutely."

He picked up a piece of cheese pizza and took a bite. We stared at him until he finished chewing. He nodded. "Of course. I'll be on a plane with Jayda on Monday morning. Anything the team needs. You don't have to ask twice. Hirsch is one of us. We'll do everything we can until this person is stopped."

That's what I liked to hear. And that was what I would miss most about the squad. It was a blow that we didn't get DNA or fingerprints off the envelope or note threatening Hirsch. But we had finally found a connection between Luna and Sarah. It was something, but it wasn't enough.

We approached the bungalow, and Vincent stopped. "You wanna take bets? Does Mrs. Weston claim he's a dirt bag or a perfect man like Matt Baldwin's wife the first time around?"

"They murdered Kyle for a reason, and it was likely because he was a dirtbag. But we shouldn't rush to judgment. Let's pull whatever we can out of Crystal Weston."

"Okay, I'll let you take the lead. You seem to be good at this."

I smirked. "Thanks, Vincent. I feel like I can continue on now that I have your approval."

He laughed, but he also blushed. I nudged him in the shoulder. "Come on, let's find out more about Kyle Weston."

The bungalow was charming, with a cream-colored stucco and tile roof. Succulents and grasses lined the path to the entrance. Kyle Weston had done well for himself living in Southern California, making the big bucks in finance. Who had he crossed who decided he needed to pay for his offences? Had it been Luna? Did she know Kyle?

After I knocked and stepped back, the door opened. A woman in her forties with dark hair and sad eyes said, "Hello."

"Are you Crystal Weston?"

"Yes."

"We're Martina Monroe and Vincent Teller, the investigators from the CoCo County Sheriff's Department. We spoke on the phone yesterday."

"Yes, of course. Please come in."

Was she still grieving the loss of her husband? Maybe he was a saint at home and a sinner elsewhere?

The home was decorated in a fashion that I had learned was called shabby chic. Mismatched but coordinated items with a bohemian flair. I couldn't imagine having the type of life where I hired a decorator or had something curated on my behalf. Maybe I should. Why didn't I? Our home could use a spruce here and there. We had family photos on the walls and Zoey's art collection, but nothing more than matching furniture and a few decorative items I had purchased over the years. Nobody would walk into the house and say, "Wow. I love what you did with the place!" Maybe it was time I did.

Crystal Weston led us to her dining table. She offered us beverages. We accepted coffee because I wouldn't get any sleep anyhow. "We appreciate you seeing us on short notice."

"Not a problem. I was just home meal prepping for the week. The kids are at a movie."

"Like my associate mentioned on the phone, we're taking a second look at Kyle's death. We think it might be connected to some others."

"You think a serial killer murdered him?" she asked, with raised brows.

"Maybe. We're trying to find a connection between the victims, but they were all killed similarly, which we can't ignore. What would be most helpful, Mrs. Weston, is if you can tell us about Kyle. What was he like? Did he have a lot of friends?

Active in the PTA at the kid's school? Did he coach little league?"

Mrs. Weston sipped on her tea and set down the cup on the saucer. "Kyle was what you'd call a man's man. I don't love the term, but more than one of his friends had described him as such. He liked to drink beer, watch football, and he pumped iron. Six days a week. His appearance was very important to him. He always dressed stylishly and was a fan of the ladies. Too much so."

"Did Kyle have a wandering eye?"

"It wandered, but it never acted, as far as I knew."

She probably didn't know. "When you say he liked the ladies too much, what do you mean? How did he act around other women?"

"He liked to flirt, especially with younger women. It was how he charmed me. We met at the restaurant I worked at. I was the server, but he flirted throughout his entire meal. The worst part? He was on a date with another woman. I knew he was a bad boy, but he was handsome. I figured it would be fun for a while, but then we fell in love. After he proposed, I assumed his eyes would stay focused on me."

"And you're sure he never had an affair?"

"Like I said, not that I knew of. There was nothing specific to make me think he had. But I'm not a fool. A zebra doesn't change his stripes."

"Did he have any enemies? Anybody who may have wanted to hurt him?"

"No, not really. He worked five to six days a week. He was good at his job and made good money. As far as I know, there weren't any issues at work. But he didn't always confide in me, either."

"Why do you say that?"

"Sometimes he would come home agitated, and he wouldn't tell me why. I didn't press."

"How did he treat you and your children? Was he kind, loving, attentive?"

"He worked a lot. He made some effort to go to the kids' soccer, basketball, and plays. That kind of thing. We had been married for a long time, and we didn't date or go out together as much anymore because he worked so much. The more successful he became, the less we saw him."

"How was your relationship with Kyle before he died?"

"It felt like we were two strangers. Ships passing in the night. He had a lot of business trips and worked a lot. I went to bed early, and he got home late."

"Is it fair to say the romance had fizzled?"

"Romance was long gone. It's tough with kids and a job and all the adult responsibility."

"I understand." And I did. Not that I had a romance to fizzle out. "You never suspected he was having an affair?" There was no romance in the marriage, yet he cared about his appearance more than average, arrived home late, and took a lot of business trips?

She shrugged halfheartedly. "I wondered. But he never slipped up, and I never found lipstick on his collar or suspicious receipts in his pockets. I guess maybe I didn't want to know."

Maybe it was easier that way. Pretending you didn't see the fault line running through your marriage. Jared and I hadn't been married long enough to fall out of love or to extinguish our passion for each other. "You said he was a man's man. Did that mean he ruled the house? Did he run the house like a dictator? Like, did he prescribe what activities you took part in or what to eat and cook?"

Mrs. Weston shook her head. "No. He wasn't home a lot, so I ran the house and took care of the kids. He was never unkind or abusive toward us. But Kyle could be short or maybe dismissive of people's feelings, like my own. He didn't like me nagging either. Nagging." She tsked. "Is it nagging to ask your husband to be home and spend time with his children? He played by his own rules. He was a jerk sometimes, but never abusive."

Interesting. Interviews at his place of work would have to tell us if Kyle was another man accused of sexual harassment or sexual assault, something that would tie him to Matt and Larry. A knock on the door directed the group's attention.

Mrs. Weston stood up. "That must be Kevin, Kyle's brother."

Mrs. Weston had been kind enough to arrange for her brother-in-law to come over to talk to us. It saved us a trip to his house across town. Apparently, Kyle and Crystal and their children were all the family he had in the area. What would he have to say about Kyle? Did Kyle confide in Kevin about any indiscretions?

A strapping man with salt-and-pepper hair and a black cashmere sweater and dark jeans strolled in. Based on photographs, he looked like his brother Kyle. Mrs. Weston had been right. He was handsome and, if he was charming too, perhaps he had flirted with the wrong woman and wound up dead. Vincent and I stood up. "Hi, I'm Martina and this is my partner, Vincent."

From the corner of my vision, I'd swear I saw a small smile form on Vincent's lips. He enjoyed being called my partner. "Kevin Weston, it's nice to meet you."

After polite handshakes and an exchange of business cards, Mrs. Weston offered her brother-in-law a beverage. He declined, and she looked over at us. "Would you mind if we spoke with Kevin alone?" I asked.

"Oh, of course not. I need to do laundry anyhow. Take all the time you need."

We thanked her, and she hurried out.

Kevin focused his piercing blue eyes on me. "So you're reopening Kyle's case?"

"We are."

"Have you found new information?"

"We have. We found other murders that are similar to your brother's. We're working with the Santa Monica Police Department to determine if there is a connection between the other cases and your brother's."

"Like a serial killer?"

"Something like that. We just spoke with your sister-in-law. She said that Kyle was a good man and treated the family decently and didn't have any affairs, no enemies."

Kevin shut his eyes and took a breath and exhaled. "And you want to know if that's true?"

"We do."

"My brother was a good man. Smart, charismatic. A bit of a ladies' man before he settled down."

Puzzling. "Once he was married, he didn't have any affairs?"

He glanced around the house, as if inquiring about his sister-in-law's location. When the coast was clear, he said, "There were a few other women. It started after he was married. I don't know, five, six years. I remember thinking it was odd that he had married in the first place. He was not one to pick just one girl. But he loved Crystal, and they seemed happy. But I think he got bored with the same dish every night, so to speak. I don't condone his behavior, but he was who he was. Are you thinking an affair could've led to his death? By a serial killer?"

There was skepticism in those sizzling eyes.

"We're just trying to understand everything there is to know about your brother. To determine if his death is connected to the others. Or if it could've been a jealous boyfriend or husband of one of the women he was seeing."

Vincent jumped in. "Or a scorned woman. Maybe a girl-friend wanted him to leave Crystal and he wouldn't."

"Like if I can't have him, nobody can?" I asked.

"Fatal attraction's not just a movie," Vincent quipped.

Kevin nodded, as if he understood what we were trying to learn. "Well, there wasn't anybody too significant, but there was one he dated for a while. She was young, and I think enamored with him and it flattered him. He thought it was just fun, and she thought it was a lot more."

"In the original investigation, you didn't mention these affairs. Why is that?"

"Well, the detectives thought it was suicide. Even though he had no reason to kill himself. He had everything, but you never really know, do you? Anyhow, they didn't ask about affairs, just enemies. And I didn't think he had any."

"Did he act strange around the time of his death?"

"No, my brother and I were close, and we told each other just about everything. The last girl he dated didn't take the breakup very well, but then it seemed to blow over. He wasn't concerned about it."

"How long before Kyle's death did the relationship end?"

"I'd say about a year."

"How long were they dating?"

"I think several months, and that's why she stands out. Most of his extracurriculars were chance encounters, but this one he saw for a while before he broke it off. He said he realized she was getting too serious about him."

"How did they meet?"

"They worked together."

"Do you remember her name?"

"It was something different. Millie, no Mila. That's right, Mila."

"Did you know her last name?"

He shook his head.

"Did he have any other significant affairs, something that wasn't just a chance encounter?" I asked, trying my darndest to not sound repulsed.

"She's the only one he dated for as long as he did. Usually the flings only lasted a few weeks or the duration of a business trip."

The perfect cover. "And do you know any of their names?"

"No. He never mentioned anyone but Mila by name."

"Is there anything else you can tell us that might help us find out who did this to him?"

"Not that I can think of. But please let me know if there is anything I can do to help. He may not have been a faithful man, but he never did anything that made him deserve to be killed."

We thanked him and made our way out of Kyle's house of lies. I couldn't wait to find out more about Mila and to interview the folks at Kyle's company. Had our killer targeted men who were misogynist cheaters or men who abused women or had treated women like playthings? If yes, the first three victims, Matt, Kyle, and Larry, would fit the profile.

31

MARTINA

The Human Resources representative at Trademark Industries testified that Kyle Weston was a model employee who had been with the company for several years. Coworkers liked him, and there were no complaints lodged against him. Was it true, or was this another Vaxxmore situation? "It sounds like he is missed."

"Oh, yes. It took us nearly a year to refill his position."

The woman seemed to be sincere, but so had Lynden at Vaxxmore. "I'm going to be brutally honest with you here, ma'am. We've done our fair share of interviews and learned corporate spokespersons aren't always straightforward with us. I want to give you a moment to reconsider your answer about Kyle Weston."

"I don't know what you mean."

"We find in times like these, people don't want to give the deceased a poor reputation if they didn't have one before. But that kind of thing comes out when we investigate. We just want to make sure that your company is being completely honest with us."

"I assure you what I say is the truth. I can provide employment records. There was never a complaint against him, and he always had the highest performance ratings. He was a valued member of our team," she said, rather incredulously.

"That's great to hear. When we spoke on the phone earlier, I had requested to interview people he worked with directly. Are they available today?"

"There's one who's on a trip, but most of them are available."

She passed a sheet of paper across the table. Scanning the interview schedule, I stopped and pointed to one name. Vincent peered over.

Mila Turner, financial analyst, one of Kyle's subordinates.

I'd bet dollars to donuts that Mila Turner was his mistress. "Excellent. This is very helpful."

"Are you ready to get started? I'll bring them in."

"We appreciate it."

She stepped out of the room and Vincent said, "Well, well, well. Ms. Mila Turner was easy to find."

"Another workplace affair gone *very* wrong?"

"It would fit. But is it too lucky that she's in the office today?"

"We didn't call them until this morning. She'd have no idea we were coming."

"True."

The first person walked in wearing a gray suit. After introductions and an explanation for our visit, Elijah Hall sat down.

"What can you tell us about Kyle?"

"Well, he was great at his job. He got along with everybody. Overall, he was a great guy, someone to go to happy hour with."

And not go home to his wife and children. "How was he with female colleagues?"

He nodded, as if he understood what we were asking. "I'm not gonna lie. Kyle liked women, but I never saw him or heard him do anything inappropriate. He had no complaints about him. And honestly, most of the girls flirted back. He was known for being the office hunk. Much to the rest of the men in the office's chagrin."

Not a harasser or criminal? "You don't think he ever crossed a line?"

"Not that I was aware of. If he had, he'd been careful. You can certainly ask the others, but I never heard a whisper of anything against Kyle."

"Was he close to any of his subordinates?"

He nodded again, as if he knew exactly who we were asking about. Which was odd, since he said he didn't know of any indiscretions. "Mila?"

"You tell me."

"I'm not sure if anything ever happened between them, but there was a lot of flirting. What I can tell you is the attention Kyle paid Mila was not unwelcome. She had eyes for him. I think most people kinda knew that. But like I said, I never saw anything inappropriate, like any touching or vulgar comments."

"Was there anybody else he was extra friendly with?"

"Sure. If she was young and hot, he had eyes for her. But again, I never saw him make a move on anybody in the office."

"Nobody at all?"

"I'm not saying he never did. I'm just saying I never saw it."

"Do you know if he had any enemies?"

"No."

"Thank you. You were very helpful."

After several more interviews with similar statements, I was ready to conclude that Kyle Weston had not assaulted or harassed anybody. Even the females we interviewed said they adored Kyle and admitted he was kind of a flirt but he never got handsy with any of them. But we still had a few more interviews and one in particular I couldn't wait for.

There was a knock on the door before it opened. A young woman with dark hair and big doe eyes entered, wearing a sharp black suit and white, crisp button-down shirt accented by a gold chain necklace. "Mila Turner?"

"Yes. I'm Mila."

"I'm Martina Monroe, and this is Vincent Teller. We're investigators from the CoCo County Sheriff's Department, and we're here because we're looking into the death of your former supervisor, Kyle Weston."

Mila had an olive complexion, but it had turned ashen. "Oh?"

"Yes, please have a seat. We'd like to ask you a few questions."

Mila was visibly nervous as she fidgeted and avoided making eye contact with us. "We're hoping you can tell us more about Kyle. What was he like to work for?"

"He was a great boss. He was really nice and fair. Enjoyable to work with."

"And what is your role here at the company?"

"I'm a financial analyst. We look at companies that are about to IPO, and we do a systematic analysis to determine their value so that they can set a stock price for the IPO."

"Sounds like a big job."

"We usually do a compilation. I do part of it and then maybe another one of our team does another part. We do multiple analyses to average out the price estimate. And then Kyle would make the final decision and communicate it to the firm."

"Fascinating."

"It's interesting work."

"Did you get along with Kyle?"

"I did."

"We've interviewed others here in the office and his family, and we were told that you and Kyle were more than a little friendly."

Her eyes grew as big as saucers. "Oh, I..."

"Were you having an affair with Kyle?"

"His family knows?" she asked, with a horrified look on her face.

"His brother knows."

She nodded.

"How did the affair start?"

"On a business trip. It was my first one since joining the company. Kyle was charismatic and smart. He was handsome and returned my attention. We were having drinks at the bar after a lecture, and one thing led to another. First, I thought it was a horrible mistake, but I kind of fell for him. I had a big crush on him before that. The cocktails simply loosened me up. You know, gave me the courage to take that extra step."

"How long did the affair last?"

"About six months."

"How did it end?"

Mila stared at the floor. "He told me he didn't want to continue. He said that he wanted to be a better man and be faithful to his wife, and so we ended things."

"How did you take the breakup?"

Staring straight into my eyes, she said, "I accepted it. I forgave him and moved on."

"When did the relationship end?"

"It was probably about a year before he died."

"Where were you on June seventh, the day Kyle died?"

"I was visiting family in Vancouver."

A solid alibi? "Do you have the exact dates of your trip?"

"I can get them to you."

"We appreciate that."

Vincent cocked his head and said, "One more thing. How did you feel when Kyle died?"

Mila swallowed. "It shocked me when I heard the news. I was still up at my parents' house. It was really shocking," she said, with very little emotion.

"We'd appreciate those dates of your trip."

"Absolutely."

I handed her my business card. "Just email the dates to me, or you can call me."

"Of course. Anything I can do to help your investigation."

She smiled, but the friendliness didn't meet her eyes.

Mila exited, and I turned to Vincent. "What did you think of her?"

"I think we need to learn more about Mila Turner."

"Exactly."

Something told me Mila wasn't being entirely truthful with us. Her smile was fake, as was her reaction to how she had felt when she learned Kyle had died. As soon as she learned we knew of Kyle and her affair, it was as if Mila's answers had been rehearsed. Had they been?

32

ANDREA

My plan of action was clear. Complete the mission. But first I had to stop the investigation. At a minimum, I had to divert attention away from the reopened murder investigations. I didn't start this, but I knew I had to be the one to end it. The other girls had chickened out. And the whole thing was Mila's idea! And now they wanted to lie low. Be cool. Forget the rest of the mission. We were not finished, and I wouldn't stop until I was. There was just one little thing in my way.

The man at the gun shop tried to convince me shooting a gun was easy as pie and even took me around the corner to the shooting range to show me how it was done. It was my first time, and I had told him so. He gave a creepy grin and said I was a "Shooting virgin." Talk about recoil.

Eye and ear protection in place, he instructed me to hold the gun in my dominant hand and steady it with the other. Standing with my feet shoulder-width apart, I took one step forward and aimed. I squeezed the trigger and jumped back. The man, likely flirting with me, laughed and said to keep steady and pull my shoulders back.

The second attempt, I kept my feet planted. And I felt powerful. Unstoppable. And that was exactly how I would be.

There were only two things stopping me from continuing my mission. Martina Monroe and Detective Hirsch. After a little research, I learned Martina was a mother and a widow. She was smart, and I could tell she cared about women. I couldn't leave her child an orphan, and I really didn't want to. I liked to think, under different circumstances, Martina and I would be friends.

Detective Hirsch, on the other hand, was a man and a police officer. Need I say any more? Who knows what he did to that poor beautiful pregnant wife behind closed doors? Did he keep her like a bird in a cage? Did he think since he was born with a penis he would be the one to dictate what she did, when she did it, and where she would go? Knocked up, she was stuck. Probably just how he wanted her — barefoot and pregnant. Wasn't that what all men wanted? To control us? To prove they were stronger? Braver? Scarier?

But they weren't. It was all a façade. I knew that because I could take any of them down with a single squeeze of the trigger. And I would.

It had taken three days to purchase the gun, putting me behind schedule. I wanted it done and over so I could move on to more important tasks.

Hat affixed, I straightened my sunglasses and drove slowly toward his house. With ice in my veins, I was ready. The patrol car parked out front and the other one heading toward my car turned that ice into a watery pool. Not only were there cops in front and driving by the detective's house, but a big beefy man was walking around the front yard. He carried himself like a police officer and had a firearm on his hip.

Sailing past the house, I continued on, as if I was innocently driving through the neighborhood. The plan was to get rid of the detective and stop the investigation, but there was no way I could take him out. It would be a suicide mission. The police had taken my threat seriously and were guarding the detective with their lives. And that wasn't part of my plan. A few blocks down, I stopped my car and screamed as I pounded on my steering wheel.

After everything I had done, it couldn't end like this.

My mission wasn't finished.

If this whole thing blew up and they figured out our mission, we'd all end up in jail. And if that was going to happen, I was going to make it count. And it wouldn't count until I was done.

Breathing even and heart rate back to normal, I realized trying to kill a cop was a bad idea. I could see that now. I was woman enough to admit it. I had to come up with a better plan. One that went off with a bang. If those other women wouldn't help me, then I would do it myself.

The others didn't have the guts to put it all on the line. That was because they hadn't endured what I had. I lost my sister. The others wanted revenge. Sure, I did too, but my sister died because of those men. They killed her. There was no way they should still be breathing. Thankfully, Matt wasn't. Matt didn't deserve water or air, and neither did Frank Musker. And I would rid the Earth of him, if it was the last thing I did.

33

MARTINA

The last forty-eight hours felt like a whirlwind. And it wouldn't stop until we solved the case. "I'll meet you in the squad room. I need to grab a coffee and talk to Sarge."

"Do you want me to order dinner?"

"It's only three-thirty."

"I'm starved."

My stomach grumbled. We had missed lunch. "You're right. Salad and pizza?"

"I'll tell them to send over our usual. We'll call it the Martina and Vincent special. A garden salad with chicken and a side of cheese pizza."

It was certainly different working alongside Vincent. He was young and fresh-faced, with a lot of energy. I missed Hirsch, but maybe Vincent was exactly what I needed to get through this investigation.

"Count me in." We only had an hour before Luna Katz was scheduled to be at the station for an interview. With the trip to Southern California, the interviews of people closest to Kyle Weston, and the flight that day, I was worn out and desperately needed all the energy I could get. Coffee, pizza, and salad would have to suffice.

Walking toward Sarge's office, my mind went back to the case. The interview with Kyle's former girlfriend, Mila Turner, wasn't sitting right with me. Could Kyle's death be a coincidence? And not at all connected to the others? It was possible, but my gut said otherwise.

Stepping up to Sarge's office door, I knocked.

"Martina, how's it going?"

"It's going and moving fast."

"Did you find anything interesting down in Santa Monica?"

"Kyle was dating a woman named Mila who worked at the firm. She says it ended amicably, but I'm not so sure."

"You think she could be our killer?"

"I don't know. Luna Katz is coming in an hour. We're prepping for the interview."

He removed his specs. "Have you been home?"

Do I look that bad? "Vincent and I came straight from the airport."

"Your mom's worried about you. She hasn't seen you like this before."

I wasn't sure I would ever get used to Mom dating Sarge, but soon I wouldn't be working with him, which might make the situation less strange. The one silver lining? "It's because she's only lived with me since I've been sober. I used to work crazy hours trying to distract myself from reality. This is a special circumstance. I won't let anything happen to Hirsch or anyone else on the team. Mom knows that, and Zoey's a trooper."

"I appreciate that. You're doing a hell of a job. I wish there was a spot for you."

The sentiment was sweet but getting a bit tiresome. If they really wanted me to stay, couldn't they make room somewhere? I wasn't exactly cheap, but c'mon. The sheriff had the power to keep my services but chose not to. "I'll be okay. And I have a feeling you won't be rid of me that easily."

He gave a knowing smile. I had suspected he was itching to ask my mom a very important question. Stranger things had happened. If Mom married Sarge, he would be my stepdad. And it would be just Zoey and me again. It was like as soon as I thought I had life figured out, God laughed at me and changed it all up.

"I'm about to call Hirsch with an update, but as far as the case, he'll be at home until we catch those responsible for the threats."

"Agreed. As I know the sheriff does too. He is all about protecting the team and will do anything he can to help. He's a good guy."

"I'm getting that impression." Unfortunately, most of my tenure at the CoCo County Sheriff's Department didn't include Sheriff Baldwin. Just when a good guy took the spot, I was out. Wasn't that how life always worked? Our experience was an equilibrium. Once tipped, it would right itself in due time. And I had faith things would be righted again soon.

"How's Vincent doing?"

"He's doing a great job. You should consider him for more detective work. He's pretty good. He catches the little nuances and inconsistencies from the witnesses. He's sharp."

"Good to know." He paused. "Take it easy, Martina."

Update to the boss complete, I headed toward my favorite machine in the building. The coffee maker. Minutes later, clutching my coffee cup like it was a lifeline because it kinda was, I met up with Vincent in the squad room. "Anything new from the research team?"

He shook his head.

"Food here yet?"

"Should be here in about twenty minutes."

"Great. Let's talk strategy."

AN HOUR and a call from the receptionist later, I set down my second cup of coffee since arriving at the station, and said, "Are you ready to meet Luna?"

"I am."

Inside one of the smaller conference rooms, a young woman with blonde hair, flawless complexion, and a winning smile stood and said, "Hi, I'm Luna."

"Martina Monroe, and this is Vincent Teller. Thank you for coming down here today." Handshakes ensued, and the vibe I had gotten from Mila was present with Luna. Too calm. Too polished.

Something told me we were lucky she came in on her own since our research team hadn't found any travel reservations for Luna. No hotel, flight, or car rental reservations. I didn't know where she'd been, but she had been untraceable. Seated, I said, "We're going to cut right to the chase, Luna. We're investigating the death of Larry Henderson, and we've been told by a few sources you had accused him of sexual assault at the holiday party. Can you explain what happened that night?" It wasn't my typical style to request a victim recount trauma, but we needed to know if the complaint had been credible.

"Well, as you said, it was at the holiday party three years ago. There was an open bar, and I'd had a few, and so had Larry. He kept coming up to me, asking me to dance. I tried to brush him off. He wasn't my type, and it was totally inappropriate. But he kept at it, saying how beautiful I looked. I continued to say thanks, but no thanks. He said he just wanted to talk. I figured it was my chance to let him have it. Say no means no. You're making me uncomfortable, that sort of thing. We went down the hall into what looked like a supply closet. When he shut the door, I realized my mistake and tried to get out of there. He blocked the door and said, 'I've always wanted to get you alone in a dark room.' And I told him, 'I want to leave. Let me out.' But he just laughed and grabbed my wrists and told me, 'Not until we're done.' I told him, 'This isn't funny. Let me go.'"

She paused, and I began to see flaws in her polished demeanor. "He said, 'Oh, it will be fun.' And I threatened to scream if he didn't let me go, and that's when he put his hand over my mouth." She stopped as tears streamed down her cheeks, as if she were reliving the incident. "And then he shoved me against a shelf, pushed up my dress, pulled down my underwear, he unzipped his pants, and he raped me." She began sobbing.

I was filled with guilt. I'd thought we could break her, and she would tell us what she had done to Matt and Larry. Our theory was the victim wanted revenge against her attacker and that may be so, but she was still a victim. She didn't seem enraged or full of fury. She seemed broken.

Vincent handed her a box of tissues, and a few moments later, she dabbed her eyes and wiped her cheeks before blowing her nose. She sniffled and said, "It was over pretty fast. After I curled up on the floor, he said, 'C'mon, I know you wanted it.' " She shook her head. "He was such a monster."

He *was* a monster. "I'm so sorry that happened to you."

"Well, nobody seemed to care when he did it."

"I'm also sorry that happened to you. How have you been able to cope with what happened?"

After feeling like a bit of a monster myself, I changed to a much softer approach with Luna.

Luna regained her composure, head held high. "I'm in therapy, and I have friends and a support group. They have helped me cope and move on. Given me purpose. Things are better at my new company."

"It sounds like you have worked hard to move forward."

She shrugged. "I have. And you know, I didn't think it would take so long to get over. Sometimes I wonder if I ever will get over it."

Trauma was difficult to conquer, and time didn't heal all wounds. Looking over at Vincent, I saw that he appeared as rattled by the testimony as I was.

Hearing Luna's account of the attack, I could almost see killing Larry as self-defense, but it wasn't. No matter how bad the bad guy was, we couldn't allow people, or victims, to run around killing people. And we knew that whoever killed Larry did so in cold blood.

Vincent nodded. "When was the last time you saw Larry?"

She averted her gaze. "I don't know. I guess maybe a month after that happened. When I left the company."

"Two years later, Larry died on September thirteenth. Where were you that day?"

She stiffened. "I was at a conference in North Carolina. It was on behalf of my new company."

"Would you be able to provide us with the exact dates and conference details?"

"I'd have to look it up, but sure. There are plenty of records. I can email them to you," she said, with eye contact and a renewed self-confidence.

"That would be really helpful. Thank you."

Vincent said, "To be honest, we're not only investigating Larry's death but also that of a man by the name of Matthew Baldwin. Did you know him?"

Her eyes brightened. "No."

"Did you know someone by the name of Sarah Nesbit?"

She nodded. "Of course. We were roommates in college. Why?"

"Matthew Baldwin assaulted her. Did you know that?"

"Was he the scumbag she worked with? She told me about a monster at work but never said his name. She told me that no one at work believed her and he just got away with it. Like he got away with everything else. Men get away with everything," she said with irritation.

"You stayed in contact with Sarah after college?"

"She was one of my closest friends. What they did to her was unforgivable."

The deeply traumatized, sobbing woman from earlier was gone. This was a woman filled with anger and an edginess.

"Where were you two years ago, March ninth? I understand if you have to check your calendar. It was quite a while ago."

"Well, that one's easy to remember. I was on a girls' trip. Hawaii," she said, straight-faced and a little smug if I was reading her correctly.

Girl's trip to Hawaii? "Would you be able to provide us with those details as well?"

"Of course."

Assuming her alibis checked out, she wasn't our killer. Yet, my gut was telling me there was more to Luna than met the eye. If Luna wasn't our killer, then who? There was more than one puzzle piece missing. And we needed to find them — ASAP.

34

MARTINA

Bright and early, I received an email from Luna Katz with her alibis. Both the details for her trip to North Carolina when Larry Henderson was killed and her trip to Hawaii when Matt Baldwin was killed. She had provided receipts and the dates. Luna was trying to be helpful or trying to clear her name quickly so we would take her name off the list of suspects. Which, frankly, we had to. But then what was niggling in my gut?

Vincent approached, looking rested. We both took a beat and went home to sleep and make an appearance with our loved ones. Sleeping in my bed, seeing Zoey, and a home-cooked meal were priceless.

"Get some rest?"

"I did. How often do you have to travel?"

"It depends. Especially as a PI, you never know where the case will take you. If it's a kidnapping or long-lost family member, it can take you across the country or a trip around the Bay Area."

"Does it get tiring?"

"It can. Especially if you're continually traveling. It's easy to get homesick, missing family and friends."

"Hadn't thought about that. I don't mind travel."

Because he was young. "Are you thinking about making investigations a permanent gig?"

"I'm weighing my options."

"Not an awful choice."

"What are your plans?"

Word about the changes to the squad had spread quickly despite efforts to keep it hush-hush. "I'm going back to my firm full-time."

"Everything is going to change. Just when this room felt like home," he said wistfully.

Indeed. "The end of an era."

Vincent looked away.

We hadn't had any lengthy discussions about the end of the squad. It was too sad and distracting. Obviously, I wasn't the only one who was feeling it. I said, "Don't worry. You can't get rid of me that easily. Inside or outside this room, we're family now."

"And who knows, maybe we'll end up working together again."

"Our firm can always use someone with your talent. You're darn good at your job, Vincent."

"I am pretty good, aren't I?" he said, puffing out his chest.

At least I got him to turn his frown upside down. "I knew I would regret that."

He gave a cocky smile before he turned serious again. "What do you make of our interview with Luna yesterday?"

"Her alibis check out. She couldn't have killed Larry or Matt. But I feel like we're missing something."

"She was too confident."

True. Guilty or not, most people questioned by the police appeared nervous. "Agreed."

"Do you think her crying act was genuine?"

"I do. That type of trauma is difficult to get past. But her demeanor changed during the interview. When she was done discussing the assault, she reverted to a poised and confident woman. An angry one. The question is, is she only angry at just Larry or other people's abusers too? She's a perfect suspect except for the fact that she has solid alibis for the two murders we liked her for."

"Not an insignificant detail. Hirsch coming in today?"

"He'll be in for a few hours this afternoon. He doesn't want to leave Kim for long. Between us, he says Kim is getting bigger by the minute. They think she might have the baby pretty soon. All this stress isn't helping."

"I'm glad he's taking time to be with her. It's more important than solving a case, you know?"

It was moments like these that I saw Vincent in a different light — thoughtful and introspective. It was as if he was a kid at heart but also an old soul at the same time. "I agree."

Before I could say another word, the door opened, and Rosemary rushed in. Her green eyes were wide and her unruly curls flowing as she hurried across the conference room. "Hey, Rosemary."

"You won't believe what I found."

"What did you find?"

"Luna Katz, Sarah Nesbit, and Mila Turner all went to UCLA at the same time, and they all shared an address. They were all roommates."

Vincent and I both stood stunned. "Are you sure?"

"One hundred percent. They all know each other, and do you want to hear another interesting connection?"

"I do." We needed all the connections we could get.

"I went through the emails that you sent me from Luna about her travel."

Was her alibi fake? "What did you find? Was it a lie?"

"Oh, no, her alibis check out. She could not have killed Matt Baldwin or Larry Henderson."

"Okay?" So then, what was the big deal?

"But when I saw the name of the resort in Hawaii Luna stayed at, it triggered a memory. One of the other suspects stayed at the same resort at the same time. And they were on the same flight."

"Girls' trip."

"That's right. Andrea Puerto and Luna Katz went to Hawaii together. They stayed at the same hotel, in the same room. I called and checked."

Andrea and Luna were close enough that they traveled together. And Mila and Luna were roommates with Sarah. "What about Mila's alibi for Kyle Weston's murder?"

A smile crept onto Rosemary's face. "You'll love this. Her alibi checks out. Mila was in Vancouver visiting family when Kyle was killed. Her parents have a house there, but it's not Vancouver, Canada. It's Vancouver, Washington which sits on the Oregon-Washington border."

We had two murders in Oregon and Washington. "Did you find a link between Mila and Danny Appleton or Scott Ogden?"

"That's our next search."

"Thanks, Rosemary."

She smiled and hurried back out of the squad room.

"Are you thinking what I'm thinking?" Vincent asked.

Unclear. "What are you thinking?"

"Larry assaulted Luna. Mila had a workplace-affair-gone-wrong with Kyle. Matt assaulted Andrea's sister, Sarah. All three connect to Sarah — and the first murder — Matt Baldwin.

This is no coincidence. And I think Andrea, Luna, and Mila know a lot more about the murders than they've told us. Like, they may be the masterminds behind all of them."

Like Hirsch, my belief in coincidences no longer existed. But what Vincent was implying — could it be true? Had Andrea, Luna, and Mila gone on a murder spree to avenge each other, and Sarah? And if so, how had they done it? And more importantly, since the last murder was only two months earlier, were they done with their killing spree?

35

ANDREA

He was a creature of habit. Lucky for me. Thankfully, I recalled Sarah gushing over how he was so fit and went for a run every morning at 6 AM on the trail near his house, regardless of whether it was light, dark, or freezing outside. From what I had witnessed, he had all the gear for the elements. Head lamp. Reflectors. The latest in tech outerwear. He had thought of everything. *Well, not everything.*

Honestly, after watching him at Vaxxmore and tracking his every move over the last few days, I did not know what Sarah had seen in him. He was boring and not *that* cute. He was kind of a nerd. It was probably some type of workplace Stockholm syndrome. It was the only thing that made any sense to me.

Having watched him, I knew when he'd be on the most isolated part of the path. I parked my car under a tree and stood near the trail that he ran every day.

Personally, I varied my routine. If I didn't, someone could watch me and anticipate my every move. And then, bam! They could take me out.

Being too predictable was more dangerous than walking into oncoming traffic. If you hang with the wrong people or make the wrong people mad. Mad enough to hurt you. *And, Dr. Frank Musker, you have made me furious.* There was never another soul I had hated like I hated him.

Wearing athletic wear to blend in, I set off into a light jog with my hand in my jacket pocket, clutching my secret weapon.

I chuckled to myself.

It was a secret.

And it was a weapon.

After an uphill segment, I stopped to run in place and waited thirty seconds before I heard the patter of a runner's feet punching down onto the gravel trail. Starting up again, I continued onward casually to bump into him for an, "Oh my gosh, it's you," type scenario.

He was easy to spot with the light strapped to his forehead. It was ridiculous, but it was dark out. I stopped and said, "Frank?"

He turned around. He hadn't even noticed me until I called his name. "Andrea?" his voice cracked.

In that moment, I knew he knew exactly who I was. "That's right, I'm Andrea. You know who I am, don't you?"

He stopped and walked toward me. "I do. The detectives told me you're Sarah's sister."

"I am."

"I'm sorry for your loss. She was an amazing young woman."

That she was, but I didn't take stock in words that exited his mouth. His lips only spewed lies and heartbreak. "You know you're responsible for what happened to her, right?"

Even on the dark trail, I could tell he paled to a pasty shade. His eyes looked sad, but I didn't think he was capable of the emotion. "I didn't know she would kill herself. I would've handled things differently if I'd known."

Shaking with anger, I said, "Would you have? It's because of you I don't have my sister anymore. Your cruelty devastated her.

Your dismissal broke her. She killed herself thinking there was nothing to stop that pain. You did that to her."

"I'm sorry for what happened to your sister. I wish things were different, but I think maybe she needed help. I wish I would've seen that she needed help. I could've helped her."

"Oh, really, you would have helped her? All you ever did was hurt her."

"Look, I'm sorry, but I don't know what else to tell you. I'm really sorry about what happened to Sarah. I truly am."

"I don't think you're sorry enough."

· He shook his head, as if annoyed with me. *Oh, he will be more than a little annoyed with me in a moment.* "Look, I said I'm sorry, but I have to go."

I pulled my hand, clutching the gun, from my pocket and pointed it at his chest. "I don't think we're done, Frank."

"Hey." He raised his hands in defense. "I'm so sorry. You're right. I am responsible for Sarah's death. I'll do anything you want. I could open a charity in her name, and I can pay you. Do you want money?"

I'd had enough of this terrible creature. I growled, "Money? You think I want money in exchange for you killing my sister? Seriously?"

He stared at me with a look of terror.

"That's right, you should be scared. Because your fate is the same as Matt's."

He shook his head, as if making the connection. "You killed Matt?"

"Not personally. A friend of mine did. We taught that monster a lesson. The ultimate lesson."

"A friend of yours killed Matt?" he asked, with confusion.

"Yes. We came up with the perfect way to honor Sarah. To snuff out the men who placed that razor blade in her hand."

"I'm so sorry. You don't have to do this," he cried.

He wasn't sorry, but he would be. Like the man at the gun shop taught me, I pulled the trigger, and he went down, face first, onto the trail. Staring down at his crumpled body, I thought, that's more like what I suspected death would look like. But like my first kill, it was almost too easy.

After a quick glance around the trail, I ran back down the hill, hopped into my car, and drove off. As I sped down the road, I thought, *I hope the wild animals get to him.*

36

MARTINA

"Hey, hey, hey. It's the big boss man. Good to see you, Hirsch," Vincent said.

I was happy to see Hirsch, too. We didn't have many days left in the Cold Case Squad room together, and I was savoring every moment. Not that after December I would never see him again. He was family.

"You, too. Martina, how's the team?"

"They're doing well. They're all working on the case. Jayda and Ross are up north interviewing the family, friends, and acquaintances of Danny Appleton and Scott Ogden. They should be back tomorrow."

Vincent said, "And Jess will be here tomorrow to discuss the FBI profile on our killer or killers." He cast a knowing glance over at me.

"Sounds like there's been a development. What's going on?"

"Come over to the whiteboard, and we'll explain."

After an explanation of the connections found between Andrea, Mila, and Luna, Hirsch said, "What about Jennifer and Marcia? They worked with Larry Henderson and didn't like him much either."

"They have alibis. They were at work at the time he died."

Hirsch contemplated it. "So, the three key people of interest are Andrea, Mila, and Luna?"

"It's our working theory. It's unusual, but it fits."

Hirsch scratched the back of his head, and I wondered if he was getting enough sleep. He said, "Like some kind of vigilante girl gang?"

"Why not? The killings didn't start until after Sarah died. Her death might have been the trigger."

Hirsch nodded. "The women have alibis for the victims they're connected to. But do they have alibis for each other's attackers, or in Andrea's case, her sister's attacker?"

Vincent and I exchanged glances. "Not yet."

We needed all three in the station for questioning.

"Do you think Andrea is the ringleader?" Hirsch asked.

Vincent nodded. "Andrea has exhibited the strangest behavior. The fact she works where Sarah worked right before Matt died is odd. We all agree on that."

Vincent was right. It was weird. Everybody grieved differently, but it just didn't seem to fit. Especially since she didn't tell anybody she was Sarah's sister. It made little sense, and when things don't make sense, it's usually because they're not true.

Hirsch pointed at Danny Appleton and Scott Ogden's photos. "Any connection between these two?"

"We haven't found anything yet, but Mila grew up in Washington state, so maybe."

"Have we checked their employment records? Maybe one girl worked with Scott Ogden or spent time at the University of Seattle, where Danny Appleton was a professor?"

Before I could answer, Rosemary entered. Hirsch eyed her suspiciously, and I realized they hadn't met. Rosemary was a recent transfer from Alameda County. She was bright and maybe in her mid-thirties, with strawberry-blonde hair and a smattering of freckles against her peaches and cream complexion. "Is this a bad time?"

Vincent said, "No, it's fine. Hirsch, this is Rosemary. She's new on the team."

Eyeing Hirsch, I said, "She's good."

Rosemary blushed. Hirsch said, "It's very nice to meet you. It seems like you have something to share."

"It's nice to meet you too, and yes. I figured you would want to know right away. Not that it's great news."

"What is it?"

"Well, we finished doing the employment searches for Mila, Luna, Andrea, and Sarah. We even looked at all the odd angles most won't see. But even though Mila grew up in Washington, she has no affiliation with Scott Ogden's company or with the University of Seattle, where Danny Appleton was a professor. There is no connection between the suspects and the last two victims."

No connections to the last two murders. Maybe it was a different killer who used the same MO? We were still missing a major piece of the puzzle. "Thanks, Rosemary."

"No problem."

"No connection to the other two. What does this mean?"

Hirsch studied the board, as if trying to make sense of everything we had learned until that point. "We're fairly certain all the murders are connected. And there was no physical evidence left at any of the crime scenes."

Vincent said, "Which is why they went cold."

"Exactly. No evidence. Which means these murders were well thought out."

A smart killer? "Absolutely."

"We don't have motives for Danny and Scott."

I explained, "Not yet. Ross and Jayda are up north right now."

"I'd be itching to hear what they find. If they don't find a connection to Sarah, Andrea, Mila, or Luna, that means..."

I finished his thought aloud. "There has to be another killer or another member of this vigilante group."

Vincent said, "Or it's none of them. Maybe it's somebody getting revenge on their behalf? Maybe there's someone in their lives who knew all of them. It's likely they have other mutual friends. A boyfriend, brother, dad, or sister who wants revenge for everything that happened to those women. We need to keep our eyes open for possibilities other than the vigilante girl group scenario. We don't want to have tunnel vision and miss something important."

"Thanks for keeping us honest, Vincent."

"Anytime. But seriously, it may be somebody else. We should check to find their mutual friends or family. Or maybe it's not even them. Maybe it's someone who's not even that close to them. One who sat quietly in the corner and plotted revenge for them."

A needle in a haystack. "That's true. Without physical evidence, anything's possible."

A sinking feeling dripped into me. Even if our theory about the vigilante girl group was right, how on Earth would we prove it? "There's no physical evidence."

Hirsch said, "Exactly. We need to keep looking at all angles."

Vincent said, "I hate these types of cases."

"What do you mean?"

"The kind where the only way we'll actually put someone in jail is if someone talks."

He may be right. "Or messes up and leaves a clue."

"They haven't messed up yet. But to be sending threats demanding we stop the investigation, they must be getting nervous."

"We should re-interview Andrea and ask her about the other women. See if we can trip her up."

"Good idea. Let's head over to her office."

"A surprise attack," Vincent said, with excitement.

"What do you think, Hirsch?"

"I think it's a good idea. Andrea seems the most likely to become unhinged. She's the oddest one, right?"

"Definitely."

"All right, well, let me know if you need me."

"Are you heading home?"

"Yeah, after I talked to Sarge, the sheriff, and a few of the team. I don't want them to forget me," he said sheepishly.

"We couldn't forget you, boss."

"Even if we tried," I said with a smile.

WE MADE A BEELINE TOWARD RECEPTION. I waved to the now-familiar receptionist, Rita. "Hello again."

Rita's smile seemed forced. "Hi. What can I do for you today?"

"We need to see Andrea Puerto."

"I haven't seen her today, but I'll call her desk."

"Thank you." We stepped back and waited for her to call Andrea to make sure she was in her office. She hung up, and we returned to the desk.

"She doesn't appear to be in her office. I've been here since seven and haven't seen her. Do you want to leave a message?"

"No, but since we're here, we would like to speak with Lynden."

"Sure, I'll call her."

Within moments of Rita's call, Lynden greeted us. Her face was pale, and she appeared shaken. "Is everything all right?"

She shook her head. "Come into my office."

With a nod, we followed her to her office. Inside, with the door shut, I said, "What's going on?"

"Something terrible has happened."

"What happened?"

"Frank's wife called. He was shot earlier this morning. He was out for his morning run, and they shot him. They think maybe a mugging. I don't know. He's at the hospital. He's in surgery. They're not sure he's going to make it."

Someone was finishing the job. Why hadn't I thought of it before? If someone wanted revenge for Sarah, they would kill both Matt and Frank. Vincent and I turned toward one another. He and I both knew Frank's shooting was connected to the five other deaths. I returned my attention to Lynden. "That's terrible. What hospital is Frank being treated at?"

"Mount Diablo."

With urgency, I said, "Thank you, Lynden," and turned to the exit.

"Wait. Do you think it's related to Matt's death?"

Absolutely. "I'm not sure."

"Oh, my. Is there anything I can do to help?"

"Would you know if Andrea Puerto called in sick?"

"I wouldn't know. Her manager might."

"Do you mind if we check the offices to see if she's here? The receptionist said she didn't think so."

"Let me check our system and see if she submitted a vacation day. If she did, it would be in the system." She sat down, still shaking, and tapped away on the keys. Moments later, she shook her head. "Not a planned vacation. You're welcome to look in the offices."

"Okay. Have you told the staff what happened to Frank?"

Tears escaped and dribbled down Lynden's cheeks. "No, I

just found out myself. This is so awful. He was such a good man."

Debatable. "We'll keep that to ourselves. We'll do a quick perusal of the facility and see if she's here."

"Okay."

We said our goodbyes and began the search, but after a quick rush around the office and conversation with Andrea's supervisor, Andrea was nowhere to be found and hadn't called in sick. She was officially MIA.

Outside the office building, Vincent said, "She's finishing the job."

"Exactly what I was thinking. We need to get to the hospital and hope Frank wakes up and can ID the shooter." Fingers crossed he would give us the answers we desperately needed.

37

MARTINA

WHILE VINCENT DROVE to the hospital, I placed a call to the Alameda County Sheriff's Department to get the name of the investigating officer for the Frank Musker shooting. After explaining our interest in the case, they gave me Detective Olivio's contact information to learn the details of the shooting. Not wasting any time, I called.

"Olivio here."

"Detective Olivio, my name is Martina Monroe with the CoCo County Sheriff's Department. I heard you're working the Frank Musker shooting. Is that correct?"

"It is."

"My partner, Detective Hirsch, and I met Frank during our investigation into the death of Matt Baldwin, and we think there might be a connection."

"Sheriff Baldwin's brother?"

"That's correct."

"What's the connection?"

"Matt Baldwin worked with Frank, and we think Matt's killer may have a grudge against Frank. We're certain the perp is still active. We'd like to come to the hospital and question Frank."

"He's not out of surgery yet."

"Are you at the hospital?"

"I am."

"We—my associate Vincent and I—would like to discuss the case with you. Are you open to us stopping by for a conversation?"

"We'll see you when you get here."

"Thanks." After ending the call, I turned to Vincent. "They're okay with us coming by."

"They sound cooperative."

"I think they will be. Hirsch has a reputation."

"Not just Hirsch."

"I suppose." The press coverage made us more notorious than I would like, but sometimes it came in handy.

WE DARTED through the hospital doors to escape the chill. Inside was slightly less cold and stank of cleaning products and sick people. I hated hospitals. And I hated being confined to a hospital bed even more.

We followed the signs to the emergency room and spotted two men in dark blue suits carrying themselves like cops. Our detectives. Next to them were two women, one middle-aged blonde and a woman in her fifties with gray hair. The women were clutching each other. Perhaps Frank's wife? Vincent and I headed toward the detectives.

They stepped away from the women. "Martina Monroe?"

I nodded. "And this is Vincent Teller. He's working the case with Hirsch and me."

"I'm Olivio, and this is my partner, Samson."

Firm handshakes ensued. "Where's Hirsch?"

"Hirsch is at home with his very pregnant wife. He's had a few threats against his life. Hand-delivered to his house. We think it was the perp who took out Matt Baldwin."

Detective Olivio gritted his teeth. "Yikes." He placed his thick arms across his chest. "And you think the same person came after Frank?"

After explaining the status of the investigation, the connection between Matt, Frank, and Sarah, as well as our current theory, I said, "So, we think taking out Frank was them finishing the job — revenge for Sarah's death."

"Does Mrs. Musker know about her husband's indiscretions?"

"According to Frank, no."

Detective Olivio let out a whistle. "Any suspects?"

"We have a few persons of interest, but no physical evidence. We're hoping Frank can ID the shooter and give us the break we need to bring the killer in."

"Who are you looking at for this?"

"Our lead theory is Sarah's sister, Andrea Puerto, was involved. She also works with Frank, and she didn't show up for work today. Didn't call in sick. We came straight here from their office."

Detective Samson said, "Sounds suspicious to me. But why the change in MO?"

"We think the killer, or killers, got nervous and thought they were running out of time to take out Frank."

"I can see it," Detective Olivio commented.

Vincent said, "What do you know about Frank's shooting?"

"He was on the trail near his house in the Oakland hills. Shot in the chest, missed his carotid artery by a millimeter. He's lucky to be alive. No witnesses. Another jogger saw him lying on the trail and called 9-1-1. Frank just got out of surgery, but he's not awake yet. Did you want to talk to the wife? She's here. She's pretty broken up, but..."

"Not broken up enough?" I asked.

Detective Olivio shrugged. "I don't know. Maybe she knew about Frank's affair after all."

"If Mrs. Musker knew, do you like her for the shooting?"

Detective Olivio waved us down the hall before he said, "She was at the top of the suspect list when we first questioned her. She said at the time of the shooting, she was home, alone."

I said, "Add the affair and you have a solid motive."

"Except we did a GSR test. She's clean. She's not our shooter."

Gun Shot Residue test ruled her out for the actual shooting, but not for conspiracy. She could have hired out the task. We couldn't rule it out. "Maybe a hit?"

"It's possible. We're still pulling financials to see if there's anything that could show conspiracy. We haven't ruled Mrs. Musker out yet."

Smart. "Do you mind if we talk to her?"

"Be my guest. I'll introduce you."

Quietly, we walked over to the grieving wife. "Mrs. Musker, this is Martina and Vincent from the CoCo County Sheriff's Department. They're investigating the death of your husband's colleague, Matt Baldwin."

She nodded, as if she understood and knew we were investigating the case. Mrs. Musker, the younger blonde, looked shaken but not falling apart. She said, "Frank told me they reopened the investigation. He said he was surprised to hear you thought Matt was murdered." She studied our faces. "Wait, do you think Frank's attack is related to Matt's death?"

An awfully quick connection. Too quick? "Do you have reason to believe that their deaths would be related?"

She let out a sigh. "Maybe."

"Maybe?" I asked.

"A few days ago, Frank told me about Sarah. I guess with the detectives coming and asking questions about Matt and his relationship with Sarah, he figured it would get out. He said he wanted to get it off his chest."

I grabbed a peek at Detective Olivio, who was probably thinking what I was. *Motive.* She just learned her husband had been cheating on her and someone shot him shortly after. "How did you take the news?"

"A mix of heartbreak and anger. I couldn't believe Frank would do that to me. After all this time. I never even suspected."

She was either a talented actress or genuine. "Did you have anything to do with Frank's attack?"

Her eyes widened. "No. I was angry and sad. But I didn't do this to Frank."

The woman next to her wrapped an arm around Mrs. Musker's shoulder. The gray-haired woman glared at us. "My sister did not shoot Frank."

"Who do you think hurt Frank?" Vincent asked.

"Maybe a mugging?" And with that, Mrs. Musker broke down into sobs.

In a few days, she had learned her husband was unfaithful with a young coworker and now he was fighting for his life in the hospital.

The sister said, "This is a very difficult time. Do you really need to do this right now?"

Detective Olivio said, "Ma'am, with these types of cases, we need to learn as much as we can as quickly as we can."

Mrs. Musker pushed her sister off and said, "I didn't try to kill Frank. Whatever questions you have are fine."

"Other than Frank's confession a few days ago, has anything strange happened lately? Did he receive any notes or threats, or did he act out of character?"

She shook her head. "No, no strange notes, no strange calls. His routine was exactly the same. He was up and out running every morning at six. After that, he'd be home to shower and head to work. Every day."

I was sure the shooter knew that. "Okay, thank you for your cooperation." I nodded to the detectives, and we stepped aside. I said, "I don't think she did it."

Detective Olivio said, "No, I don't think so either. But I'm certainly interested in talking to Andrea."

"We need to find her first. When we do, we'll call you."

"Sounds good."

A doctor in blue scrubs with tired eyes approached Mrs. Musker. We hurried back over. The doctor said, "Frank is in recovery. But we placed him in an induced coma. His injuries are pretty grave. It could still go either way. He could be here awhile."

Detective Olivio said, "When will you know if he's gonna make it?"

"The next twenty-four hours are critical."

"Thanks, doctor."

The doctor turned his attention to the wife.

I had heard all I needed to hear. We had a shooter on the loose, and we needed to find him or her before they tried to kill someone else. *Someone like Hirsch.*

38

MARTINA

ON THE WAY to Andrea Puerto's home, I called Hirsch to update him about Frank Musker and told him to stay away from windows until we could locate the shooter. He thought I was being overprotective, considering the safety measures already put in place. Maybe so, but it needed saying.

Vincent pulled up in front of a townhouse with dark brown trim. "This is it. This is Andrea's house."

"Backup should be here any minute." With Andrea potentially armed and dangerous, I wasn't taking any chances.

The house was on a cul-de-sac with identical brown and beige townhomes. The sun had been down for hours, and no neighbors were out walking the dog or out for a jog. With no car in the driveway or movement visible near the Puerto residence, my hopes weren't high we would find Andrea inside.

Two patrol cars pulled up, and we popped out of the car. Black-and-whites blocked the driveway, and within moments, the uniformed officers were out of their cars and headed toward us. "Officer Olsen, good to see you. Vincent and I will go in the front."

"You got it. We'll take the perimeter."

With a nod, we hurried toward the front door. The porch light illuminated it. Curtains closed, no lights appeared to be on within the house. I knocked three times.

Met with silence, I knocked again.

No response.

I yelled out, "CoCo County Sheriff's Department. Please open up."

Nothing. The only sounds were the swishing of uniform blues rushing around the yard. Andrea wasn't there.

Without a beat, I pulled out my cell phone and dialed Andrea's number.

Straight to voicemail.

"No answer." Shoving the phone in my jacket, I waved over Officer Olsen and his partner.

He ran up and said, "No movement around the yard. No car in the garage."

Vincent said, "She's not here. But I bet I know where she is."

Of course. "The cabin."

Vincent said, "Exactly. It makes sense."

Officer Olsen looked puzzled. "What cabin?"

"Andrea's family has a cabin in Lake Tahoe. Andrea has told us she likes to go there." Which I still couldn't wrap my head around.

Officer Olsen said, "We can call in a team if you want to head over tonight. Forecast shows snow in the Sierras. The drive may require 4-wheel drive or chains. It would be faster to call over to the local PD and have them check to see if she's there. Or keep an eye out until you can make the drive."

"Smart. I'll call over."

"If you need any help, let us know. Otherwise we'll head back."

There was no reason to keep them around. With no

evidence Andrea was the shooter, we didn't have a search warrant to go inside. We were simply trying to find her.

"Go. I'll call over to Tahoe PD and get eyes on her before making the trek."

"Good luck and be safe."

"Thanks. Have a good night."

Officer Olsen waved over the rest of the team, likely to give the update, before he jogged back to his vehicle. I supposed if Andrea had been there, it would have been too easy.

Vincent said, "Let's call the team on the way back to the station and get contact details for local PD. We don't want her running around Tahoe armed and dangerous."

I reminded him, "If she's the shooter."

"But you think it's her."

My efforts to improve my poker face hadn't paid off. "My gut says it's her, but I'm not sure. I have been wrong before."

Vincent harrumphed.

"I have."

"Yeah, maybe once out of a million times," he said.

"You drive. I'll make the calls. If they find Andrea, I want them to monitor her until we can talk to her."

"You got it, boss."

Was Andrea holed up at the cabin, or was she out hunting? We didn't know if she was done with her murder spree or just getting started.

39

MARTINA

BRIGHT AND EARLY THE next morning, I stared at the murder board, reexamining the details of the case. There were still several unknowns. We knew the murders of Matt, Kyle, and Larry were most likely related to Mila, Luna, and Sarah, as was Frank's shooting. But we had nothing tying the crew to Danny or Scott's death.

If Mrs. Musker hadn't hired someone to kill her husband, the only logical scenario, to me, was that whoever was seeking revenge for Sarah's death was finishing the job by attempting to murder Frank.

My gut screamed it was Andrea. Thankfully, the locals confirmed Andrea's SUV was in the driveway and that there were lights on inside the cabin. During surveillance, they observed lights off at two in the morning. Someone was at the cabin. Someone who drove Andrea's SUV. There was no actual sighting of Andrea, and therefore we couldn't be 100% certain it was her. The locals agreed to keep watch until we could drive out to question her, or if we could connect her to Frank's shooting, they would go in and arrest her.

Vincent said, "What do you think?"

What was I thinking? I wanted to question Luna and Mila further. But I had to be careful not to show our hand too early. "I'm hoping Jayda and Ross will come back with something we can use."

"That would be nice."

There weren't a lot of investigative details around the deaths of Danny and Scott. Both MEs had labeled their manner of death as undetermined, uncertain if the heroin overdose was accidental or not. There were no signs of homicide, but there were also no signs of drug use between the two. Which meant the investigators likely hadn't dug too hard. With no leads, the detectives had given up, or so it seemed.

The door squealed open. "Just the two I was hoping to see."

Ross said, "Good to be back."

"Please tell me you have something good."

With a coy smile, he said, "We found some interesting things and are delighted to share those details with you."

My pulse quickened. "Need any coffee or anything else before we get started?"

"Not for me. I'm fully caffeinated."

Jayda said, "Same here."

"Okay, well, here's the murder board."

"What's this? There's a sixth?" Jayda asked.

"He's not dead yet, but they shot him yesterday morning."

"And he works at Vaxxmore?" Ross asked, brows raised.

"And had an affair with Sarah, Andrea's sister, the one who killed herself."

Nodding, he said, "You think the sister did it?"

"We have no evidence, but it's our current working theory. We're working with Alameda County on the investigation."

Jayda shuffled behind him and said, "Well, at least we can start filling in some blanks. Starting with Danny Appleton, the professor at the University of Seattle. Another ladies' man, or should I say students' man?"

"Had affairs with students?" I asked.

Jayda said, "Affair is a little too friendly a word."

"What do you mean? What was the nature of his relationships?"

"He was a known perv. And one woman submitted a complaint against him."

"What for?"

"She said he assaulted her during his office hours. She complained to the school, but they said they couldn't do anything about it because Appleton denied all allegations. There were no witnesses or physical evidence."

Another suspect. And maybe a connection. Fingers crossed. "Sounds like a motive to me. I'm assuming you have a name."

"Rita Pagano."

A name was a positive step forward. "Do we know what happened to Rita? Did she end up graduating? Is she working and living her best life?" One could dream.

"Not exactly. She made the complaint her senior year, and apparently, she was so distraught about the incident, she ended up dropping out of school."

Vincent said, "He ruined her life. Definitely motive."

In full agreement, I said, "Any idea where Rita is now?"

Ross gave a sneaky grin. "I thought you'd never ask. But before we tell you, let's talk about Scott Ogden."

My pulse rate skyrocketed. They had something. I could feel it. "Okay, tell us about Scott Ogden."

"He works in pharma, like your other victims. Most people insisted he was the greatest guy on Earth, but, like our friend Matt Baldwin, there were a few who didn't think he was so great. His nickname from some of his female coworkers was

Scott Ogler — as in he ogled the younger women. His wife all but confirmed he was a dirtbag."

Jayda said, "A real class A jerk."

"Who are the folks who weren't so fond of Mr. Ogler?"

"There were a few. But one of the folks at his job remembered there was an intern several years back who was quite vocal about what she thought of Scott's behavior. Would you like to guess what her name is?"

My heart pounding, I said, "Rita Pagano?"

"Exactly."

"What was the timeframe?"

"About five years ago. It was the summer between her sophomore and junior year at the University of Seattle. Ogden was her boss for the internship."

"And I'm guessing Scott Ogden was never called out for his behavior by the company?"

"You got it."

Looking at Jayda and Ross, I knew that wasn't all they had to say. "What's the punchline?"

"Our gal Rita Pagano just so happens to work at..." Ross tapped on the board next to the letters V-A-X-X-M-O-R-E.

My mouth dropped open. "The receptionist."

"That's correct. She's currently the receptionist at Vaxxmore Pharmaceuticals."

A grin flashed across Vincent's face. "I know how I'm spending the rest of my morning."

Andrea. Mila. Luna. Rita. Were there more? "Anything else?"

Jayda said, "That's it."

"No way the spouses of Ogden and Appleton could be possible suspects?"

"Neither spouse seemed terribly broken up about their dead husbands, but they both had alibis. One lady was at the spa, and the other one was at the kid's school at the time of their husband's death. The original investigators searched the house for any signs of heroin and found nothing, and they did a thorough look at financials. No sign of a hired hit."

The missing link was missing no more. All we had to do was prove it. And we would do just that, starting with a visit to Rita Pagano.

Pacing the living room, I couldn't shake the feeling I was being watched. We didn't get a lot of traffic on the road in front of the cabin, but based on my account, a car had passed our driveway at least once an hour since my first cup of coffee. Was it the police? A lost tourist? If it was the cops, why didn't they venture to the front door and talk to me? It was irksome. But then again, maybe something else was going on in the area that had nothing to do with me. That must be it.

There wasn't anything to worry about.

Not anymore.

Even if they rushed in and broke down my door, they were wasting their time. My mind couldn't understand why the investigators wasted so much energy trying to find who killed some of the most vile creatures on the planet. It was such a waste. Why didn't they spend their precious resources on looking for bad people who did horrible things to the innocent and undeserving? Where were their priorities?

Matt was the sheriff's brother. If he wasn't, would they still be spending their time and risking their lives to find out what really happened? Hopefully not. Was the sheriff just as awful as Matt? Probably. I read the news. I knew that the last sheriff was a killer and locked up in a prison cell for his crimes. Were there any good men?

No.

I hadn't ever met one.

So, no, I didn't feel bad I had eliminated Frank.

Not at all.

As far as I was concerned, I'd done the world a favor.

The world didn't need any men who tormented, took, used, and broke beautiful people. Why did they do it? What made men monsters? Was it because they wished they could be like the beautiful people but could never be? They were sad and pathetic and deserved to burn in hell.

Shaking, I realized I hadn't eaten since arriving the day before. Back in the kitchen, I pulled bread from the refrigerator, popped two slices into the toaster, and waited. Toast was all I could handle.

My nerves were scrunched up in a ball. Having forgotten my Xanax, it forced me to self-soothe. It wasn't going well. But it would be fine. I would be fine. The toast popped, and I jumped. I needed to calm down.

Dry toast in my belly, my nerves settled and my breathing slowed. Just a little low blood sugar and my mind moving too fast. Easily fixed.

My phone vibrated in my hand, and I looked at the screen. With surprise, I said, "Hey, what's up?"

"Where are you?"

"I'm resting."

Did she just sigh?

"Well, I'm at work, and everyone's asking where you are. Did you call your boss to tell him you wouldn't be in?"

The plan was to email him, but the task had completely slipped my mind. "Can you give him the message that I'm out sick? I think it's the flu. It's going around."

"Andrea, what did you do?"

"Just tell him I have the flu. It's fine."

"No, I mean Frank. Did you shoot Frank?"

"How could you ask me that? I'm not crazy."

"Andrea! You did, didn't you? Have you lost your mind?"

She was really getting on my nerves. How dare she question me? "No, I haven't lost my mind. I'm perfectly lucid. But I'm now wondering if you have, in fact, lost your mind."

"We had a plan."

She had some nerve. I cut her off. "Yeah, we had a plan and then you abandoned it. But the mission was not complete. It is now complete."

That shut her up.

How dare she come at me all holier than thou? She had done dirty deeds just like the rest of us. And she was judging me?

"You should email your boss."

"Can't you just tell him for me?"

"Don't you think it would be weird if he heard it from me?"

I rolled my eyes. "Fine. I'll email him." I honestly didn't think anyone would even notice. People were in and out of our office so often, especially the lawyers. A day off wouldn't make any difference. "Why do you even care?"

"Because they were looking for you."

"Who?"

"The investigators."

"The investigators are looking for me?"

"No. I mean yes. I have to go."

She ended the call, and I stared at my phone. They were

looking for me? What did they know? A darkness took over my thoughts. What if one of the girls talked? What if they confessed? Would they do that? No. Yes? To save themselves? It was the only way the cops could pin it on us. They had abandoned the mission — had they abandoned me too?

41

MARTINA

RITA WHISPERED something and then abruptly hung up the phone. With my most friendly smile plastered on my face, I approached. "Hello."

"Hello. How may I help you?"

She asked it as if she didn't know who we were.

"You're Rita, correct?"

She blanched. "Yes. That's right. You have an excellent memory. How can I help you?"

"We're here to see Lynden."

"Is she expecting you?" Rita stuttered, and it was obvious our presence unnerved her.

"No, she's not." I stared deep into her dark eyes. She froze in place before a slight shaking of her head, then picked up the phone.

"Lynden, the investigators from the sheriff's department are here to see you. Okay." She hung up the receiver and said, "Lynden said she'd be out in just a moment."

"Great." I stepped closer. "Your full name is Rita Pagano, correct?"

She stiffened, and I could tell she was trying to compose herself. "That's right."

"How long have you been working here?"

"I started in April, so it's been seven months now."

A month before that, they killed Danny Appleton. "And you like working here?"

She nodded. "Everyone's really nice."

"That's good to hear."

Lynden emerged from the door to the offices and approached, wearing one of her beige suits. "Ms. Monroe, what can I do for you?"

"We would like to speak to you privately."

She nodded before ushering us into the office area. We stopped her before she could take us all the way back to her office. "Lynden, have you heard how Frank is doing?"

"He survived the night, which is a positive sign."

"Good. We're here to question your receptionist, and we need to do that in a conference room. Can you arrange that for us?"

Lynden cocked her head. "About Frank?"

"About a few things. She doesn't know we're planning to interview her, and we would like for you to bring her to us. We assumed you would need to have someone fill in at the front desk." We understood that an unmanned lobby could be trouble, and we were trying to keep a low profile.

"I appreciate that. Is there anyone else you need to talk to besides Rita?"

"No, just Rita, for now. We would also like a copy of her employment records."

"Okay."

A few steps down, inside a small conference room, she said, "Let me speak with someone to take the desk, and then I'll fetch Rita."

Lynden hurried off, and I turned to Vincent. "Rita must know why we're here."

"Well, at the very least, she must know it's not good news for her."

"Her nerves are a giveaway."

The door opened, and Rita stepped inside with Lynden behind her. "If I can get the two of you anything, please let me know. I'll be right outside."

The door shut, and I said, "Have a seat," as I watched her every move. I was hoping to unnerve her, to get her talking.

She sat down and said, "What can I help you with?"

"As you know, we're investigating the death of Matt Baldwin."

"I wasn't working here when he was. I didn't know him."

"We're not just investigating the death of Matt Baldwin. We're also investigating the deaths of Kyle Weston, Larry Henderson, Danny Appleton, and Scott Ogden. And we believe you knew both Danny Appleton and Scott Ogden."

Her mouth dropped open.

She wasn't expecting that.

"Did you know Danny Appleton?" Vincent asked.

"Are you talking about Professor Appleton?"

"Yes."

Fidgeting, she said, "Then, yes, he was my professor."

"When was the last time you saw him?"

With a flicker of anger in her gaze, she said, "When I left school. I haven't seen his face since, and I can't say that I'm sorry about that."

Another victim. "We understand you accused Professor Appleton of assault."

"Yeah, because he did."

I swiveled in the chair, staring her down. "Why did you leave the University of Seattle?"

"After the attack, I was in a bad place. I was terrified of leaving my house. And eventually I'd missed so much school I fell behind. Knowing I wouldn't be better any time soon, I dropped out."

"I'm so sorry that happened to you."

And although I knew Rita was a suspect, I didn't need to press too hard about the details. The look in her eyes told me the assault had occurred. All of our suspects — Andrea, Mila, Luna, and Rita — were victims who had already been pushed too far, leading them to take drastic action. It was understandable, but that didn't mean it was acceptable. "How are you coping now?"

"I've been in therapy for a long time and that helps. But I'm still trying to reclaim my life. Before it happened, I was majoring in chemistry, and I had planned to go for my PhD. I wanted to go into research, but now I'm a receptionist because of Danny Appleton," she said with venom.

Danny Appleton had not only assaulted her, but in her eyes, he had also destroyed her dreams. Was it enough to push her over the edge — to make her kill? I'd seen people kill for far less.

"And you have had no contact with Danny Appleton since you left the university?"

"That's correct."

"Where were you on May seventh?"

"If it was a weekday, I was here at work."

It was an alibi that could be verified. Surely, Vaxxmore would have better attendance records for the receptionist, the person who greeted everyone who entered the building, better than their lawyers and scientists working in the lab. "I'm sure we can ask Lynden for those records."

"She'll have them. I haven't missed a day of work since I started."

Another airtight alibi. Vincent said, "Any plans to go back to school?"

Vincent was good at keeping the young ones at ease.

She nodded. "I lost my scholarship when I dropped out, so I've been working to save up money to go back."

Like the other three, she was smart. She was capable. And I bet they thought they had planned the perfect crimes. "During your undergraduate years, you had an internship?"

"I had two."

"Can you tell us about those?"

"The first one, as you may know, since you're asking about Scott Ogden, was at Milton Biotech. The second one was after my junior year, the year before my life fell apart. That one was at Geneman Pharma."

"And what happened with Scott Ogden?"

"What do you mean?"

"Some of our detectives talked to his coworkers, and they said you weren't very fond of him."

"There was nothing to be fond of. He ogled all the young women. He made gross comments about our bodies and insisted women shouldn't be in science. Ogler said they should be at home, pregnant and making their man's dinner. He was a classic creep. You say he's dead too? Good riddance." She crossed her arms and leaned back in her chair.

No love lost there.

She definitely had a motive to kill Scott Ogden, but I had a feeling she had an airtight alibi for that one too. "Where were you on September third?"

"That was a Monday. I was here. Lynden can check those records for you."

Her attitude was defensive and a little cocky. She hated both Danny and Scott, and had a motive for revenge along with solid alibis. Just like the others. My only question was how did she meet Andrea, Mila, and Luna? Was she a latecomer to the group?

"Do you know Andrea Puerto?"

"Yes."

"How did you meet her?"

"Mutual friends. She actually got me the job here."

Now we were getting somewhere. "How long have you known her?"

"A few years."

"How did you meet? Which friend introduced you?"

"It was so long ago I don't remember who it was."

Seriously? Rita didn't want us to know how she knew the others. She divulged Andrea got her the job, which was something Lynden would have told us anyhow.

Vincent said, "Where did you work before Vaxxmore?"

Rita said, "Starbucks."

"Which one?"

"In Lafayette."

Glancing at Vincent, I could tell his wheels were spinning, and he was on to something. "Where were you two years ago, March ninth?"

Rita's eyes went black. "I would have to check my calendar."

Trying to maintain my poker face, I said, "Where were you two years ago, June seventh?"

"Again. It was so long ago, I can't remember."

Vincent stepped in. "And I'm guessing two years ago, on September thirteenth, you would have to check your calendar too."

"That's right."

"Well, you've been really helpful, Rita. We appreciate you taking the time to talk to us today."

"If there's nothing else, I should get back to the front desk."

"That's all, *for now*."

She winced as she got up and exited the room.

"It's them, Vincent. I'm telling you, it's them."

"You won't get an argument from me."

My gut was screaming these four women killed five men and likely shot Frank.

Lynden could confirm Rita's alibis for Danny and Scott's murders. We weren't surprised. She didn't kill those two, but that didn't mean she hadn't killed one of the others. The only thing left to do was prove it.

42

HIRSCH

It felt natural to be back in the office, but I was also anxious about being away from Kim. She had her parents with her and a half dozen officers keeping any undesirables away. But it was my wife and my child, who I needed to protect. Having a threat against my family was my worst fear. This time, we had the sheriff's department protecting us, but what about next time? Confined to our home, Kim and I had spent a lot of time discussing the future.

Everything was changing, including my perspective on the job. Unsure of what the right career move was, I had a hard time thinking I could walk away from law enforcement. It was part of who I was. But if they put me back in homicide, I would have to come up with an alternative path. I didn't want to leave my family at the ring of the telephone because a body had dropped. And that was the life of a homicide detective. The final decision hadn't been made, but I was thinking my days at the CoCo County Sheriff's Department were numbered.

The door opened and I glanced up. Martina grinned. "Hey, partner."

Vincent added, "Hey, boss."

"Good to see the two of you."

Martina leaned against the desk. "We kinda missed you around here."

"It's good to be back, even if only for an hour or two."

"Jess will be here in about fifteen minutes. I'm looking forward to what she has to say."

Special Agent Jessica Holley of the FBI was a friend of Vincent and had helped us tremendously in the past with her profiling skills. We were fairly certain we were on the right track with the four suspects we had identified. But it would be nice to have the FBI tell us we were, in fact, narrowing in on the perpetrators — a dangerous group of angry women.

From all accounts, they had the right to be angry, and they had the right to be heard when they were treated with violence and misogyny. But it didn't make it okay for them to kill five men. "Me too. This latest development is wild. I don't think I could've dreamed up the scenario. Four women taking revenge on men who wronged them and their loved ones. I guess you can only push some people so far."

Martina sat down next to me, clutching her coffee. "Indeed."

Vincent said, "I'm going to grab some coffee before Jess gets here. Can I get you anything?"

"No, I'm good. Thanks."

Vincent scurried off. Martina said, "How are things at home?"

"Kim's having a hard time getting around."

"She'll have that baby any day now. How are you feeling about it?"

"I'm excited, terrified, and not sure what to do about the job."

"What are you currently thinking?"

"If they move me back to homicide, I may put in my papers."

Her brows shot up. "Retirement?"

"If I'm back in homicide, I'll be working all hours of the night. I need something else, Martina. I might take some time off. Adjust to family life and decide what's best for the family. I can explore other options. I have money saved and can take my time." Other than the house purchased a few years ago, I didn't spend a lot of money. I didn't have a new flashy car and didn't take many vacations. Before Kim, my life was comprised of work, with a side of work.

"We always have a spot for you at Drakos."

"I've considered something along those lines."

"You can decide which cases you want to take and how much you want to work. With your background, you could work security or do background checks."

The most boring of all activities. Although, I had to admit, boring was better than dead.

"Is your plan finalized?"

The door creaked opened. "We'll talk later."

I nodded.

We stood up to greet Special Agent Holley, who had walked in with Vincent. After hellos and handshakes, the four of us sat around the conference table. Special Agent Holley said, "I was just chatting with Vincent on the latest developments." She set down a folder and continued, "The actions fit with the profile."

"So, we're on the right track?"

"Yes. It could definitely fit with the act of a vigilante, but I think it's more than that. I don't think it's just righting a wrong against one person. I think this person wants revenge against all men. She hates men and doesn't trust them. She thinks all men are the enemy. What's very dangerous about this profile is that although it may have started out as personal vengeance, it likely won't end there."

Vincent said, "Scary."

She nodded. "You can say that again. I also think this person may be mentally unstable."

Considering what she'd said, I inferred, "Is that why she targeted me and not Martina?"

"Exactly. This person, or persons, is very dangerous and won't stop until she is stopped. Here's the complete report, but that's the gist of it. You have a woman or women out for revenge. One of them's unhinged and won't stop with just the initial targets. These are highly coordinated attacks. There's not a trace of evidence, and they're well-planned. The perpetrators had the means to pull off these kills. It wasn't cheap. You're looking at an educated woman or women with financial means. Age ranging from twenty-five to forty."

"No middle-aged vigilantes?" I asked, half-joking.

"Not in this case."

Taking this all in, I found it interesting, and it fit what we had theorized. But it also made me think of my future and how much I would miss these types of meetings and working with the FBI to take down a dangerous killer.

"How close is the profile to your suspects?"

Martina said, "Dead on. We have three scientists and a lawyer with ages between twenty-seven and thirty-seven. They each have solid alibis for the victims they are connected to. We think they must have taken turns or swapped to distance themselves from the men they killed."

Agent Holley nodded with a smile. "Yes. These are methodical, well-planned out attacks, except for Frank. With no evidence and no connection to the victims, it's almost like a murder for hire plot, but there's no money exchanged because they're bartering. You kill my guy and I'll kill yours. No paper trail. It's really quite smart."

Special Agent Holley wasn't wrong. Martina said, "Our next step is to request alibis for all the murders from the women to match up killer and victim. If we find opportunity, we know we're right."

I reminded the team, "But there still isn't any physical evidence. It's just a theory."

"That's the tricky part. We have to break one of them."

Special Agent Holley said, "You'll want to go hard at the most mentally unstable one. The one who broke their MO and shot Frank. Do you know who that would be?"

"Yes. Andrea. Sarah's sister."

"Work her. Manipulate her. She might break."

"You think we have enough to get them down here?" Martina asked me.

"The connections are just a theory. And we don't know how Rita fits with the others except for the fact she currently works with Andrea. Did she know Sarah? If we could connect her to Sarah, we could argue they all knew her and when she died, they colluded to get revenge. For now, we should try to get them down to the station without a warrant. If they refuse to talk, we'll revisit and talk to the DA."

"Wait a second," Vincent said. "I'll be right back." He ran out of the room.

Special Agent Holley said, "Vincent's gonna Vincent."

Martina said, "Indeed."

"You two have the most interesting cases."

The thought made me smile. "We get that a lot."

"I hope they keep you two together for a long time."

My heart sank.

Special Agent Holley cocked her head. "What's wrong?"

She was a profiler. "They're disbanding the Cold Case

Squad at the end of the year. It's likely they'll put me back in homicide, and Martina will go back to her firm."

"A travesty. But I'm sure the two of you will find a way back to each other. They can't split up a team like yours for long."

Admittedly, I hoped that was true, but I didn't know how.

Vincent rushed back in. "It's what I thought."

Martina, impatiently, said, "What?"

"Rita had an internship her junior year of college at Geneman Pharma. Guess who else had an internship at Geneman Pharma at that same time?"

"Who?"

"Mila."

An important connection. They all led back to Sarah. "Rita must have known Sarah, considering her besties were Mila and Luna."

Special Agent Holley said, "Sarah's death triggered the murder plot."

Martina nodded. "That's what we think. Based on the timeline, the first death occurred just under a year after Sarah died. These four ladies need to be stopped yesterday."

Agreed. A bunch of man-hating vigilantes running around shooting and poisoning people wasn't something we could have. I only wished I was out there with the team tracking them down. But I knew my priorities, and I knew they could do it without me.

And that was almost worse.

43

MARTINA

FRESH OFF THE phone with the district attorney, I knew what we needed to do, and fast. Since our four suspects Andrea, Luna, Mila, and Rita, either didn't answer their phones or agree to come to the station, we needed to force them down there. As in, talk to us or we'll arrest you for obstructing justice. But according to DA Greggs, the only way to do that was to get more than a hunch and a theory. We had motive and possibly means, but we didn't have opportunity. We needed to prove the four women didn't have alibis for all the five victims. It would be a mix and match game. And we needed to win.

Since Greggs gave us the order, it had been all-hands-on-deck to call and get employment and attendance records for all four women, hoping to at least have days where they couldn't be alibied by their workplace. From there, we would need to place them either in the vicinity of the crime scene or at the very least prove they weren't somewhere else during the time. We needed gaps.

Pacing the squad room, I waited for the final sets of records from Mila and Luna's employers. Thankfully, we had Rita's and Andrea's, and we could begin developing theories.

The door flung open, and Rosemary rushed in and waved a piece of paper in her hand. "I've got both of them. Let's map it out."

Wasting no time, I rushed over to the whiteboard. Under each of the victims' names and the date of their deaths, Rosemary finished recording the names of the women who had either been between jobs or had recorded personal time off with their employers.

Vincent stepped back. "Hot damn."

And like that, the picture was complete. "Incredible."

"For sure. It's interesting all the deaths occurred on a weekday."

"They were solidifying their alibis with work and planned holidays, including travel records. If we hadn't found all the victims and the connections between the women, these murders would have remained unsolved."

"Smart," Rosemary added.

Vincent said, "Not smart enough."

"Thank you so much, Rosemary. There was no way we could have put this together without the research team."

Rosemary blushed. "Well, I'll get back. We still need to pull surveillance, travel records, and financials." She hurried out.

Vincent said, "Now to get them down here. We need to break one of them."

The theory we had crafted was good, but it wasn't evidence, and I knew it would be nearly impossible to convict based on it. "I'll call Greggs. It's not enough to charge them with murder, but it's enough for an obstruction charge if they refuse to talk to us."

Thank the lord for small favors. At that point, we needed a shovel full. We could not get this far and *not* bring justice for the victims and their families.

44

MARTINA

With the threat of arrest, our suspects had been more cooperative except for Andrea, who hadn't answered our calls. But with Tahoe PD stationed outside the cabin, she wasn't going anywhere. They had confirmed her location when the patrol team caught a glimpse of her when she stepped outside for a few minutes before spotting the officers. At that point, she flipped them the bird and hurried back inside. She knew we were watching her. Would it make her paranoid enough to talk to us and tell us everything we wanted to know?

According to the FBI profiler, Andrea was our best bet for a confession. We would let her sit and stew while we talked to the others. Not only that, but I wanted to drive out there for a face-to-face. Preferably after she was arrested for Frank's shooting so I could transport her back to the Bay Area. Frank was in stable condition, but the doctors weren't comfortable taking him out of the coma. We needed him to wake up in order to identify his shooter. We believed it was Andrea, and if we were right, it would allow us to keep her in custody until we had her talking about the five murders.

Were we banking too much on the idea that Andrea would

be the group's one mistake? Maybe. But we were running out of options. The other three had agreed to meet at the station for official questioning. Was it coincidence that Mila just happened to be in the Bay Area for a long weekend? I didn't think it was a coincidence. Our vigilante girl gang was in the hot seat, and they knew it.

SEATED across from Rita and her lawyer, I recognized him from a previous case. Sam Honey was very expensive and very good at his job. Our last exchange was friendly, as we negotiated his client's plea deal that brought in a serial killer. "Rita, thank you so much for coming down today. I imagine you're very busy."

"No problem," she said, her hands folded neatly in her lap. She wore a cream-colored cable-knit sweater and jeans, dark hair pulled up in a messy bun. Casual but put together. The look highlighted her youth. She was only twenty-seven years old. She should have been working in a research lab and partying with friends. Instead, she was a murder suspect. It was a shame.

"What questions do you have for my client?"

"For starters, I'd like to know where she was two years ago, specifically the week of March 7-10."

Rita blinked. Mr. Honey whispered into her ear and then sat up with a smug look on his face. Rita said, "Visiting friends."

"Where?"

"Washington state."

"What friends?"

"Mila Turner."

Each other's alibi. "Where did you stay while you were visiting with Mila in Washington?"

"I was staying at Mila's house in Vancouver, Washington. You can ask Mila. She'll tell you where I was."

"How did you get there?"

"I drove."

If what she said was true, there would be no electronic record of her travel. It was a floppy alibi, but as much as it couldn't be proven, it would be just as difficult to disprove. It was as if they had thought of everything, but not absolutely everything. They couldn't have.

Both the lawyer and Rita sat smugly, with a look as if they were untouchable. It was time to fluster Rita.

I leaned over. "I'm not sure Mila is a great alibi — all things considered."

"With all due respect, Ms. Monroe, your opinion on whether Mila is a good alibi is irrelevant. My client has answered all of your questions. If there's nothing else, we will be leaving."

Staring at Mr. Honey and back at Rita, I wondered how Rita had afforded an expensive lawyer. She worked as a receptionist and, according to her earlier interview, she had been saving up to go back to school. Had she used her college fund to pay for Mr. Honey? Doubt filled my mind. No. The lawyer had to be funded by Andrea or the others.

"Just one." Focusing on Rita, I said, "We know that you and your friends, Mila, Luna and Andrea, were involved in five murders. Matt Baldwin, Kyle Weston, Larry Henderson, and two pretty personal to you, Danny Appleton and Scott Ogden. We will prove that the four of you murdered these men in cold blood. First degree murder. Conspiracy to commit murder. That's a lot of years in prison. But whoever talks first will get the best deal. With that being said, Rita, is there anything you'd like to say?"

The lawyer stood up. "This is preposterous. My client is

innocent of these ridiculous charges. If there are no more questions, Ms. Monroe, we're leaving."

"No more questions. We'll be in touch."

Mr. Honey nodded at Rita, and I watched as they exited the interview room.

Vincent turned to me. "Well, Rita's not gonna talk."

No kidding.

An officer poked his head in. "Yes?"

"Mila Turner is here with her lawyer."

"Bring them in."

WELL, I'll be a monkey's uncle. If I had doubts if the women were colluding before, those doubts were gone. Mr. Honey, escorting Mila, said, "Ms. Monroe. Long time, no see. It's so good to see you."

Not even a full minute had passed. Any hope I had that one of them would break evaporated. "Indeed. Hello, Mila. Please have a seat."

Vincent and I shared a glance of defeat.

"Mila, thank you for being so accommodating and coming down to talk to us."

"Of course. I want to do anything I can do to help your investigation," she said with a sickly smile. All the suspects were victims, but in their attempt to defeat the monsters, they had become them. Something had broken inside them, and I wasn't sure it could be fixed. "Where were you two years ago, the week of September 9th through the 14th?"

Mila nodded, as if she expected that very question. Of course she did. "I was at home visiting my parents."

"In Vancouver, Washington."

"Yes, as a matter of fact." She said as if it surprised her I knew she was from Vancouver.

"How did you travel from Santa Monica to Washington?"

She batted her long lashes. "I drove. Don't like planes."

"It's quite a long drive."

"It is, but it's scenic. Helps the time fly by."

Of course. "And your parents will verify your visit?" Of course they would. They were her parents.

Mila shut her eyes. "Unfortunately, they've since passed."

"When did they pass?"

"My mother passed a year ago and my father six months ago."

No one to verify. How to disprove? "I'm sorry for your loss. Is there anyone else who could verify the visit?"

She shook her head. "No."

Vincent said, "Mila, did you kill Larry Henderson?"

Mila stared deep into my eyes and froze. I'd take that as a yes. Mr. Honey said, "If there are no other questions, we're done."

"We will prove that you and your friends killed Matt, Kyle, Larry, Danny, and Scott. You will go to jail. First one who talks gets a deal." I had no authority to follow through with the promise, but I was confident we could arrange it.

Mr. Honey smiled, like he'd won the battle. "I'll take that as a no. We're done here. Let's go, Mila." Off they went.

Stewing in the conference room, I said, "I don't think we're going to get anything from them."

Vincent said, "It's doubtful."

"We need Frank to ID Andrea. She's the key. I can feel it."

The officer stuck his head in.

I sighed. "Bring them in."

AS EXPECTED, Luna walked in with Mr. Honey like she was walking on air. She was quite the actress, as were the others.

Mr. Honey's grin was infuriating. "We need to stop meeting like this."

Ignoring his arrogance, I said, "Luna, thanks for coming down."

Seated, she looked fresh-faced and angelic. "Of course."

"Luna, I'd like to know where you were between May 5th and 9th and September 1st through the 4th."

She said, "I was visiting friends."

"Which friends?"

"I was visiting with my friend Andrea Puerto. Right here in the Bay Area."

With raised brows, I said, "You were visiting her in the Bay Area — where you live?"

"It was an old-fashioned girls' sleepover at Andrea's. We watched movies, ate junk food, and gave ourselves facials and manicures. Girl stuff."

"Both weeks?"

She nodded. "We enjoyed the first one so much, we did it again."

A total fabrication if I had ever heard one. I glanced at her lawyer. "You're a busy man."

"I am."

"Do you want to tell your client what we know, or should I do the honors?"

He flung his hands in the air. "Are you referring to your ludicrous claims that you think my clients are cold-blooded killers? You're really reaching."

"Am I?"

He nodded.

Vincent said, "Luna, did you kill Danny Appleton and Scott Ogden?"

Luna's mouth dropped open, and she swiveled toward her lawyer.

"That's right, Luna. We know everything. First one who talks gets a deal. This is your opportunity."

Mr. Honey whispered to his client and then stood up. "We're done here. C'mon, Luna."

As they started to exit, I said, "You know, Andrea shot Frank. And as soon as he wakes up and IDs her, it's all over."

Luna's face twisted, and Mr. Honey turned to me. "It was a pleasure to see you, Ms. Monroe." And with that, they were gone.

Alone, Vincent said, "I sure hope Frank IDs our gal."

No kidding. These women needed to be stopped. Who knows how far they would go? If the FBI profile was correct, it may be just the beginning.

45

ANDREA

Staring out the window, I knew the mission was complete. There was no more fighting. No more worrying. No more wondering when they would come for me. I shut the curtains, headed back to the kitchen, and refilled the tumbler on the counter with Rey Sol tequila. The sun-shaped bottle with its golden hue and knowing smile had been purchased for the occasion. For that special moment when we had completed our mission. It was supposed to be a celebration.

It wasn't supposed to end like this.

Mila, Luna, and Rita had freaked out when they were told if they didn't willingly go to the sheriff's station for questioning, they would be arrested.

An emergency call was held.

As usual, I was the calming voice to tell them it would all be okay. That I would foot the bill for the best criminal defense attorney in the state, if not the country. With Mr. Honey, there was no way they would see a day of jail time. They thanked me and told me anything I needed was mine. But when I asked them to provide me an alibi for Frank's mishap, they all said they couldn't and that I should have stuck to the plan. And to have thought of an alibi before shooting Frank. The only one even remotely apologetic was Rita. But even she wouldn't come through for me. She wouldn't have my back like I had hers.

They'd abandoned me.

I should've known. It wasn't the first time. We had all agreed we wouldn't stop until the mission was complete. But no. They left me alone to finish what they had agreed to do. Why was I surprised? I had always been a bit of a loner. The only person who didn't make me feel alone was Sarah. Why had I been so stupid to believe we were a team? It turned out it was every woman for themselves.

With nearly half the bottle gone, I picked up the glass and shut my eyes as I guzzled half of it down. Eyes squeezed shut, my throat burned, and my belly warmed.

I didn't know why they left me the way they did. I had always told them if anything were to go wrong, I had the means to take care of it. To take care of them. It was the same promise I had made to Sarah when she had been tormented daily by Matt and devastated by Frank. I told her no matter what, I would take care of her and she would be okay. Like her friends, I guess she thought my assurance wasn't enough. I wasn't enough.

After a deep breath, I picked up the glass again and finished it. I steadied myself on the counter before stumbling into the living room and plopping down on the leather sofa.

Once my mind stopped spinning, I wondered about the purpose of life. There didn't seem to be one. If I lived, if I died. No difference. If the monsters lived or died. None of it mattered. None. Of. It. The world just kept spinning with no regard for anything or anyone.

They'd turned on me.

I was a fool.

Dumb enough to have trusted Mila when she approached me at Sarah's funeral. Mila said, "We should get together and talk about how to honor Sarah's memory."

The idea was noble. Sarah deserved to be honored. I knew Mila was good friends with Sarah, so I trusted her. Stupid. In this life, there was only one person you could trust.

Pointing at my chest, I said, "Me. That's who I can trust."

Lying in the very spot Mila had sat and told me the plan, I laughed. We thought it was the perfect plan. It would have been if they weren't traitors. I'd hesitated at first, not sure I had it in me. But I saw how it was the ultimate way to honor Sarah.

We'd done it. We'd honored Sarah. Why didn't I feel better? I felt worse. So much worse.

I thought I was tough, a warrior delivering secret justice, but really, I was just a sad, pathetic loser with no reason for anything. The only people who would even miss me were my parents.

I had accomplished everything and ended up with nothing.

My anger had fueled me for so long, but it was gone and replaced with despair. I thought taking Frank and Matt's power would empower me. But it hadn't. There was no closure, no joy, and no longer a camaraderie between the others and me.

It was too much to face this terrible world where men told us what to do, what to wear, how we should look, how we should behave, what careers to have — it was too much. It was their world. And as far as I was concerned, they could have it. There was no fight left in me. *Put a fork in me. I'm done.*

I lifted myself off the couch and toddled toward the stairs. I held on to the banister, peered below, and contemplated my last act before descending the steps.

In the hall, I continued on to the bathroom and pushed open the door to the room in which I'd found my sister dead in a pool of her own blood. The only person who ever cared for me — my only genuine friend. Sarah discerned there was nothing more for her and the only way to end her suffering was to take her own life. I didn't understand it before.

Head bowed, tears poured from my eyes. Mesmerized by the droplets on the blue tile, I knew it was time.

46

MARTINA

THE MOMENT I hung up the call, I grabbed my keys from my backpack. "Let's go. Frank's awake."

Without another word, Vincent and I dashed out of the station and into the parking lot. In such a rush, I forgot to grab my scarf and gloves. It was freezing, and the wind was unforgiving. I jogged toward my car, then slid inside. Vincent did the same. I rubbed my hands together to generate warmth before starting the ignition, while reminding myself to stay calm and drive carefully. Being distracted would only get us into a car accident, and that was the last thing we needed.

On the road, Vincent said, "Did the officer say if Frank said who killed him?"

"All Olivio said was that Frank was awake."

Besides a wish and a prayer, Frank waking up and telling us Andrea shot him was the key to prosecuting the case. It would provide the compelling evidence we needed to prove our theory that Andrea and the others were involved in the murders. Offering a reduced sentence would be our bargaining chip to Andrea in exchange for her testimony against the others. Fingers crossed.

Not a single one of the other women gave us anything we could work with to prosecute. Everything they told us had been ambiguous. I was sure it was how their lawyer had instructed them to answer our questions. Sam Honey was every prosecutor's worst nightmare. He didn't care if his clients were murderers, drug pushers, or pedophiles. He defended them all.

Parked in the visitor parking lot, we were hurrying through the automatic doors on our way to reception when I stopped in my tracks. "Is that Hirsch?"

"Yeah. Was he meeting us?"

"No."

Hirsch stepped forward, revealing the very pregnant Kim sitting in a wheelchair. Without a word, I made my way over with a ridiculous grin.

"Hirsch."

He glanced over at me with a look I had never seen before. Terror? "Hey. Kim's in labor."

"Wow. Kim, how are you?"

With wide eyes, she said, "The baby's coming. Good."

"You're going to do great."

Hirsch said, "What are you doing here?"

"We're here to see Frank. He's awake."

Hirsch nodded.

"But you don't need to worry about that. I'm so happy for the two of you, and I hope everything goes really well. I'm sure it will." While I said a silent prayer for the baby and her parents, Kim started her breathing exercises and clutched her belly. Hirsch gritted his teeth and checked his watch.

When the contraction passed, I was about to say goodbye and good luck, but a nurse wearing pink scrubs came out holding a clipboard. "Kimberly Hirsch?"

Hirsch said, "We're here."

I patted him on the shoulder and said, "Good luck." Then I hurried back to reception. "We are here to see Frank Musker. They moved him from the ER."

The receptionist said, "Okay. Let me check." After a few clicks that seemed to take hours, she said, "He's in room 421."

After providing our information, we slapped our visitors' badges on and bolted toward the elevators. Inside, Vincent said, "I can't believe Kim is about to have the baby. Right now!"

"I know. I can't wait to meet her. There's nothing like holding a newborn in your arms."

The elevator dinged, and the doors opened. We charged toward the room. It was easy to spot, considering there was a uniformed officer standing outside the room. After showing our credentials, we entered. Sure enough, there was Frank lying in a hospital bed. I didn't envy him.

On one side was his wife, and on the other was Detective Olivio. I waved. "Hi, Frank."

He whispered, "Hi."

"How are you feeling?"

In a low voice, he said, "Like I've been shot."

Fair enough. "Well, I hope you have a speedy recovery."

Detective Olivio said, "He's not sure about the shooter."

"It's fuzzy. It was dark."

Eyeing Detective Olivio, I nodded. "Do you remember seeing someone before they shot you?"

He nodded.

"Do you remember if they said anything to you?"

Frank was about to talk but paused and cocked his head ever so slightly. "Yeah." He nodded. "A lot."

Well, I liked the sound of that. "Was it a male or female voice?"

"Female. She was yelling at me."

C'mon. Tell me it was Andrea.

He winced, as if his wounds were causing him discomfort. "She said it was all my fault." He squeezed his eyes shut. A moment passed, and he said, "It was Andrea."

"Andrea Puerto?"

He nodded. "Yeah, Sarah's sister."

Mrs. Musker gasped.

"And she said it was all your fault. Did she say anything else?"

"She said it was my fault and that I would end up like Matt. I asked her if she killed Matt, and she said a friend did it."

I exchanged glances with Vincent. "Did she say which friend?"

"No."

Andrea had confessed and then shot him and left him for dead. It was the mistake we had been hoping for. "And then what happened?"

"I told her I was sorry. I don't remember anything after that."

Because she had shot him and left him lying in a pool of blood.

"And you're sure it was Andrea?"

"Definitely. It was her."

Peeking over at Mrs. Musker, I could tell she was in shock. In a matter of a few days, she had learned her husband had been unfaithful, and that affair had nearly killed him. I did not envy her either.

"Thank you, Frank."

The three of us exited, and Detective Olivio said, "You have eyes on Andrea?"

"Tahoe PD is outside of the cabin as we speak."

Detective Olivio said, "I'll get a warrant. I'll let you know when it's ready. You can give Tahoe the green light to pick her up."

Finally.

ARREST WARRANT APPROVED and faxed to the Tahoe Police Department, my phone buzzed. "We're at the front door. We've knocked several times and identified ourselves. Nobody's answering."

"Can you see inside?"

"All the curtains are closed."

Curtains drawn. She wasn't answering the door. "Can you hear any movement inside at all?"

"No."

"And you're sure she's in there?"

"Yes. We haven't taken our eyes off the cabin."

What was Andrea up to? Considering her location and its significance, I said, "She could be in danger. The cabin is where her sister killed herself. She might do the same."

"Sounds like she could be in danger. We're going in. I'll call you when we know more."

Frustrated and worried, I prayed she hadn't taken her life. Was there a way she could have escaped?

Minutes later, my phone buzzed. "What did you find?"

"She was inside. She tried to kill herself but still has a pulse. It's faint, but it's there. Paramedics took her, and they're on their way to Tahoe General."

Slight relief flowed through me. But we weren't out of the woods yet. "How does it look?"

"It's not great. I'll follow the bus to the hospital and give you an update once we know more."

"Thank you."

Was this Andrea's plan the entire time? Kill the men who had taken her sister's life and then she would take her own? Or was that a recent development? Had she concluded that there was nothing left to live for? Saddened by the thought, I knew that in this case, there were no winners. At best, we could only serve the most bittersweet kind of justice.

47

MARTINA

Fighting exhaustion, I refused to take a break and allow time to pass by and our lead suspect to slip away. After a four and a half-hour drive through the mountains and into the snow, Vincent and I stood outside Andrea's hospital room waiting for the local police department to come out and brief us on her condition. Vincent said, "Do you think she'll talk?"

"I have no idea."

"She's clearly in a vulnerable state. We might push her hard enough to get her to talk."

"She may feel she has nothing to lose, considering she tried to end her life. It would be great to put the case behind us and go home, get some sleep, and meet the newest addition to the Hirsch family when she arrives."

"Hirsch with a baby. It's crazy, right?"

When I first met Hirsch, he was newly divorced and determined to live a solo life dedicated to the job. Three years later, he was married and would become a father at any minute. That was life for you.

A uniformed officer and a doctor, I presumed, based on his

white lab coat, emerged. The doctor, with bushy hair and a sharp nose, ushered us down the hallway. "I'm Dr. Theodore."

"Martina Monroe and Vincent Teller. We're investigators with the CoCo County Sheriff's Department. What's her condition?"

"Like your colleague may have told you on the phone, we don't want to move her yet. She is currently under a psych evaluation. Physically, she's fine. She's going to make it. It was lucky they found her when they did. Another minute or two and it would've been far too late. Mentally, that's a different story. The psychiatrist who has evaluated her thinks she may have had a psychotic break. And likely one or more undiagnosed mental health issues."

"How is her demeanor?"

Dr. Theodore said, "She mumbles and talks about the meaning of life a lot. Says there is no point. When I have questioned her, sometimes she is lucid and others delusional."

"What does that mean for us?"

"You may have to take whatever she tells you with a grain of salt. Whatever she says could be fact or fiction or somewhere in between."

I didn't love the sound of that. Not that we wouldn't have to corroborate everything she would tell us, anyway. But this didn't make me feel any better about the situation. "Can we talk to her now?"

"Yes. She's medicated to level out her mood. She's awake and knows where she is, and she is aware of what happened."

"Thank you."

The doctor nodded and scampered down the hallway.

Turning to Officer Jameson, I said, "Have you tried talking to her?"

"She didn't want to talk to me. I asked her why she tried to hurt herself, and she started yelling at me. Something about how

I probably beat my wife and should be dead. Men are monsters and statements along those lines.”

“She’s not very fond of men.”

He tittered, “Yeah, I got that.”

“We’ve met her a few times. Hopefully, we’ll have better luck.”

Vincent and I trod over to the first bed. Andrea was propped up in it, staring at the TV. “Andrea.”

She turned her head to look at us. “Ms. Monroe,” she drawled, as if the medication was hitting her hard. Had she purposely ignored Vincent? Maybe that was for the best.

“How are you feeling?”

“Just great.”

Sarcasm at its finest. “Do you think you could answer some questions for me?”

“Oh, I’m sure you have lots of questions for me.”

On the stand, Andrea would make a terrible witness. I held up my voice recorder. “Are you okay with me recording the conversation?”

“Yes. Fine by me.”

This would be interesting. “First, we would like to ask you about Frank Musker.”

She rolled her eyes. “What about him?”

“Well, they found him shot on a trail near his house.”

She frowned. “So sad.”

I wasn’t a psychiatrist, but I had to agree with the professionals here. Something was not right with Andrea Puerto. Was it the drugs or something else? “Good news. Frank survived.”

Andrea shut her eyes and exhaled in frustration. “What *great* news.”

“It is good news for Frank. But I’m afraid he’s identified you as his shooter.”

“Apparently not a very good one.”

An admission? It wouldn't hold up in court unless she was cleared by a psychiatrist, but hopefully we could prove she was the shooter without her confession. "Did you shoot Frank?"

"I did. Obviously, I should've practiced more. They say practice makes perfect."

"Why did you shoot Frank?"

With a deranged look in her eyes, she said, "You know why."

I did. But I wanted her to say it. "Can you tell me again?"

"He killed Sarah's soul and broke her heart. And then she took her life because of him. He did that to my innocent, beautiful, and brilliant sister. He deserved to die, and I'm not so happy he's alive. And one day, I hope he rots in hell. It's where he belongs."

"Where's the gun you used to shoot him?"

She laughed. "You'll never find it. I threw it in Lake Tahoe. It was the first thing I did on my way up to the cabin."

"What about the clothes you were wearing? Where are they now?"

Detached from the seriousness, she said, "Fireplace. Gone. Covering up crimes is so easy. Sometimes killing is too."

Not great news for the case.

Vincent eyed me and then said, "Speaking of killing people and how easy it is, do you want to talk about Matt Baldwin?"

She stuck her tongue out. "Yuck. I'd rather not. But I could."

"Do you know how he died?"

"I sure do."

"We know it wasn't you, Andrea, but we think you know who did it."

She nodded exaggeratedly. "Yep, I do. World, you're welcome. Not that anything really matters."

Vincent said, "Who killed Matt?"

"I suppose I could tell you. Like I said, nothing really matters. They abandoned me. I have nothing left. It was all a perfect plan. A mission. A purpose to this wretched life. I thought I could finish it on my own, but clearly, I couldn't. Since Frank is *still* alive."

"Who killed Matt? Was it Rita or Mila?"

She grew serious and looked at Vincent and then me. "You know, under different circumstances, I think you and I would be friends. You're smart. I like that."

Which meant we were right. "So, who was it? Rita or Mila?"

"Okay, okay. I'll tell you everything."

I glanced at Vincent, and he shrugged. "We're listening."

"Okay, I'll tell you everything. What do I get?"

Lucid. "You could avoid the death penalty."

She lifted her wrists.

Point taken. "We could offer life in prison, but at a nicer prison. Minimum security." It was a bluff. If she was going anywhere, it was likely to be a mental health facility.

She shrugged. "I guess it doesn't really matter. But you should know, they're weak. They're not strong. I thought they were. They should go somewhere nice, too."

This one would be for the books. "Can you start at the very beginning? How did it all start?"

Andrea nodded. "It started with Sarah. For years, Matt Baldwin tormented her. He was so gross. And then she fell for her icky boss, Frank. I saw through all of his lies, but Sarah was head over heels. I tried to tell her he would never leave his wife. She was young and ambitious. She was bright, and I'm sure he loved that about her. He called her his angel. *Gross.*" She stuck out her tongue again. "And then, as was inevitable, he dumped her in the trash. He broke her, and I couldn't put her back together. I felt so powerless. It was torture watching her go through it. And you know what? When Sarah died, something died inside me, too."

I had no doubt. "I'm so sorry Sarah and you had to go through that. It's not fair."

"No, it's not. And when Mila came up to me at Sarah's funeral and said she had a plan to honor Sarah's memory, I was interested. A few weeks later, Rita, Mila, Luna, and I met at the cabin. It was there each of them shared their stories of men who hurt them, damaged them, and ultimately broke them too. They wanted revenge, and I wanted revenge for Sarah and for all the women. All the ones who had been treated like they were less than human. Less than men. Men who acted like the only purpose for women was to look pretty, smile, and to please them. Men who dictated how we act and look and be. That's who I wanted to save. I couldn't save Sarah, but maybe I could save a few others." She picked up a plastic cup from the side table and sipped through the straw.

After placing the cup down, she continued. "We came up with a plan. It was a brilliant plan until you and your partner came along and reopened Matt's case. To be honest, I didn't know Matt was related to law enforcement until it was too late. I may even have reconsidered if I had known." She waved her hands in the air, as if to say, "too late now." "So, the plan. It was perfect. We would each take out each other's targets so that there was no connection, no motive. And it worked. We had a rotation. We left no evidence anywhere."

"How did Rita kill Matt?"

"Ah, you got it. Well, easily. Mila bought the drugs from someone she knew in the Los Angeles area. Mila and Luna went to UCLA and already had the recreational drug hook up. Mila had seen a true crime show on TV where a man almost got away with killing his wife because he poisoned her cereal with heroin." She started laughing maniacally. "That's how we should've known it wasn't perfect. The man *almost* got away with it." She continued to laugh.

Vincent and I exchanged looks once again.

She calmed and continued, "Yeah, well anyway, Mila bought the heroin, and we devised a way to kill them. Since everyone had worked with their targets, they knew their habits. We knew where they went each day. Before we took them out, we watched them for a few days, to ensure their routine hadn't changed. Matt was the first. We were so nervous before Matt's death. We didn't know if the plan would work. Anyway, Mila brought the drugs, and we put it in little white packets, so it looked like sugar. Rita showed up at the coffee shop he went to every day, and while the coffee sat on the counter waiting for him to pick it up, she poured the packet in and replaced the lid. She said she even talked to him. He said, 'Oh I think that's mine,' and Rita said, 'Oh, I'm so sorry. I added sugar. Is that okay?' He said, 'Of course it's okay. I would accept sugar from a pretty lady any day.' *Gag.*"

"We reviewed all the security footage outside of the coffee shops. I didn't see Rita."

"Are you sure about that? We knew there were cameras. We wore disguises. Put on some lipstick, maybe a hat, a wig, and a new style of dress and presto, a new woman. Women can change their appearance in a snap. Thanks to the billion-dollar beauty industry that makes women continue to spend money and time and endure pain to look *just right* for men."

The FBI profile fit Andrea to a tee.

"How did Matt's death go down?"

"Perfectly. We met at the cabin. She said it was so easy, like it was nothing. She couldn't believe it."

Because nobody would suspect a pretty young woman

would poison a complete stranger. That's how they got away with it because women are seen as soft and nonaggressive because that's how they are told to be. "And you want to tell us about Kyle Weston?"

"Kyle was my kill," she said with a smile, as if remembering fondly. "I did almost the same thing as Rita. But I was more bold. The week of, I studied his habits and convinced a sixteen-year-old barista to let me serve Kyle. I wanted to see his eyes when he drank it. I told the barista I was surprising my boyfriend and that it was an act of love. The barista hesitated, but after I flashed some cash, he agreed."

The way she spoke of the murders, she was right. It was almost too easy to kill a stranger. And all of them would have gotten away with it if Andrea wasn't drugged and talking to us. Listening to the details, I knew there was no way we would've been able to prove any of it. "And Larry?"

"Larry was Mila's kill. She said she stood outside his car and watched him die. I think she liked it. Larry was a creep. I heard all the stories from Luna. He deserved it. They all did."

She said it is as if trying to convince us that everything they had done was perfectly okay.

"And so I'm guessing Danny Appleton and Scott Ogden were killed by..."

"Luna. She heard how easy it was and offered to do both of them. She was already going up north to visit some friends and stayed at Mila's parents' house since it was empty. Luna did the same as the others. Followed routines, wore a disguise, and drugged their morning brew."

We'd have to check all the video surveillance to confirm everything Andrea was saying. If we could prove it was Mila, Luna, Rita, and Andrea on surveillance, it should be enough to convict. Even if Andrea took back her confession.

"And that was the end of the list?"

She shook her head. "Nope. Frank was the last one. We saved him for last because we didn't want two people from the same company being murdered and the cops being able to connect it to Sarah."

"Was shooting him the plan?"

"Well, that's where things fell apart. You people were already re-investigating and interviewing us. The others wanted to call everything off. Lie low. Do nothing. Let the case run cold."

"So, how did things fall apart?"

"They wanted to end the mission without killing Frank. They said we had to cut our losses and be proud we took out the first five. That wasn't good enough for me. Frank deserved to die."

"Where did you get the gun?"

"At the gun shop. I waited three days and there you have it. Have gun, will shoot."

"You had to shoot Frank because your pals bailed on you?"

"That's right. In the end, we're all alone."

I had never considered myself to be alone because I had Zoey and my mom living with me. I had Hirsch and the squad and the Drakos team. But one day, Zoey would grow up, go off to college, get married, become independent. Mom would probably marry Sarge and move in with him, and then I would be alone in the house. Maybe Andrea had a point.

Was it time to date again? My previous attempt was a disaster. Perhaps it was time I tried again. Because it was true. None of us wanted to end up alone. "How did that make you feel?"

"Well, I'm here, aren't I?"

She felt betrayed and alone.

"We appreciate you talking to us, but may I ask why you're telling us all of this?"

"Why not?"

"Well, honestly, if you didn't tell us, you would be charged with attempted murder on Frank, but we couldn't prove the others."

"Either way, I'm going to prison."

"Does that bother you?"

"Not anymore. The way I see it, every woman lives in a prison. Men are the guards, telling us how to look, how to behave, what careers we should take, and how many children we should have. Being born female is a life sentence. Behind bars, I won't have to worry about what clothes to wear, what makeup to buy, or what color and cut will be sexy enough. I don't have to be frustrated that I make only 82% of every dollar a man with my same job is making. In prison, I'll finally be free."

Andrea hated men, or perhaps the world that men had created.

It was difficult to find the right words to say in a moment like this. Andrea wasn't completely off base about how women were treated in our society. It didn't mean it was okay to kill men or to take vigilante justice so far. There were right ways to do things and there were wrong ways to do things, and murdering five men was the wrong way. Had she forgotten that there had been progress for gender equality? And the world needed women like her who were smart and talented to continue to fight for women's rights. We didn't need to kill, but we needed to keep fighting. Instead of helping the cause, she had hurt it. It was a shame they had been so blinded by rage to understand how they could have actually helped other women. "Who sent the letters to my partner, Detective Hirsch?"

"I did. I was hoping you'd stop the investigation so we could continue our plan."

"Did you think threatening or killing a police officer wouldn't bring on the full force of the sheriff's department?"

She shrugged. "You know the stats on police officers' families, right? At least 40% are abused. At least. I just figured he was probably one of the 40%, so I would do the world and that pretty blonde a favor. Has she had the baby yet?"

"Not yet."

"Well, good luck to her."

Filled with disgust that Andrea could be so callous toward Hirsch, someone she didn't even know, I said, "For the record, Detective Hirsch is one of the best men I have ever known. He has never treated a woman as less than equal. Kim is a lucky woman for having a husband like him, and he will make an amazing father to his daughter. Not all men are terrible."

"If you say so. I'm tired and don't want to talk anymore."

"No last words?"

"I'm glad they're dead. And I'm glad they can't hurt anybody else. I'm glad I could take some of my power back. And I'm looking forward to prison. To being free of all the shackles placed upon me and my fellow sisters. Who knows, maybe I'll even eat a donut."

And that was a wrap. "Thank you for talking with us, Andrea. We appreciate it."

She smiled. "I'm free, and soon, Luna, Mila, and Rita will be, too."

Out in the hallway, we met up with Officer Jameson. "Did she talk?"

"Oh, yeah. She had a lot to say." We filled him in. "We'll keep in touch. When she's ready, we'll need to transfer her to CoCo County."

"Sounds good. Have a safe trip back."

We shook hands and made our way to the parking lot. Before I could even say the words, Vincent said, "I'll call the team. We'll have everyone on deck, sifting through video footage. We will prove these ladies are guilty, and they won't kill anyone ever again."

It was difficult to feel joy knowing that these women's lives would be over soon. Instead of thriving, they would be imprisoned with felony records. Their lives would never be the same. It was a shame they had felt so powerless against men that they figured the only way to make a difference was to take a life. Five lives.

48

MARTINA

With only a few hours of shut-eye, I paced the squad room while Vincent stood in front of the whiteboard, arms crossed, studying everything we had put together so far. All we needed was the surveillance video evidence to arrest Mila, Luna, and Rita and close the case. With it, Hirsch and the squad's safety would be secured. And maybe we could all get a full eight hours of sleep. Wouldn't that be something? Not to mention, I was dying to meet the baby. She was born at midnight. Everyone was healthy, happy, and in love.

Overjoyed for Hirsch and his family, I couldn't help but remember the day Jared and I brought Zoey home from the hospital. It was a joy I hadn't felt since. The connection to another human being, not just my little girl, but to Jared, too. We were a family. Bonds that could never be broken.

On the drive back, Vincent had convinced his team to pull an all-nighter to make sure we had everything we could get, as fast as we could. We were all itching to pull the trigger on the arrest warrants. The research team included. It had been a long, tiring case. I was ready for a break.

Vincent explained to me in simpleton terms how the team would use facial recognition software to make positive identifications. The computer would make the task faster and more reliable than human eyeballs alone. Even with technology, there were four women who had to be identified against five different men covering several hours of footage — at least an hour before and after, when we thought the men entered the coffee shops before their deaths.

The team was exceptional and had gone above and beyond for Hirsch and the case. When it was done, we would celebrate.

Vincent said, "Are you excited to see Baby Hirsch?"

"I am. They're still in the hospital, and I would love to give them the gift of knowledge that the people threatening their family are locked up and not able to hurt anybody."

"Talk about a one-of-a-kind gift," he said with a smile.

Vincent excelled at adding a little levity to our jobs right when we needed it.

The door creaked open. Linus and Rosemary entered with a laptop in Rosemary's hand. She said, "We've got all four."

Holding back tears of relief, I said a quick and silent prayer full of gratitude.

Rosemary sat the laptop on the table and powered it up. She pulled up the first screen, showing us how the facial recognition software matched Rita's face to a woman wearing a blonde wig and large-framed sunglasses and walking out of the coffee shop five minutes after Matt Baldwin. Next was footage of Andrea, in full disguise — red wig and sunnies, entering the coffee shop twenty minutes before Kyle Weston entered and exiting ten seconds later. And then Mila, wearing a long, blonde wig and sunglasses at the scene of Larry Henderson's poisoning, three minutes before he entered and thirty seconds after. And then Luna following the near-exact routine at both crime scenes for

Danny Appleton and Scott Ogden. None of the women would have been recognizable without the facial recognition software.

Too in awe to speak, Vincent said, "That's it. Let's call Greggs."

"Excellent work, Rosemary and Linus."

I pulled out my phone and called DA Greggs to tell him what we had found.

"Nice work."

"Will it be enough to prosecute?"

"It's not perfect, but between Andrea's detailed confession, even if she recants, and placing each woman at the scene of the crime in disguise, it's enough for a warrant and should be enough to convince a jury. But it still lacks physical evidence. It could go either way. Submit for the arrest warrants, and you'll be good to go."

"Thanks, Greggs."

Another win for the Cold Case Squad. Our last?

Shaking it off, I said, "I'll update Sarge. We'll need to submit for the arrest warrants. Thank you, all of you. I've never worked with a better team." Tears beginning to form, I said, "I'll be back."

All the prayers and hard work paid off. These women would no longer be a threat to others. Not that I could stop thinking about Andrea and all the things she had said during her confession. She wasn't entirely wrong, and I felt terrible that they had endured so much trauma. This job would be easier if all the criminals were soulless monsters who deserved everything they got. But I had found in this job there was far more gray than there was black-and-white.

At Sarge's office, I performed an obligatory knock on the open door. He was wearing a T-shirt and a ball cap. It wasn't his typical attire, but then again, it was the weekend, and he'd come in to support the team. Any other time, it would've been Hirsch, but he had a little baby to take care of. "We got them."

Relief showed on his face. "Thank goodness. All four?"

"The facial recognition software identified all four women, Andrea, Rita, Mila, and Luna. All corroborating Andrea's confession."

"Excellent."

"I talked to Greggs. We can submit for arrest warrants and pick up Mila, Luna, and Rita. If you could help with that, we can go get them."

"I'll take care of the warrants and have a fresh team execute them. You and Vincent have been working nonstop. You need a break. Plus, I've heard Zoey is dying to meet the baby."

"It's true."

"Why don't you go home? Give your daughter a hug and go meet Baby Hirsch. And give Hirsch the good news."

"Thanks, Sarge."

It felt weird not going to arrest our suspects. Hirsch and I had a tradition. Along with backup, the two of us would arrest our suspects so we could look the perps right in the eyes as Hirsch snapped the cuffs on them. It was one of the most satisfying aspects of the job. Without Hirsch, though, I didn't really see the point. We would have plenty of time to question them once they were in custody.

Sarge said, "I'll call the team. We'll take care of everything. Go get some rest. Great work."

I nodded and treaded back to the squad room to tell Vincent that Sarge and the team would handle the situation from here on out.

"Are you going to the hospital to see Hirsch?" he asked.

"I'll stop at home first and see my girl. And then I'll call Hirsch to make sure they're up for visitors."

"I would love to see the baby too, but I'll let you two have first dibs."

I was going to miss Vincent. "Thanks. I'll let them know. And good work out there. I don't think we could have closed this one without you."

"I'm pretty sure you could do anything, Martina."

I gave him a pat on the shoulder and left the Cold Case Squad Room — *one case closer to saying goodbye.*

49

MARTINA

It devastated Zoey to hear they wouldn't allow non-sibling children in the maternity ward and that she'd have to wait until Kim, Hirsch, and the baby were at home. But in some ways, I was glad it would be just me. It would give me the chance to talk to Hirsch and tell him that the case was closed. I decided not to tell him over the phone in the event he had questions. Plus, I wanted to buy some time so that by the time I saw him, all the suspects would be in custody.

As I approached with flowers in one hand and good news in the other, I knocked on the door. The sight of Hirsch holding a tiny bundle in his arms nearly took my breath away. He looked up with a smile and a look in his eyes that told me he experienced that joy of becoming a parent for the first time. Something that fills you up like you can't describe. It's a moment that makes you believe there is good in the world and humanity isn't doomed. It's magic.

Walking over to Kim, I said, "Hi, there."

"Hi, Martina."

I set the flowers down on the table next to her bed. "How are you feeling?"

"A little sore. I'm glad labor is over. But I'd do it again in a heartbeat."

Yeah, that's pretty much the sentiment I knew well. Hirsch stood up. He looked like a giant compared to the baby. "Congratulations to both of you. To all of you. I can't imagine a more beautiful family."

Hirsch said, "Thank you, Martina."

And then he stared down at his baby girl with a pink, squishy face, and said, "Audrey, this is your Auntie Martina. She's the strongest and bravest lady I know. And I think you're gonna love her."

And at that point, I thought Hirsch was trying to make me cry.

He said, "Do you want to hold her?"

"I do." He handed her to me, and I stared down at baby Audrey. Her eyes were open wide, as if she was already aware of the world around her. I whispered to her, "Hello, Audrey. You've got two awesome parents. Not to worry, you're in excellent hands. And always remember, the entire world is yours for the taking. Don't let anyone tell you otherwise."

She made a gurgling noise. I liked to think she understood what I was saying to her. I leaned over and inhaled the scent of her newborn head and shut my eyes. Baby powder and heaven.

I glanced over at Kim and Hirsch. "She's perfect."

With a smile that practically took over his entire face, Hirsch said, "She is, isn't she?"

Hirsch was a proud papa, and Kim was a radiant new mother.

A few moments later, Audrey wiggled and fussed. Kim smiled and said, "It's feeding time. She's a hungry girl."

Not wanting to let her go, but knowing I had to, I placed Audrey into Kim's arms, then stepped over to Hirsch and pulled him outside the door. "You have a gorgeous family, Hirsch."

"It's pretty spectacular, isn't it?"

"Yes, it is."

"Any word on the case?"

He was a new beaming father and wonderful husband, but he was still Hirsch, and it didn't surprise me he wanted details on the case. Even though time passes and we grow, we can't change who we are at the core. "We have a full, albeit drugged, confession from Andrea that detailed how they pulled off every one of the murders. We could corroborate her story, so even if she recants, we have some evidence. All four women have been arrested and are currently locked up."

He nodded his relief. "It's over." He paused, perhaps knowing that it was over in more than one way. "I've submitted for paternity leave. I'll be out until the new year."

Which meant we had just worked our last case together.

With one new beginning, a life so precious and perfect, another thing ending came close to something a lot like that. "And what will you do after that?"

"I'll have to decide whether to put in my papers and move on or wait and see if other opportunities open up." He gave me a look, as if he wasn't telling me everything.

In the years we worked together, I had learned Hirsch was a sneaky one. But usually he only held back information when he thought it was the right thing to do.

"It's all gonna work out, Martina."

And I believed him because Hirsch was a good man, and he wouldn't say it if it weren't true. A bona fide pragmatist and the best partner I'd ever had. Trying to maintain my composure, I said, "This isn't the end, Hirsch."

He smirked, as if he had a secret. "Most certainly not."

THANK YOU!

Thank you for reading *Her Last Words*! I hope you enjoyed reading it as much as I loved writing it. If you did, I would greatly appreciate if you could post a short review.

Reviews are crucial for any author and can make a huge difference in visibility of current and future works. Reviews allow us to continue doing what we love, *writing stories*. Not to mention, I would be forever grateful!

Thank you!

ACKNOWLEDGMENTS

I'm always asked what inspires my stories and this is usually the spot where I explain it. But *Her Last Words* wasn't inspired by one case or one story or one experience. This story idea that has been festering in my brain for five years, comes from a collection of stories and experiences. Some my own, some from others. Some ripped from the headlines. There is no shortage of inspiration for this topic. (She belts out a silent scream.) All I have to say is to all of the men and women who inspired this story, I hope karma finds you sooner rather than later.

On a more positive note ... Hi!

First and foremost, many thanks to my readers. If it wasn't for you, I wouldn't get to have the best job in the whole wide world. If I could bake each of you a dozen cupcakes I would.

I would also like to extend my deepest gratitude to my Advanced Reader Team. My ARC Team is invaluable in taking the first look at my stories and spreading awareness of my stories through their reviews and kind words.

To my editor Paula Lester, a huge thank you for your careful edits and helpful comments. And many thanks to my proof readers Becky Stewart and Ryan Mahan. To my cover designer, Odile, thank you for your guidance and talent.

To my friends and family and, of course, the official spokesdog of H.K. Christie and Keekstar Media, Charles "Charlie" T. Snickerdoodle, thank you for supporting me in every crazy little thing I do.

ALSO BY H.K. CHRISTIE

The Martina Monroe Series —a nail-biting crime thriller series starring PI Martina Monroe and her unofficial partner Detective August Hirsch of the Cold Case Squad. If you like high-stakes games, jaw-dropping twists, and suspense that will keep you on the edge of your seat, then you'll love the Martina Monroe crime thriller series.

The Selena Bailey Series (1 - 5) — a suspenseful series featuring a young Selena Bailey and her turbulent path to becoming a top-notch private investigator as led by her mentor, Martina Monroe.

The Val Costa Series —a gripping crime thriller with heart-pounding suspense. If you love Martina, you'll love Val.

The Neighbor Two Doors Down —a dark and witty psychological thriller. If you like unpredictable twists, page-turning suspense, and unreliable narrators, then you'll love *The Neighbor Two Doors Down.*

A Permanent Mark A heartless killer. Weeks without answers. Can she move on when a murderer walks free? If you like riveting suspense and gripping mysteries then you'll love *A Permanent Mark -* starring a grown up Selena Bailey.

***

For H.K. Christie's full catalog go to: **www.authorhkchristie.com**

At **www.authorhkchristie.com** you can also sign up for the H.K. Christie reader club where you'll be the first to hear about upcoming novels, new releases, giveaways, promotions, and a free e-copy of the prequel to the Martina Monroe Thriller Series, *Crashing Down!*

ABOUT THE AUTHOR

H. K. Christie watched horror films far too early in life. Inspired by the likes of Stephen King, true crime podcasts, and a vivid imagination she now writes suspenseful thrillers featuring unbreakable women. When not working on her latest novel, she can be found eating & drinking with friends, walking around the lakes, or playing with her favorite furry pal. She is a native and current resident of the San Francisco Bay Area.

To learn more about H.K. Christie and her books or simply to say, "hello", go to **www.authorhkchristie.com**.

At **www.authorhkchristie.com** you can also sign up for the H.K. Christie reader club where you'll be the first to hear about upcoming novels, new releases, giveaways, promotions, and a free e-copy of the prequel to the Martina Monroe Thriller Series, *Crashing Down*!